SHERLOCK HOLMES

FOOTSTEPS IN THE FOG
AND OTHER STORIES

Kel Richards is a best-selling Australian author. His crime novels and children's books have sold over 120,000 copies, and are now published in the UK as well as Australia. Before turning to writing he was a leading radio and television journalist; a compere of 'AM' (on ABC radio) a senior reporter on 'Nationwide' (on ABC television) and host of his own interview and talk-back shows ·on commercial radio. He is married with two children.

Books by Kel Richards

Sherlock Holmes Tales Mysteries
The Curse of the Pharaohs
The Vampire Serpent
The Headless Monk

The Ben Bartholomew Mysteries
The Case of the Vanishing Corpse
The Case of the Damascus Dagger
The Case of the Dead Certainty
The Case of the Secret Assassin

The Mark Roman Mysteries
The Second Death
The Third Bloodstain

Non-series Thrillers
Moonlight Shadows
Death in Egypt
An Outbreak of Darkness

Verse
Domestic Bliss and Other Verse
The Ballad of Two Sons

Children's Books
Father Koala's Nursery Rhymes
Father Koala's Fables
Father Koala's Fairy Tales

Non-fiction
The Vanishing Corpse Study Guide
Hospitality Evangelism (with Barbara Richards)
Free for All (with Phillip Jensen)

Audio Books
Kel Richards' Radio Follies
The Fridge Dwellers
How to Raise a Responsible Teenager (with Brian Cade)
What Has God Ever Done for You?

SHERLOCK HOLMES

FOOTSTEPS IN THE FOG
AND OTHER STORIES

Kel Richards

based on characters and incidents created by
Sir Arthur Conan Doyle

BEACON BOOK

A Beacon Book

First published in Australia in 1999 by
Beacon Communications Pty Ltd
PO Box 1317, Lane Cove NSW 1595

National Library of Australia
Cataloguing-in-Publication data
Richards, Kel
Sherlock Holmes: footsteps in the fog and other stories

ISBN 0 9587020 6 3

A823.3

Typeset by Beacon Communications, Sydney
Printed in Australia by Australian Print Group

Cover photograph: Sarah Richards
Cover design: Sydney Design Studio
Font: Baskerville Old Face

CONTENTS

FOREWORD

The *Encyclopedia Mysteriosa* says: "Not simply the greatest and most famous of fictional detectives, Sherlock Holmes is quite possibly one of the most famous personages, real or fictional, in the history of the world."

In other words, there are few people on this planet who have not heard of the name: "Sherlock Holmes".

When and where did you first encounter the world's greatest detective? On television? In one of the many movies? Or, perhaps, in the original stories by Sir Arthur Conan Doyle? I first encountered Holmes on radio—in a famous series of programs starring Sir John Gielgud as Holmes and Sir Ralph Richardson as Watson. I was ten years old at the time.

The next Christmas my parents gave me (at my insistence) a copy of *The Complete Sherlock Holmes Short Stories* by Conan Doyle (in the red-covered John Murray edition). That book is still on my shelves. Next I came across the legendary series of films made by Universal International, starring Basil Rathbone as Holmes and Nigel Bruce as Watson, when they were screened on late night television. (At the time it struck me as odd that Rathbone and Bruce did not have knighthoods: after all, anyone who plays Holmes and Watson *should* be knighted—"Sir Basil" and "Sir Nigel" have a nice ring to them, don't they?)

Then there was the time I went to see some awful movie of no interest whatsoever, because it was part of a double feature and the supporting attraction was the Hammer Films production of *The Hound of the Baskervilles* with Peter Cushing as an excellent Holmes.

Since then, the movies and television productions have

kept on coming (although the quality varies somewhat). The stories, however, stopped with the death of Sir Arthur in 1930. And that was a situation no good Sherlockian could abide. No new Sherlock Holmes stories? Why, it hardly bears thinking about! Hence, many dedicated Sherlockians have (in recent years) rushed in to make up the deficit by writing new stories featuring the world's first and greatest, consulting detective (of course, the quality varies somewhat).

Nicholas Meyer, Julian Symonds, H R F Keating, Michael Moorcock, Edward D Hoch, Henry Slesar, L B Greenwood, Frank Thomas, Val Andrews, David Stuart Davies, Laurie R King and countless others have contributed new adventures to the canon.

This is the noble band (a rather speckled band, perhaps) that I have volunteered to join. After all, what is the point of being both a writer and a Sherlockian if one does not write of Sherlock?

One question to be addressed is the correct length for a Sherlock Holmes story. In his introduction to a collection of G K Chesterton's "Father Brown" detective stories, Ronald Knox writes: 'What is the right length for a mystery story? Anybody who has tried to write one will tell you, I think, that it should be about a third of the length of novel. Conan Doyle uses that formula in *A Study in Scarlet*, and in *The Valley of Fear*, filling up the rest of the book with a long story which does not really affect the plot.'

Knox is, of course, quite right. Which is why Conan Doyle wrote many more Sherlock Holmes short stories than novels—56 short stories against four novels. And the latter he did not even call "novels" but "long stories" (all four of them are rather shorter than most popular novels, even with the interpolated stories to which Knox refers). In pursuit of this "ideal length" I have untaken to write stories in the vicinity of 20,000 to 25,000 words. The problem then is how to package and publish these.

Since many juvenile novels are about that length, the first three tales in this series (*The Curse of the Pharaohs, The Headless Monk* and *The Vampire Serpent*) were published as slim individual volumes aimed at the juvenile market. But they were never really juvenile stories, and this was reflected in sales—or lack thereof (mind you, I read Conan Doyle before my eleventh birthday).

Hence, this new solution—three tales together making up a full-length book, addressed to their proper readership: true Sherlockians everywhere. If you like them let me know, and there will be more.

Best wishes, and good detecting,
Kel Richards

The Waters
of Death

In November of 1895 Holmes and Watson tackled the case Sir Arthur Conan Doyle called "The Bruce-Partington Plans". By the time the case was over it involved two mysterious deaths, assorted spies and foreign agents, and secret plans for a new fighting submarine. Needless to say, Holmes solved the mystery surrounding the deaths and recovered the stolen plans.

But why need the matter have ended there? New submarines have to be built and tested as well as designed— and can we expect desperate foreign powers to abandon their attempts to learn Britain's naval secrets?

The result is that, with Christmas drawing close, Holmes and Watson are dispatched to the wilds of Scotland for a sequel to "The Bruce-Partington Plans" that they could never have anticipated.

1

'The battle is not over yet,' said Mycroft Holmes, as he entered our rooms in Baker Street, brushing the loose snow from his shoulders.

'What battle?' I asked, as I helped him out of his coat, and then poured him a hot cup of tea.

'The battle to save the most important naval secret of this nation,' said Sherlock Holmes, as he waved his elder brother to take a seat by the fire. We were only two weeks away from Christmas, and the weather was bitterly cold.

'You mean the secrets of the Bruce-Partington submarine?' I asked.

Mycroft scowled at me for even speaking aloud the name of that most secret of all government projects.

'But I don't understand,' I continued. 'The spy Hugo Oberstein is under arrest, and the stolen plans have been recovered.' I was referring to the case that I have recorded elsewhere under the name of *The Bruce-Partington Plans.* It was an adventure that began when Mycroft, a senior government adviser, as well as my friend's older brother, called us in to investigate the loss of the plans and the death of a junior clerk from the naval office.

'What else,' continued Sherlock, 'can have brought Mycroft away from the narrow world of his private club and his government office? I presume that the foreign power that hired Oberstein to steal the plans has not given up?'

'Precisely,' muttered Mycroft, as he settled his bulky frame into the cushions of the armchair. 'Having failed to secure the plans, they are now attempting to sabotage the submarine itself.'

'You mean the thing has already been built?' I asked in amazement.

'It was built some time ago,' Mycroft explained quietly, 'and is now undergoing testing—under the strictest security, of course.'

'Where is this testing being done?' asked Sherlock Holmes.

'Not in the open sea,' replied Mycroft. 'There it could too easily be observed by foreign ships. It is being tested in Scotland—in Loch Ness. The tests had been going well, but—despite a blanket of absolute secrecy—the vessel has now been damaged. Sabotaged.'

'Do you believe this sabotage is connected with the

attempt to steal the plans of the submarine from the naval office here in London?' I asked.

Mycroft rubbed his several chins thoughtfully before replying, 'Unlikely, Dr Watson. I am inclined to suspect a separate operation—perhaps paid for by the same foreign power, or powers, determined to either discover the secrets of the Bruce-Partington submarine, or else to put it out of operation forever.'

Taking a sip of tea, Mycroft leaned back in his armchair and then continued, 'This has been the most jealously guarded of all Government secrets. You may take it from me that naval warfare becomes impossible within the radius of a Bruce-Partington's operations. Thanks to your efforts, brother Sherlock, attempts to steal the plans have been thwarted. But now the prototype vessel itself is under attack.'

'And you wish me to investigate?' asked the great detective, his steel grey eyes hidden behind half-closed eyelids.

'You are the one man who can clear the matter up,' growled Mycroft, setting down his teacup on the small table at his elbow. 'If you have a fancy to see your name in the next honours list—'

Sherlock Holmes smiled and shook his head.

'I play the game for the game's own sake,' said he. 'But the problem certainly presents some points of interest, and I shall be pleased to look into it.'

'Excellent!' cried Mycroft. 'There is a small Navy cutter—*HMS Drake*—currently moored at Victoria Dock, that is leaving on the morning tide. I am counting on you and Dr Watson being on board. *Drake* will take you directly to Inverness at the head of the Moray Firth. You'll be met at Inverness docks by a carriage from Forgill Castle.'

'Why Forgill Castle?' I asked.

'Because the Duke of Forgill has very kindly provided his family home as a base for the British Navy's secret operations at Loch Ness.'

'Who is in charge of the testing program?' Sherlock inquired.

'The entire naval operation is under the supervision of Commander Lethbridge-Stewart, but the testing itself is being directed personally by the inventors of the submarine—Sir James Partington and Professor Nigel Bruce. There are other people involved—naval officers and engineers—but you'll meet them when you arrive. You are free to leave on tomorrow morning's tide?'

'Most certainly,' said Sherlock Holmes. 'And now, brother Mycroft, I must tell you of my conditions for undertaking this investigation.'

'Conditions?' spluttered Mycroft. 'This is for your country!'

'Nevertheless, there are certain conditions.'

'Such as?'

'You will join us here for Christmas lunch, two weeks from tomorrow—to celebrate the success of our venture. And furthermore, you will provide one fine, plump goose for Mrs Hudson to roast for our Christmas lunch.'

'A goose? That's all you want?'

'But it must be a particularly fine, plump, tender goose. Mrs Hudson has already prepared one of her rich Christmas puddings, but a goose is required if the meal is to be truly memorable.'

'Very well. I shall be here with the goose on Christmas morning. And now I must be off—there are urgent matters awaiting my attention at Whitehall.'

'Two weeks?' I said to Holmes as I closed the door

behind Mycroft. 'Will that be enough?'

'If we can't solve the problem in two weeks then it cannot be solved at all. Now, since we have an early start in the morning, I suggest a relaxing evening.' With those words Holmes took up his violin and began to play.

The next morning, as a pale, grey sun began to creep over the horizon, *HMS Drake* slipped her moorings and began steaming down the Thames towards the North Sea. Holmes and I stood on the forward deck, watching the ghostly, foggy outlines of city buildings slip past. Holmes was wearing his long, grey travelling cloak and deerstalker cap, while I relied on my bowler hat, a thick woollen scarf and my old Army greatcoat to keep out the morning chill.

During the morning Southend passed on our port side as *Drake* turned towards the north, and whatever strange mystery awaited us beneath the dark waters of Loch Ness.

2

Holmes and I travelled light—a single carpetbag sufficed to hold our belongings. The Duke of Forgill's coachman, a giant of a man named Angus MacRanald, dropped our bag into the baggage compartment of the Duke's coach, and then, with a grunt that was less than a welcome, opened the coach door for us.

The journey by sea from London had been uneventful, and all my attempts to get Holmes to speculate on what might be happening at Loch Ness had been unsuccessful.

'Never speculate in advance of the facts, Watson,' he had said repeatedly, 'it is a capital mistake.'

A minute later the wheels of the coach were rumbling over the timbers of the Inverness docks, and we were on our way to Forgill Castle on the shores of Loch Ness.

As the coach rattled along the rough road I asked Holmes, 'Do you know anything about Loch Ness?'

He leaned back against the leather upholstery, rested the tips of his fingers together and closed his eyes as he said, 'It's 22 miles long and about a mile wide. It's part of the Great Glen which runs like a deep crack right across Scotland, from one coast to the other. In fact, it's one of three lochs—or lakes—that nestle in the Great Glen.'

'Very big is it, this Loch Ness?'

'Surveyors estimate that it's almost a thousand feet deep and contains over 250,000 million cubic feet of inky black water. Its mean depth is approximately twice the mean depth of the North Sea.'

'Ideal place to test a secret submarine then.'

'Precisely so, Watson.'

After travelling for some time we passed through the town of Dores, and rattled on down the dusty, rocky road. The shoulders of the road were covered with slowly melting snow, and the air was bitterly cold. The loch was visible from the road as a broad expanse of black water, nestling among hills that towered a thousand feet over it.

Later that afternoon—and 36 hours after leaving London—we rattled through the tiny village of Forgill and came to a halt before the impressive gates of Forgill Castle.

The blood-red light of the setting sun made the ancient stone castle look even more impressive, and rather sinister. Angus MacRanald lifted the iron knocker on the giant timber gates, and pounded it down with a crash that seemed to echo from inside the castle. Several minutes later the gates were opened by an elderly, sour faced butler. He accepted our bag from MacRanald and ushered us inside without saying a word.

We followed the butler down a wide, dark hallway. Then he threw open a heavy door and stood back, indicating that we should enter. As he did so he announced us, saying, 'The gentlemen from London, your grace.'

The room we entered was a library, lined with leather-bound books from floor to ceiling. At the far end of the long room, gathered around a blazing fire, was a group of three men.

Advancing towards us was a grey-haired man wearing a dinner jacket and a kilt of Royal Stewart tartan.

'Mr Holmes, Dr Watson—welcome to Forgill Castle. Step up to the fire and warm yourselves after your journey.'

'It certainly is jolly cold,' I agreed as the butler took our coats and we followed the Duke of Forgill across a vast Turkish carpet to the huge stone fireplace.

'These two gentleman,' said the Duke, 'are Sir James Partington and Professor Nigel Bruce.' Both men were wearing dinner suits. One was tall and thin with brown hair and a shaggy brown beard. The other was shorter and stouter, with white hair and a thick white moustache.

'How do you do,' I responded. 'My name is Dr Watson, and this is Mr Sherlock Holmes.'

'Sherlock Holmes!' exclaimed the tall thin one. 'We're delighted to see you! Aren't we Professor?'

'Absolutely. I say, jolly absolutely. Been beastly, the things that have been happening. Absolutely beastly. But now that you're here, everything's all right, what?'

'Thank you for. your expressions of confidence, gentlemen,' said Holmes. 'I'll do everything in my power to justify them. Perhaps you should begin by telling me exactly what has been going on.'

'Of course, yes, of course,' muttered the stout one. 'Sir James—why don't you fill Mr Holmes in on the problems?'

As the Duke of Forgill offered us comfortable seats close to the fire, and ordered a pot of hot coffee from the butler, Sir James told his story.

'Tomorrow you'll see the vessel that Professor Bruce and I have invented. It's unlike any ship that has ever sailed on any ocean—or under any ocean for that matter. Our vessel is a narrow, steel-hulled craft, exactly 48 feet long and 8 feet wide at its broadest point. When travelling on the surface it's powered by a small, oil-burning steam engine, but when underwater it's driven by an electric motor running off storage batteries.'

9

'What form of attack does your submarine employ?'
Holmes

3

While this conversation was going on, there were other events happening, out on the loch—events of which I learned only much later.

A local fisherman named Donald Taggart was rowing his small wooden dinghy along the edge of the lake. He had spent the night drinking in the village inn at Forgill, and was now rowing back to his cottage on the shore of the loch.

His head was swimming from the whisky he had drunk, and he stopped for a while to rest his oars and catch his breath. As he did so he noticed a disturbance in the middle of the loch. In the bright, blue moonlight he could plainly see that the water in the middle of the loch was in a state of commotion. At first he thought it was two ducks fighting, and then realised that the area of the disturbance was too wide.

Taggart broke out in a cold sweat, grabbed the oars and began to row as hard as he could. For a moment the moon disappeared behind clouds. When it reappeared the disturbance in the water had moved closer.

He heard the sound of splashing, and then large ripples began to rock his small, wooden boat. Taggart shipped his oars and sat very still, hoping that by remaining still and silent he would not attract the attention of whatever was down there, in the loch.

The water settled back down again, and for several minutes the loch remained calm and still. Cautiously Taggart placed his oars back into the inky waters and began to row. As he did so he felt a thump on the bottom of the boat, and a moment later his whole dinghy was lifted up out of the water. The fisherman fell back into the bottom of the boat as it rocked unsteadily on whatever was supporting it.

Terror filled his voice as Taggart screamed aloud. Then whatever was underneath the small boat submerged, and the boat itself dropped back into the water. The terrified man grabbed both oars and rowed as hard as he could.

Five minutes later he reached the shingle beach in front of his cottage. Leaping into the shallow water he pulled his boat high up onto the beach, and then ran towards his house.

He found his teenage daughter Sarah sitting in front of a blazing fire, knitting a woollen shawl. She turned around to see her father standing in the doorway, pale and shaken.

'Father,' she scolded, 'you've been drinking again. You know what mother would say if she were still alive.'

'It's not the drink, girl,' mumbled Taggart, as he slammed the cottage door closed, and staggered towards the fire to warm himself and stop his trembling. 'It's not the drink that has done this.'

'What is it then?'

There was a long pause before Taggart replied, 'It was the beast.'

'You saw it?'

'Well ... not exactly saw it, girl. It was underneath my boat,' explained Taggart, his voice dropping to a hoarse whisper. 'Right underneath. Lifted me out of the water and then dropped me back again.'

'Is this the whisky talking?' asked Sarah, laying aside her

knitting. 'Or did this really happen?'

The fisherman took out a large red handkerchief with white dots, and wiped his pale forehead. 'Let's go and take a look at the dinghy,' he said, after a moment's silence.

Carrying a flickering hurricane lantern Donald and Sarah Taggart walked the short distance from the cottage to the narrow shingle beach. There the small, wooden boat was lying on its side. Sarah knelt down and ran her fingers over deep, fresh scratches in the bottom of the hull.

'Well, you certainly didn't imagine it,' she said to her father. Then, turning towards the inky black waters of the loch she added, 'There is something out there. What it is I can't begin to guess—but there is something.'

While these events were happening Holmes and I were sitting down to dinner at Forgill Castle. In addition to the Duke, Sir James and Professor Bruce, we were joined at the dinner table by three of the Naval officers— Commander Ralph Lethbridge-Stewart, Captain Harry Sullivan and Lieutenant Philip Benton. Sullivan and Benton were two of the crew members of the experimental submarine.

'Tell Mr Holmes and Dr Watson about what happened last week,' said the Duke, as he carved thick, juicy slices from a haunch of roast venison.

'Jolly odd it was, actually,' said Sullivan. 'I was at my command post, in the centre of the vessel, and Benton here was at the helm. Suddenly the nose went down and we began a rapid descent.'

Holmes leaned forward listening intently. The candlelight caught his lean, hawk-like profile, and I could see his steel grey eyes gleaming with interest.

'Captain Sullivan shouted an order,' said Benton, taking up the story. 'He told me to pull the nose up. Well, I tried, but the ship refused to respond to the helm. It was as if we had been caught in a strong current, and our electric motors were powerless to pull against it.'

'Except that there are no currents that pull straight downwards in that fashion,' explained Commander Lethbridge-Stewart. 'At least, to the best of our knowledge there are none.'

'What happened next?' Holmes asked.

'I felt the pressure on the helm suddenly ease,' said Benton. 'The vessel started to respond to my movements of the main wheel and the depth levers. For a while it did, at least.'

'And then it happened again,' Sullivan added. 'I saw the wheel start spinning through Benton's fingers as the vessel went out of control and began a crash dive towards the bottom of the loch.'

'Jolly nasty moment,' I remarked.

'It certainly was, doctor,' agreed Sullivan. 'For several minutes I thought we had breathed our last. It happened several more times—the nose of the vessel diving as we lost control, and then coming up again. Finally the disturbances ceased and we floated to the surface.'

'Then we were able to turn off the electric motors—which are not very powerful—start the steam engine and bring the ship back to the castle's jetty,' concluded Benton.

'We used the crane to haul it out of the water,' explained Lethbridge-Stewart, 'and found the submarine had been sabotaged.'

'As I explained before,' continued Sir James, 'on the outside of the vessel are tubes that carry the wires operating the steering controls. Those tubes had been torn off.'

'And you didn't notice the damage before you took her out?' asked Holmes.

'Well, when she's sitting deep in the water, it's not the sort of thing you would notice,' explained Captain Sullivan. 'The damage only became apparent when the crane lifted her out of the water.'

'So,' continued Holmes, 'you can't be certain whether the submarine was damaged while it was tied up at the jetty or while it was out in the loch?'

'I suppose we can't,' Benton agreed. 'But surely sir, you're not suggesting that the damage was caused by an attack out in the loch.'

'Nonsense!' snorted Professor Bruce. 'For that to happen there would have to be enemy agents with their own submarine somewhere out there in the loch. Preposterous! You can't really believe that, surely?'

'I form no conclusions until all the facts are in my hands,' Holmes replied quietly. 'And at this stage I am ruling out no possibilities.'

4

After making arrangements to inspect the submarine immediately after breakfast, Holmes and I were shown up to our rooms and retired for the night.

My room was on the side of the castle that overlooked the loch. I changed into my nightshirt and blew out the candle. As I was about to climb into bed, I pulled back the curtains to take a look at Loch Ness in the moonlight.

The waters of the loch were calm, with barely a ripple disturbing the placid surface. The moonlight painted a pale blue path across the still waters. As I watched, a dark shape passed through the reflected moonlight. For a moment I thought that what I was looking at was the hull of an upturned rowing boat, and I feared that one of the locals had come to grief in a boating accident.

As the object—whatever it was—drifted out of the beam of moonlight and into the darkness, a second one appeared. It too passed down the loch, sending out shallow ripples as it moved, and disappeared into the darkness. What had I seen? Two dark humps? Floating logs? Mats of rotting vegetation? I couldn't be sure.

I stood looking at the mysterious loch until the bitter cold of the December night forced me to abandon my vigil and climb beneath of the covers of a warm bed.

While I slept there were other events afoot, of which I was to learn later.

The little village of Forgill was plunged into darkness. All lights were extinguished and the inhabitants slept peacefully in their beds. Or, almost all the inhabitants. One dark figure slipped past a cottage, and crept in stealthy silence towards the back of the village inn.

There the man waited in the darkness, smoking a pipe, until the clock in the village church chimed 2 am. A few minutes after the clock had finished chiming a second dark figure slipped out of the back door of the inn.

'You kept me waiting long enough,' whispered the first. 'I've almost frozen to death.'

'Keep your voice down! I had to wait until I could be sure that everyone was asleep. Do you have it?'

'Not yet. But they have their strange boat out of the water, undergoing repairs. That should give me a chance to get my hands on it.'

'When do you think that will be?'

'I can't be sure. Meet me here two nights from now. And bring the money you promised. I won't hand it over until I see the money.'

'I'll be here, and I'll have the money—never you fear.'

With those words the two dark figures ended their whispered conversation, and crept off in their separate directions.

In the morning, after a breakfast of hot porridge and hot coffee, Commander Lethbridge-Stewart led Holmes and me around the high stone walls of Forgill Castle until we were standing on a tumble of rocks, on the very edge of Loch Ness itself.

'As you can see,' said Lethbridge-Stewart, 'the castle has been built right up to the water's edge. Just beyond where we're standing, extending from the rear wall of the castle is the jetty, and just a little further beyond that is the crane that we use to raise and lower the submarine for repairs. Follow me.'

He led the way over the rocks under the shadow of the great, stone wall. A moment later the wooden jetty came in sight, with a large, marine crane bending over it—looking like a strange, primeval bird of prey. Hanging in chains from the crane was the long, sleek, black hull of the submarine.

Standing on the jetty, supervising operations, was Captain Sullivan. Beside him were two men we had not yet met. As we followed Lethbridge-Stewart across the timber planking of the jetty he introduced the two strangers as Graham Kirton, a naval architect, and Jock Munro, the engineer on the project.

We all shook hands, and then the engineer, Munro, began explaining the damage that had been done to the underwater vessel.

'You'll notice, Mr Holmes, that there are one inch steel pipes along both sides of the submarine. These pipes are packed with grease, and steel cables run through them controlling the steering apparatus of the vessel. Well, you can see for yourself what damage has been done to those pipes. Although, what would have had the strength to do that ...'

His voice trailed away in puzzlement. The pipes were twisted and bent into fantastic shapes. Sections of the pipes were missing completely—torn away from the brackets that welded them to the steel hull.

Holmes stepped forward and grasped one piece of bent and twisted piping. Seizing it firmly with both hands he tensed his muscles and tried to bend it back into shape.

'There's no point in trying to ...' began Munro. But then he stopped in amazement as the metal shifted and straightened under Holmes' powerful grip.

'Well, I never,' murmured the engineer. 'You obviously have more power in those long, thin hands of yours than I would have thought possible. Here, Mr Holmes—wipe your hands on this rag.'

'What was the point of that?' I asked Holmes as he cleaned his hands.

'The point Watson was to discover for myself just how much effort would be required to twist and tear those pipes. And as you saw for yourself, the answer is—a great deal.'

We then walked further down the jetty, closely examining the blackened steel hull of the submarine.

'Well, what do you think, Mr Holmes? Dr Watson?' asked Lethbridge-Stewart, a note of pride in his voice. 'In her own strange way she's quite a vessel isn't she?'

'Most impressive,' I muttered. 'Most impressive indeed.'

A cold, December wind was whistling off the loch, carrying a damp chilling spray, as Holmes pulled out his pocket lens and began examining the hull more closely.

'Mr Munro,' said Holmes, calling the engineer to join us. 'What do you make of these scratches?'

Jock Munro borrowed Holmes' lens and examined a long series of shallow, parallel grooves in the steel hull.

'I don't know what to make of them, Mr Holmes,' he said at length, 'and that's the honest truth. I've only seen marks like that once before in my life.'

'And when was that?' I asked.

'When I was serving in the South Seas—on a Navy frigate operating out of Sydney, Australia. On that occasion the marks had been caused by the attack of a giant shark.'

19

5

'A giant shark indeed!' sneered Commander Lethbridge-Stewart. 'Sometimes, Jock, your imagination takes my breath away.'

'I was just making a comparison, sir. That's all.'

'I should hope so. I certainly hope that you're not suggesting there might be a giant shark in Loch Ness?'

'Certainly not, sir,' said Jock Munro respectfully, and then he added under his breath, 'the water is too cold for a shark—that's why.'

Lethbridge-Stewart showed us the circular hatch in the top of the submarine, through which the crew members entered.

'It takes four crew in total,' he explained, 'a helmsman, an engineer, a weapons officer, and a commanding officer.'

'How well guarded is this vessel?' asked Holmes, as the wind whipped his long, grey travelling cloak around his tall, lean figure.

'We have a two man patrol walking around the walls of the castle both day and night, Mr Holmes,' said Captain Harry Sullivan. 'To be honest, we hadn't felt it necessary to post a guard on the jetty beside the submarine. We were quite confident that our operations here were a well kept secret.'

'A false confidence as it turns out,' muttered Lethbridge-Stewart bitterly.

'You suspect a foreign power of this sabotage?' I asked.

'Who else could it be, Dr Watson?' Sullivan responded with a shrug of his shoulders.

'In that case,' I continued, 'have there been any strangers in the neighbourhood in recent days? Any foreigners?'

'No foreigners,' said Sullivan. 'The only stranger in the district is a retired bishop—and you couldn't find anyone more English than Alfred Milton. He's staying at the local inn.'

'A bishop, eh?'

'A missionary bishop. Retired from somewhere in New Guinea, or so I gather.'

'So, where do we begin to look for the saboteurs?' I asked Holmes.

'You sum up the problem nicely, Watson. We shall begin in the village—perhaps some of the locals have noticed other strangers or foreigners in the district. Hello—who's this? Were you expecting visitors, Lethbridge-Stewart?'

I looked in the direction indicated by Holmes, and saw one of the local fishing boats approaching the jetty.

'Ah, that's only Taggart,' explained the Commander. 'He has an agreement to supply the castle with fresh fish.'

On board the small fishing boat were a weather beaten man and a teenage girl. Certain similarities between their facial features suggested that she might be his daughter, and this, indeed, turned out to be the case. Jock Munro caught the rope the girl threw up to the jetty, and made it fast. Then the two of them climbed out, carrying a large, wicker basket between them.

'Good morning to you, Commander,' said the fisherman, with a respectful nod of his head, then he glanced in our direction as suspicion clouded his face.

'Morning Taggart,' responded Lethbridge-Stewart. 'These two gentleman are guests at the castle—Dr Watson and Mr Sherlock Holmes.'

'Sherlock Holmes? The detective?' cried out the girl, a delighted expression on her face.

'At your service,' Holmes replied, with a polite nod of his head.

'Pa, tell them what happened last night. It's just the sort of thing that would interest a detective, like Mr Holmes.'

'Hush, girl,' her father snarled, looking embarrassed and annoyed. 'We'll no be bothering the gentlemen.'

'If something unusual has happened,' remarked Holmes, 'I'd very much like to hear about it.'

It took a good deal of insistence on Holmes' part before the fisherman, Donald Taggart, for that was the man's name, would narrate the events of the night before. When he did so it was reluctantly, and with ill grace.

'How do you account for what happened?' asked Holmes, when the man had told his story.

'I can't account for it at all, sir. Loch Ness is a strange place. It always has been. Strange things happen here. It's best not to try to explain them. And it's best not to be on the Loch, late at night, and full of whisky. What happened to me was my own fault, and I'll take care that it doesn't happen again.'

'How do you explain it?' Holmes asked again, turning this time to Sarah Taggart, the man's daughter.

'There's something in the Loch, Mr Holmes, of that I'm certain. Some creature. There have been a number of strange incidents. People don't like to talk about them, but they happen all the same. What happened to Pa last night is only the latest.'

'Quiet girl! You talk too much,' snapped her father. 'Now help me with this basket—we have fish to deliver to the castle.'

With that they left, carrying the dripping wet basket between them—the man clearly pleased to escape from our company, the girl rather more reluctant.

'You'd do well not to pay too much attention to the local superstitions, Mr Holmes,' remarked Lethbridge-Stewart, with an indulgent smile.

'I have a favour to ask, Commander,' said Holmes.

'I'll do what I can. What's the favour?'

'I would like to travel on this submarine, when it's repaired and fully operational again.'

'Do you think you'll learn anything important in that way?' asked Captain Sullivan.

'I'm not certain,' Holmes responded, rubbing his long chin thoughtfully. 'But it may well be there are certain pieces of information that can be acquired in no other way.'

'In that case, Holmes, I'd like to come too,' I volunteered.

'Good old Watson,' said Holmes heartily.

'Well, I suppose there's no reason why not,' Lethbridge-Stewart said slowly. 'What do you think, Harry?'

'It should be safe enough, sir,' replied Sullivan. 'Mr Holmes and Dr Watson can take the positions usually occupied by the weapons officer and the engineer—and we'll take them for a short run in the Loch.'

'Splendid—that's settled then,' said the Commander, rubbing his hands together.

'And now, Watson—how about a walk in the morning

sunshine?' suggested Sherlock Holmes.

'Certainly, Holmes. Where to?'

'To the village, Watson. You and I are going hunting for spies and saboteurs.'

6

The morning was filled by a thin, bleak sunshine that did nothing to ease the bone-chilling winter cold.

'Will we really find the saboteurs we are looking for in the village, Holmes?' I asked as we walked down that narrow, solitary country road.

'Quite possibly not, Watson. But the local villagers may have knowledge that is useful to us.'

On one side of the road on which we walked was a rocky, heather covered slope leading down to the inky black waters of Loch Ness. On the other side was a rising slope of rugged ground, filled with long grasses, heather, exposed boulders and stunted trees, known as Tulloch Moor. This ground rose to a peak called Dun Dearduil. Although we didn't know it at the time, as we walked from the castle to the village we were being watched from a rocky crag on Dun Dearduil.

The watcher was a thin, rat-faced man with a thick, black beard. He lay on a shelf of exposed rock holding powerful field glasses to his eyes. He was spying on our movements, and on all the comings and goings at Forgill Castle—as he had been doing for the past month. He was wearing a heavy tweed Norfolk jacket, with stout boots and leather leggings that came almost to his knees.

'So, it is them,' he muttered to himself. 'I had expected them to arrive sooner or later.'

He raised the field glasses to his eyes and watched for several minutes. 'The program of attacks will have to be speeded up,' he thought. Then he pulled a small notebook out of his pocket and scribbled a hasty note.

By the time he resumed his vigil, Holmes and I had walked around the curve of the road and had vanished from his sight. The watcher rose from his hiding place, brushed the loose dirt and leaves from his jacket, and began making his way down the narrow track that led from the top of the hill.

As he walked he thought what a pleasure it would be if, as well as disabling the submarine, he could also kill Sherlock Holmes.

All this we were unaware of at the time—although it wasn't long before we discovered that we were both in deadly danger.

We entered the small village of Forgill, walked past several, neat little cottages with highland flowers growing in their front gardens, passed the old stone church—or the kirk, as the locals called it—at the centre of the village, and stopped in front of the local inn. There, sitting on wooden benches in the pale sunshine in front of the mellow stone walls of the inn, was a group of local fishermen.

Holmes quickly introduced us, and engaged them in conversation about strangers or foreigners in the district.

'Strangers? I don't think so, sir,' replied one man, who appeared to be the spokesman for the group. 'As for foreigners ... well ... I suppose there might be some foreigners with the circus.'

'There is a circus in the district?' Holmes asked.

'Aye. They passed through here a month ago.'

'And they haven't returned?'

'Not yet, but they said they would. I spoke to a man on one of the circus wagons, and he told me they were on their way to Fort William, and then would be working their way back up the lochs.'

'Aye, that's so,' chipped in another man. 'My cousin told me they've already been at Clunes, and Kilfinan, and Invergarry.'

'Most interesting,' Holmes remarked quietly, staring into the distance through half closed eyelids.

'And there've been no other strangers or foreigners?' I asked.

'None at all, Dr Watson,' replied the first man as he lit his pipe.

Just then a short, stout man emerged from the front door of the inn. He had a thick mane of grey hair, and a round, florid face.

'Good morning, gentlemen,' he said cheerfully. 'Would you two gentlemen be Sherlock Holmes and Dr Watson by any chance?'

We acknowledged that we were.

'I'm delighted to meet you both,' he said heartily, as he shook our hands. 'I've read your stories in the *Strand Magazine*, Dr Watson. And as for your exploits, well, even in the wilds of New Guinea we had heard of your reputation, Mr Holmes.'

Holmes' vanity was always pleased by news of the spread of his fame.

'Allow me to introduce myself,' the man continued. 'My name is Alfred Milton—formerly Bishop of Madang in New Guinea, now retired.'

'A Lutheran bishop?'

'Whatever makes you think that? No, Church of England—that's me. Always have been, always will be.'

'What brings you to this part of the world, Mr Milton?' Holmes asked.

'Childhood memories. Some sixty years ago I passed through the Great Glen when touring Scotland with my aunt and uncle. The memory has stayed with me all through the years. And I made myself a promise that one day I would come back and see Loch Ness again. And here I am.'

'How long have been in the district?' asked Holmes.

'Let me see now ... a month or so, I would guess ... perhaps a little more.'

'And how much longer do you intend staying?'

'A few more days. Perhaps a week,' replied Milton.

'You have now satisfied your childhood curiosity?'

'That I have, Mr Holmes—that I have.'

At this point the conversation was interrupted by the sound of running feet. We looked up and saw young Sarah Taggart hurrying down the narrow village street towards us, with her father not far behind.

'What's up, lassie?' asked the fisherman we had been talking to, taking the pipe out of his mouth and hurrying towards her.

'It's ... our ... neighbour,' she puffed, gasping for breath.

'Robbie Stevenson? The water bailiff?'

'Aye.'

'What about him?'

'He's missing,' said Donald Taggart, as he caught up with his daughter. 'Out on the Loch somewhere—and missing.'

'How do you know?' asked genial old Alfred Milton.

'I went to take him some eggs this morning,' explained

Sarah Taggart, 'and his housekeeper told me he had not been home all night. She said she was beginning to worry. Apparently he went out in his boat about sunset, heading towards the centre of the Loch, and he hasn't returned. Well, because of what happened to Pa the other night, we thought ...'

'Quite right, lassie,' interrupted one of the fisherman.

'Come along lads, we'll have to mount a search.'

7

As the fishermen ran towards their boats moored at the town jetty, Holmes and I volunteered to join the search party. We ended up in the same boat as the two Taggarts—father and daughter.

Donald Taggart and I pulled on the oars, while Holmes took up a watching position in the stern of the boat, and young Sarah did the same in the bow. The fishing boats spread out in a broad pattern across the width of the Loch—slowly moving towards the western end.

We had not rowed far when a cold, white mist began to rise from the surface of the inky, black water. I was glad to be rowing, for the exercise kept me warm, and counteracted the chilling influence of the cold, white fingers of mist that lifted themselves from the Loch and seemed to wrap themselves around us.

Before long the mist was so thick we could not see the other boats.

'Does the mist always rise as quickly as this on Loch Ness?' asked Sherlock Holmes.

'Aye, that it does, Mr Holmes,' grunted Donald Taggart as he pulled on his oar. 'You have to have a good sense of direction to be a fisherman on this Loch.'

As we rowed we could hear the voices of the other

fishermen in the other boats as they called, 'Robbie! Robbie! Can you hear us? Where are you lad?'

But the other boats were all invisible in the spreading, thickening mist, and the disembodied voices floated across the water like the cries of lost souls.

'This Robbie Stevenson who has gone missing,' began Holmes.

'The water bailiff? Aye, what about him?' said Taggart.

'How well did he know these waters?'

'He knew the Loch as well as any man living, Mr Holmes.'

'Then he couldn't have got lost? Or been taken by surprise by the weather conditions?'

'Oh, the Loch can take anyone by surprise, sir,' grunted the fisherman, as he continued rowing. 'Loch Ness can be dead calm at one moment, and filled with waves that can smash your boat to pieces half an hour later. It's the Great Glen, you see—it acts like a funnel in the way it tunnels the wind down onto the water.'

'Stop your rowing,' shouted Sarah from the bow of the boat. 'There's something ahead in the water.'

Taggart and I rested our oars in the water and let the boat drift. A moment later Sarah said, 'It's only some matted weed floating on the surface. You might as well start rowing again.' Her voice sounded disappointed—and worried.

The voices of the other searchers became fainter and fainter as they spread out across the Loch. 'Robbie! Robbie, lad, can you hear us?' they shouted—dim voices from invisible people lost in the deep, white mist that filled the air and filled our lungs, and chilled us to the very bones.

'How can you be sure we won't get lost in this wretched mist?' I grunted between strokes on my oar.

'I can't be,' admitted the fisherman beside me. 'But I have a fair idea of where we are.'

'Pa's being modest,' said his daughter loyally. 'He has the best sense of direction of any fisherman on the Loch.'

'What was that?' snapped Holmes urgently.

'Your ears are sharper than mine, Holmes,' I said. 'I can't hear a thing.'

'Listen!' he said.

Taggart and I stopped rowing, rested on our oars and listened.

'There it is again!' insisted Holmes.

'I didn't hear a thing,' I admitted.

'Quiet. Listen,' said the fisherman beside me.

The four of us sat very still, as the boat slowly rocked up and down on the gentle swell. Somehow the heavy mist seemed to have deadened our sense of hearing as well as our sense of sight. Then the sound came again—and this time I heard it.

It was a deep throated cry. Perhaps more like a rumble than a cry.

'Have you heard that sound before, Mr Taggart?' asked Holmes.

'Aye, sir, that I have. And I don't like it at all.' His voice was trembling as he spoke.

'It's the water kelpies,' whispered Sarah Taggart quietly.

Then it came again. This time it was a deep throated roar—and there was no avoiding the note of menace in that sound.

There could be no doubt about it: there was an animal, a very large animal, somewhere in the waters of Loch Ness—and it was not very far away from us.

At that moment, in a small, secret boatshed, at the far

western end of the Loch, a meeting was going on that was to have a profound impact upon us before too long.

The man who had been spying on us from the peak of Dun Dearduil was meeting with one of his confederates.

'Is it now fully active?'

'As far as I can tell, it is,' replied the short, nervous man who was with him.

'Can you control it?'

'Only very slightly. It will respond to certain sounds and certain smells—but not always.'

'Can you make it more aggressive?' asked the rat-faced man, with the thick, black beard.

'We can use the high-pitched underwater whistle that we trained it with.'

'What effect will that have?'

'I can't be sure. But if we use it repeatedly it might become more agitated, more active, and more likely to attack.'

'Then try it. We must speed this process up.'

'Yes, sir.'

I was to learn of that deadly planning meeting only much later. While it was going on, I was out in a small fishing boat on Loch Ness with Sherlock Holmes, and Donald and Sarah Taggart, listening to a savage animal, whose roar echoed across the waves towards us.

'What is it?' asked Holmes, in his quiet, calm voice.

'It is the creature,' replied Taggart, his voice little more than a murmur.

'What creature?' I asked, feeling alarmed.

'The creature of the Loch. What Sarah called the "water kelpie". Very few folk have heard its cry and lived to tell the tale.'

Just then its roar came again—but this time it was further away, and growing fainter as we listened.

'It's leaving us,' gasped Sarah, in a hopeful whisper.

The next roar was little more than a dim echo from some great distance across the water. 'Yes, child, you're right,' muttered Donald Taggart. 'God has taken mercy upon our souls.'

'Upon our bodies, more likely,' I said. 'If that thing has teeth to match its roar, I wouldn't fancy meeting it up close.'

Further discussion of what we had heard was prevented by Sarah's sudden cry of alarm, 'Wreckage ahead—in the water.'

Once again the fisherman and I lifted our oars and let the boat drift. A moment later we heard the clunk of something solid hitting the side of the boat. With some difficulty Sarah pulled it out of the water.

Holmes clambered forward to examine what she had found.

'This is part of a boat,' he said. 'It's certainly no ordinary driftwood. Start rowing again—but slowly.'

Over the next ten minutes we found a dozen small pieces which were all that was left of a timber rowing boat. Then something soft thudded against the side of our craft. Holmes leaned forward over the gunwale to look at it, then he said, 'Sarah, you had better go to the seat in the stern of the boat, while I pull this body on board.'

Sarah did as she was told, then Holmes, Donald Taggart, and I pulled on board the soaking wet body that was all that was left of the missing man.

'Is this Robbie Stevenson?' asked Holmes.

'Aye—that's him. Or what's left of him,' affirmed Taggart.

'What killed him, Watson?' Holmes asked, turning towards me.

I knelt down in the boat and conducted a cursory examination.

'Impossible to say,' I responded after a few minutes. 'The body has been too badly mangled to be able to tell.'

8

Back at the town jetty Holmes and I stood back and watched as a group of the local fishermen lifted Robbie Stevenson's remains out of Donald Taggart's boat, and laid the corpse on the village's stone jetty.

As we stood and watched a tall, broad-shouldered man made his way through the crowd of onlookers.

'Ah, Dr Cameron,' said one of the fisherman. 'You'd better look at this—and tell us what killed poor wee Robbie.'

The doctor put his medical bag down on the flagstones and made a brief examination of the corpse.

'I'll have to conduct an autopsy, lads,' said the doctor as he straightened up. 'Take the body along to my house—I'll conduct a proper examination there.'

Stepping forward I introduced Holmes and myself.

'Mr Holmes, Dr Watson—I'm delighted to meet you,' said Dr Cameron, shaking our hands.

'Doctor,' said Holmes, 'I wonder if you would be so kind as to allow Watson here to be present at the autopsy.'

'Of course! Of course! I am more than happy to welcome Dr Watson as a professional colleague.'

We arranged to meet at Dr Cameron's surgery in half an hour and then he departed to complete the last of his morning rounds. Holmes and I made our way back up to the main street of the small village, walking in thoughtful silence.

We were interrupted by the shrill sound of a loud female voice.

'I knew he was doomed! Anyone who goes out onto the Loch at night is doomed—doomed!'

Standing before us was a most unusual woman. Wrapped in half a dozen shawls of different colours, she had a mass of unruly hair with wild flowers in it, and a wild, wide-eyed expression on her face.

'The creature has returned to the Loch, and we are all doomed!' she continued in her strange, shrill voice.

We were standing in the small square in front of the village inn, and one of the local fishermen tugged at Holmes' elbow and explained quietly, 'That's Constance White. Some people around here say that she's fey—that she has the second sight, you understand.'

Holmes turned towards the woman and began to speak, 'Miss White? My name is ...'

'I know what your name is good sir,' she interrupted. 'I know that you are an outsider, and that you have joined the other outsiders who are disturbing the spirit of the Loch.'

'How do you know?' asked Holmes gently.

'Because I have seen it!' cried Constance White, in a loud shriek.

'Seen it?' I asked.

'I have seen the creature.'

'This is most interesting, m'dear,' I continued. 'Tell us more about it.'

'It is older than time and darker than night. Its green scales drip with the slime of the secret caves at the bottom of the Loch. Its jaws are filled with a thousand teeth that are sharper than razors. Its eyes are blood red, and it looks upon the sons of men with a consuming hatred.'

'You saw this?' I asked.

'In a vision,' she cried. 'I saw it all in a vision.' With a swirl of her skirts Constance White spun around and walked away, still talking loudly to herself.

'She's balmy, Holmes,' I remarked. 'Absolutely potty.'

'Quite possibly, Watson. Or, equally possibly, what we've just seen is a very clever form of "madness". Which it is remains to be seen.'

'Well, I think she's potty.'

Just then Dr Cameron arrived, having completed the last of his morning rounds, and I accompanied him to his surgery to conduct the autopsy on the poor unfortunate Robbie Stevenson.

While we were doing this, Holmes returned to the castle alone. What happened when he got there, he told me about later.

'Ah, Sherlock Holmes! Just the man I'm looking for,' said Commander Lethbridge-Stewart as Holmes entered the library. Also in the room, standing by the big fireplace, was the Duke of Forgill.

'You have news for me?' inquired Holmes.

'I have indeed,' replied the Commander. 'Jock Munro tells me the repairs to the submarine will be completed by dusk, and that Captain Sullivan will be able to take the ship out first thing tomorrow morning.'

'That is good news.'

'Precisely. And in the light of your earlier request, I am now offering you and Dr Watson places on board the submarine for tomorrow morning's cruise.'

'Thank you, Commander. I accept with pleasure.'

'You don't mean to say that you intend travelling on the damned tin sardine, do you?' interrupted the Duke of Forgill, turning his back on the fire.

'That is exactly what I intend,' replied Holmes.

'Take my advice, Mr Holmes,' said the Duke earnestly, 'and forget any such plans.'

'Why do you say that?'

'You may dismiss me as a superstitious Scotsman—and, undoubtedly I am—but after the death of Robbie Stevenson I fear the Loch is not a safe place.'

'In what sense.'

'When I was just a wee bairn, growing up in this very castle, my old nurse used to tell me stories about the creatures that dwelt in the Loch. I've never fully believed in such tales, but I've never been able to fully forget them either. The Loch is very large, and very old, and it's peat-filled waters are as dark as night. Anything could be down there. I have come to the conclusion that these submarine tests should be moved to a safer locality. And I strongly advise you not to travel on that wretched vessel. Not tomorrow, and not at any time.'

At that point I entered the room, having just returned from Dr Cameron's surgery.

'Ah, Watson,' said Holmes, avoiding the necessity of responding to the Duke's advice. 'What news from the autopsy?'

'Stevenson was attacked by some animal—there can be no doubt about that.'

'Fascinating. And did the autopsy suggest what kind of animal the attacker might be?'

'Unfortunately not. Something very large, but unlike any creature that either Cameron or I had come across before. You see, there were no teeth marks on the body. Instead, there were strange, round, red marks, interspersed with razor-like cuts and scratches. On top of which. every bone in the dead man's body was broken.'

'Every bone?'

'Exactly, Holmes. That poor man was crushed to death.'

9

Something ancient was moving beneath the waters of the Loch. Its thoughts were the dark thoughts, the simple thoughts, of an ancient creature out of the primeval past. It knew every part of the Loch as well as it knew every scale on its twisted claws. And somewhere in the dark recesses of its simple, ancient brain, it knew that all was not right. All was not as it should be.

Silently and powerfully it moved through the black waters at the bottom of the Loch. But its dark thoughts were troubled. Its ancient home—its home since the dawn of time—had been invaded. Its slow and primitive thought patterns were coming to understand that it was no longer alone in the Loch. There was something else in these waters—something alien.

Its huge, sinuous body twisted and turned with discomfort. This was its home—and its home had been invaded. The ancient thing in the Loch trembled with anger. The alien would have to go. It would have to be driven out of the ancient creature's territory. The creature's huge body settled into the mud at the bottom of the Loch and brooded on dark and terrible thoughts.

That afternoon Holmes and I again visited the small village of Forgill.

'Why have we come back again?' I asked Holmes, as we entered the cosy, wood-panelled front room of the village inn.

'Because our task here is to find and stop those who are behind the spying and sabotage.'

'Gentlemen!' cried a hearty voice behind us, interrupting our conversation. We turned around to find Dr Cameron approaching.

'Well, have you given any further thought to the findings of our autopsy? What did you make of the results?' he asked as he took a seat at our table.

'I don't know what to make of it,' I remarked, while Holmes maintained a thoughtful silence. 'Do you really think there might be some sort of creature out there in the Loch?' I asked.

'The locals certainly believe so,' replied Cameron. 'In fact, they have held that belief for many years. The first recorded sighting of the beast goes all the way back to the 6th century when the Abbot of the Isle of Iona wrote a biography of St Colomba. In that book he tells how the saint arrived on the banks of Loch Ness and found some men preparing to bury a friend who had been bitten to death by a water monster while he was swimming.'

'Like Robbie Stevenson?' I suggested.

'Perhaps. At any rate the saint ordered one of his own monks to swim across the Loch. The monster heard the splashing and swam towards him, at which point—according to the old book—the saint made the sign of the cross and commanded the creature to go away.'

'And ...?'

'And the terrified monster obeyed.' Dr Cameron took a sip from his glass of stout and then resumed his story, 'Of course there are many local legends and folktales. For instance, folk here talk about the "water kelpies". Well, "kelpie" is the local word for "faerie" so you can make of that what you will. And for many generations, going back for centuries, local fisherman have had tales about what they call "water horses". But, of course, these things may be mere legend.'

'What do you think, doctor?' asked Holmes, a glint in his steel grey eyes.

'What I think is that my own father once saw it. Or saw something.' He took another sip and then continued. 'It happened 25 years ago. He told me that he saw something that looked like an upturned boat, but moving at great speed, wriggling and churning up the waters.'

'What about yourself—have you ever seen it?'

'Not I. But I have a patient, a crofter named Alex McDonald who claims to have seen the beast—not once, but twice. The first time he was out fishing with a friend. They were up at the north end of the Loch, not far from an old quarry, when they noticed two black humps about half a mile away.'

'Could have been anything,' I remarked.

'Possibly,' agreed Cameron, 'but Alex had a much more definite sighting several years later. He was driving his farm cart towards Loch End at about lunchtime. He came to a spot in the road where the trees were very short and leafless, and this gave him a good, clear view over the water. There, about 600 yards away, he says that he saw, quite clearly, a neck and head sticking out of the water by about 3 feet. It was dark brown or black, he told me, and the head was flat. He moved his cart further down the road for a better view, but by the time he stopped again the thing had disappeared. He could see many miles up the Loch towards Urquhart Bay and, he insisted, there were no boats in sight. He was very sure of what he saw. He told me he waited there for another hour and a half to see if the thing would reappear.'

'And did it?'

'No, it did not. And there are other stories. I'll tell you something Donald Taggart told me many years ago—when he was a young man, long before Sarah was born. It's an incident he never talks about now, but he told me all about it at the time. It seems that Donald and a friend were standing on the stone jetty at Foyers, just a little further around the Loch from here. The water was calm and there wasn't a boat in sight. Suddenly, about 300 yards off shore, there was a great churning of the water—more commotion than a fish could make—then a five foot length of neck appeared with spray flying everywhere. Donald told me at the time that he observed it for 20 seconds as it began to move away before diving back beneath the water in a sort of curious sideways motion.'

Our only response was silence, so Dr Cameron continued, 'Fifteen years ago I treated some children, two girls and a boy, who had been frightened by the sight of a large animal on the land ...'

'On the land?' I repeated, puzzled.

'Indeed. They described an animal the size and colour of an elephant waddling down the slopes and into the Loch. They said it disappeared underwater.'

'You clearly have a theory of your own,' said Holmes. 'So, perhaps, doctor, you would be kind enough to share it with us.'

'Well, I believe,' said Cameron in a conspiratorial tone, leaning across the table towards us. 'I believe there is something in the Loch: a surviving plesiosaurus—or, rather, a small family of them—trapped in the Loch 7,500 years ago when it became cut off from the sea by local volcanic activity. You see, my theory is that back in the Jurassic period these plesiosaurus-like creatures used Loch Ness as a breeding ground. As it slowly changed from saltwater to freshwater they evolved with it.'

Our strange conversation with Dr Cameron came to an abrupt end when two strangers walked into the inn and demanded a drink. They were both dark haired, unshaven men with vicious, unpleasant faces.

'From the circus,' whispered Cameron, nodding over his shoulder to where the two men stood at the bar. 'They went through here with their wagons some four weeks ago.'

A hush had fallen over the inn, so Cameron lowered his voice even more to add, 'People around here don't take kindly to strangers.'

10

Back at Forgill Castle, as I learned later, Angus MacRanald, the Duke's coachman, was at that time making his way around the high, stone outer wall of the castle, towards the water's edge.

When he reached the tumble of boulders lapped by the black waters of Loch Ness, he dropped down into the shadows and moved ahead slowly and cautiously. The sun had set and thick clouds filled the sky. He had to grope his way forward carefully in the dark.

At last he reached the timbers of the jetty. He stood up and looked around. He could see and hear nothing—except for the faint lapping of ripples against the wooden piers of the jetty. He moved silently and cautiously down the jetty towards the submarine, which had been lowered by the crane back into the water.

MacRanald reached a point where he could hear the dull thuds of the underwater ship bumping against the jetty. With only the sound to guide him in that pitch blackness he reached into his pocket and drew out a heavy spanner.

As he clambered up the side of the floating submarine, his spanner clattered noisily against the metal plates, and suddenly there was a voice from the end of jetty demanding, 'Who's there? Who is that?'

Angus MacRanald froze where he was. But again the voice came, 'I know you're there. And I must warn you that I'm armed.'

'It's only me—the coachman,' shouted MacRanald in reply.

'Oh, I see. It's you, is it?' Angus recognised the voice as belonging to Professor Nigel Bruce, one of the two inventors of the strange vessel.

A moment later there was the flicker of a match, followed by the lighting of a candle.

'You gave me quite a start,' said Bruce, as he approached. 'It's my turn to stand guard, you see. With my trusty 303 Lee Enfield rifle, I was sitting with my back against one of the piers, but the wind blew out my candle, and then, well, I think I must have dropped off to sleep.'

'It's a good thing I came and woke you up again,' growled MacRanald.

'Yes ... yes, I suppose it is. I say, why did you come?'

'His grace asked me to come and see if there was anything I could fetch for you. A nip of whisky to keep out the cold, perhaps?'

'Sounds very nice, I must say. But on the whole I suppose I'd better not. I'd just fall asleep again, what? Thanks all the same.'

'I'll be getting back to the castle then,' snarled MacRanald as he turned and left.

'Strange fellow,' muttered Bruce to himself, as the coachman departed.

As Holmes and I walked back from the village to the castle that night, we were whipped by an icy wind that blew off the Loch. For some time we had to find our way up the road in complete darkness, then there was a break in the clouds, and pale blue moonlight lit the way and made our journey easier.

'The moon was a ghostly galleon, tossed upon stormy seas,' I quoted.

'What was that, Watson?'

'Oh, nothing Holmes. Just a bit of poetry I picked up once.'

The wind-whipped cloud moved on and the moon disappeared once more.

'We're almost at the castle, Holmes. Another quarter of a mile and we should be standing in front of a nice, blazing fire.'

'Quiet, Watson!'

'What is it, Holmes?'

'Didn't you hear it?'

'Hear it? I'm afraid I didn't hear a blessed thing. Except for this screeching wind, of course.'

'Quiet. Listen carefully.'

We both stood still and listened. When the wind died a little I could hear something: the sound of shrubs and bushes being pushed aside—or, possibly, trodden under foot.

'What is it, Holmes?'

'I'm not sure.'

'Could someone have followed us from the inn?'

Then there was a definite thump, as of something large and soft on the roadway, and I became aware of a smell—a strong odour of dampness and slime.

'Quiet, Watson—if we don't move it may not notice us.'

'Whatever you say, old chap.'

There was a small break in the clouds, and for just a few seconds the road was lit by pale blue light. In those few seconds I saw something stretched across the road ahead—a trunk or a neck, followed by a grey slimy body, at least six feet high, moving across the road in jerks, like a caterpillar. Then the moon was gone, and we were plunged into utter darkness once more.

'What on earth was that, Holmes?'

'Sshh Watson. I'm not sure we want to attract its attention.'

Attract its attention? Suddenly I realised what Holmes was saying—we had no way of knowing how hostile this creature would be on land. We both stood as still as we could, frozen to the spot.

As we stood there, the wind tugging at our coats, I became aware that the smell was getting stronger, and that I could now hear the sound of heavy breathing. Each breath seemed to end in a grunt, and the sounds were getting louder all the time.

'Run, Watson!' yelled Holmes. 'It's heading this way.'

I turned and ran.

'This way,' shouted Holmes. 'There's a light—head towards the light.'

There was dim light coming from the window of a cottage in the distance. I ran towards it. Behind me I could hear a loud weight crashing through the undergrowth, crushing trees each time it moved.

Within a few minutes we were at the cottage door, and the sound of the creature was moving away in the other direction. I knocked at the door as a puffed Holmes reached my side.

'Why, Watson, my dear chap,' he said, 'you're white and trembling.'

Just then a loud splash told us that the creature had returned to the Loch.

'You need a hot cup of tea to settle your nerves, old

chap,' said Holmes, just as the cottage door opened.

As it turned out we had arrived at the cottage of the Taggarts. It was Sarah who opened the door. Seeing two frozen, trembling travellers shivering on her doorstep she ushered us inside, and made us a pot of hot tea.

As we stood in front of the fireplace, drinking our tea, we told them what had happened.

'Aye, I'm not surprised,' said Donald Taggart, with a shake of his head. 'And you'll not be surprised to learn that this is not the first time this sort of thing has happened.'

'But does it happen often?'

'Very rarely, Mr Holmes,' replied the fisherman. 'Until recently, that is.'

'Something has stirred up the water kelpies,' said Sarah, in her quiet, serious voice.

'Must be the submarine,' I suggested. 'What do you think, Holmes?'

'I think all of this needs more investigation—urgently,' he replied, grimly.

11

The next morning dawned cold but clear. There had been a light snowfall over night. After a breakfast of hot porridge and hot coffee Holmes and I joined the team on the jetty preparing for the first voyage of the prototype Bruce-Partington submarine after its repairs.

'Brisk morning,' I remarked to Captain Sullivan, slapping my arms against my side to keep warm.

'Certainly is, sir. And it won't be any warmer on board, I'm afraid. It's always well advised to be warmly dressed for submarining.'

Having been previously advised about this, Holmes and I were dressed in our warmest travelling clothes.

As I stood on the wharf watching the narrow, steel vessel bob up and down in the slight swell I asked, 'Are you sure this contraption is entirely safe?'

'I've taken it out a dozen times in the last month. It's cramped and uncomfortable, but I'm quite convinced it's safe.'

'Having second thoughts, Dr Watson?' asked Sir James Partington.

'Certain not. No, most certainly not. I was just inquiring as to whether it had been ... fully repaired, that's all.'

'I can vouch for the repairs, sir,' said Jock Munro. 'You'll have a bonny voyage—you've nothing to worry about.'

'We'll just take you and Mr Holmes out into the centre of the Loch, dive to a reasonable depth, and run the ship around a few times. Then we'll bring you straight back here.'

'Who is coming with us?' asked Holmes.

'I will be in command, as usual,' explained Sullivan, 'and Lieutenant Benton will be at the helm. You, Mr Holmes, will be seated beside me, in the place usually occupied by the weapons officer, and you, Dr Watson will be at the stern, where Jock would normally sit as the engineer.'

'Is it quite safe going out without an engineer?' I asked. 'I mean to say, leaving the weapons officer behind I can understand, but the engineer ...'

'It's only a short jaunt, Dr Watson. We'll be quite safe without an engineer for this short run out and back.'

Jock Munro made his final inspection, and then the round hatch on the top of the vessel was opened and Lieutenant Benton clambered aboard. After a moment we heard his muffled voice call out, 'All set down here, sir.'

'Right, Mr Holmes,' said Captain Sullivan. 'You follow Benton—he'll show you were to sit.'

A moment later Holmes' tall, thin, athletic frame disappeared into the hatchway, and Sullivan turned to me. 'Now you doctor.'

I climbed up the short ladder on the jetty, and lowered myself through the hatch. I was disconcerted by the way the submarine kept rocking and pitching. As I grabbed for a firmer grip Sullivan called out, 'I'm afraid it's not very stable on the surface. That's because it doesn't have a keel. You'll find it's much more stable once we've submerged.'

Bracing myself against the pitch, I climbed down the short, steel ladder into the hull.

It was very cramped and dark, and smelled strongly of hot oil.

'Welcome aboard, Watson old chap,' said Holmes cheerfully. 'Careful where you put your feet.'

The submarine was, in effect, a steel tube, and, although this tube was eight feet in diameter at its widest point, it was so cluttered on the inside with equipment, controls and attachments that it was impossible for a man of average height, such as myself, to stand upright at any point.

'If you move towards the stern of the vessel, Dr Watson,' said Lieutenant Benton, 'you'll find a position just ahead of the main engines. That's the engineer's place, and that's where we've put you for this voyage. I hope that's okay?'

'Oh, fine . . fine,' I muttered as I ducked around pipes, levers and handles, and made my way to a steel chair that was bolted to the floor. Around this chair was a belt made of canvas webbing.

'Have you found the safety harness, doctor?' called Benton from his forward position. 'Good. Strap yourself in please. That's just a safety precaution.'

Sullivan followed me down the ladder and took his position beside Holmes, and immediately behind Benton.

'Cast off!' shouted Sullivan, up through the still open hatch. We heard the rattle of ropes, and then the submarine drifted free from the jetty. Benton operated some controls and the slowly ticking steam engine behind me increased its revolutions. Soon we were steaming slowly towards the centre of the Loch, with the hatch above us still open, and water occasionally spraying in.

'Are you going to close the hatch?' I asked.

'Soon, doctor—very soon,' Sullivan replied. 'Let's get fresh air in for as long as we can. You'll appreciate it later.'

Before long the swell had increased, and the submarine

was pitching in several directions at once. The amount of water splashing in through the open hatch began to increase rapidly.

Sullivan released his safety harness, climbed the short, steel, ladder, pulled the hatch closed, and locked it down tightly. As he did so Benton turned a dial and the interior of the vessel was illuminated by a dull, yellow glow.

'What type of light is that?' I asked.

'It's an incandescent lamp, doctor,' replied Benton, 'running off its own storage battery. It only gives light for 15 minutes at the moment, and is one of the major restrictions on our operations underwater.'

'Prepare to submerge,' ordered Sullivan, as another wave hit the ship and set it rocking back and forth.

Benton busied himself with the levers and wheels in front of him. Behind me the wheezy pumping sound of the steam engine ended, and was replaced by the quiet whirr of an electric motor. Slowly the sounds of the waves faded as the submarine began to settle beneath the surface.

Several minutes later Sullivan announced, 'We're now fully submerged. Normally this vessel would operate not far below the surface. After all, its targets are enemy ships that are on the surface. However, for test purposes we have taken this submarine to greater depths than it would ever need to approach under operational conditions.'

'And it has stood up to the strain?' asked Holmes.

'Admirably,' replied Sullivan, 'in fact ...'

His remarks were interrupted by a sharp crack, that was followed by a jet of water pouring into the vessel from the bow section, just ahead of Lieutenant Benton.

'What's happened?' snapped Sullivan.

'It appears to be the two-way valve that's broken open, sir. We're taking water fast. I'm trying to get us back to the surface, but the controls are not responding. We're heading straight to the bottom'

12

Sarah Taggart was in the front garden of her father's cottage when she caught a glimpse of Constance White, crossing the road not far away, and heading towards a clump of trees.

'That's strange,' thought Sarah. She hurried into the cottage, wrapped a shawl around her shoulders against the chill December winds, and returned to the front garden. Constance White could still be seen in the distance, between the trees, walking up the slope towards Tulloch Moor. Sarah decided to follow the woman, and discover what she was up to.

Sarah crossed the road and slipped in amongst the sparse trees that dotted the moor. Keeping her eyes on Constance White she moved quickly from tree to tree, and from one clump of heather to the next. Constance never looked back, and appeared to be quite unaware that she was being followed.

The wind whistled and Sarah pulled her shawl closer around her shoulders. Ahead of her Constance White appeared to be unaware of the chill wind, and just kept steadily walking, higher and higher up the moor.

Sarah had always had strange feelings about Constance. She knew the older woman was respected by some in the villagers for having what they called the "second sight". But the minister at the local kirk had taught Sarah not to put her faith in such occult powers, but rather in the Creator God who had made the world and all the powers in it. For that reason, Sarah had always felt a bit uncomfortable about Constance White and her claim to be a clairvoyant.

The higher up the moor they went, the thinner and sparser the trees became. Sarah had to crouch down to ensure that she was not seen. However, up where she was, on the high moor, although the undergrowth was thin there were large outcroppings of bare rock, and Sarah found that she could hide behind these, and slip quickly from rock to rock.

After nearly an hour of walking on the moor Constance stopped and looked around—almost as if she was expecting to find someone there. Sarah ducked down behind a large boulder and stayed carefully out of sight while Constance surveyed the horizon.

On board the Bruce-Partington submarine Captain Sullivan spoke calmly but urgently as he issued orders.

'We have to blow the ballast tanks. Benton open the canisters of compressed air into the forward tanks. Dr Watson, near your right hand is a large brass wheel—turn it fully clockwise as far as it will go.'

'Righto,' I said as I applied my strength to turning the wheel. The water was getting deeper in the vessel, and was now almost up to our knees. As I struggled with the wheel I discovered Holmes at my side. He also grabbed the wheel and together we turned it for three and a half turns until it would go no further.

As we turned it I heard a hissing sound, as of gas being released.

For a moment the ship rocked back and forth unsteadily, and then it began to sink again.

'We're still sinking, sir,' pointed out Benton, unnecessarily.

'Keep calm, Benton—keep calm,' urged Sullivan. 'All right—the ballast tanks are having trouble competing with the water coming in. We have to do more to block off the broken valve. Dr Watson—there should be some oil rags near the engines just behind you.'

'Yes, here they are.'

'Benton—fetch those rags and stuff them as hard as you can into the launch tube with the broken valve.'

Holmes carried the bundle of rags down the short length of the submarine and helped Benton push them firmly into the opening that was gushing water.

I slumped back into my seat wondering to myself, 'Is this it? Am I to die in a steel tube at the bottom of Loch Ness?' And then I asked myself, 'Am I ready to die? Am I ready to meet God?' And the answer was a firm and clear, 'yes.' I had often had conversations with our local minister, the Reverend Henry Bunyan, Rector of St Bede's on Baker Street, about how we can be friends with God. And I was trusting myself entirely to God's own Son, Jesus Christ to be by my side as my defence lawyer, when I stood in judgement before Almighty God.

As these thoughts went through my mind I felt my muscles relax. 'Even here,' I thought, 'deep beneath the inky black waters of Loch Ness, we are not out of the hands of God. He is here, and He is still in control. If He wants to save our lives in this desperate situation, then He can and He will.'

At that moment the electrical equipment just behind my back emitted a shower of sparks and went dead—the electrical motor stopped and the incandescent lamp went out. We were plunged into pitch blackness.

Up on Tulloch Moor Sarah Taggart waited patiently. After half an hour her patience was rewarded as she saw, by peeping around the edge of the rock behind which she was hiding, a tall man walk up the slope towards Constance White. He was a thin, rat-faced man with a black beard. He wore a heavy tweed Norfolk jacket with stout boots and brown leather leggings that went almost up to his knees. On his head was a grey, soft felt hat with a wide brim.

It was obvious that this was the person Constance had been waiting for. They stood close together engaged in quiet conversation. Sarah wished she could hear what they were saying. Dare she creep any closer and try to listen? Very slowly and cautiously she left her hiding place and began to creep forward, step by step.

Constance White, and the man she was talking to, were so engrossed in their conversation that they appeared to be utterly unaware of anything around them. Emboldened by this, Sarah crept even closer. Unfortunately, she was looking at them so closely that she failed to look where she was putting her feet. As she took one more step she slipped on loose gravel and fell noisily into the heather.

'Who is there?' demanded the man. A moment later he was towering over Sarah. He held a long-barrelled revolver in his hand. He pointed the revolver at Sarah as he said, 'Someone has being spying on us! This girl is a spy—she must be shot.'

13

'Keep still, and try not to breathe too deeply,' said Captain Harry Sullivan.

With the engines stopped, all was silent on board the Bruce-Partington submarine—except for the shallow breathing of four men, and the water sloshing around our legs.

'What has happened to the valve?' asked Sherlock Holmes quietly.

'I'm completely puzzled,' Sullivan replied. 'It's worked perfectly on every other trial.'

'And since it's part of the weapons system,' added Benton, 'we weren't even using it on this voyage.'

'It has never leaked before?' persisted Holmes.

'Never,' said Sullivan firmly.

'What does it mean, Holmes?' I asked.

'It almost certainly means sabotage, Watson.'

At that moment the submarine lurched to one side.

'What's that?' I asked nervously.

'That, doctor,' replied Benton, 'is good news. I think we're starting to rise.'

'Yes, you're right, Benton!' said his captain. 'We've stopped sinking, and I think we're slowly rising. But only very slowly. So, the question is: will we reach the surface before the air runs out?'

After that we stopped talking to preserve the air—and we waited!

Up on Tulloch Moor, Sarah was staring into the barrel of a .45 calibre revolver.

'Who is this girl?' growled the man holding the gun, speaking over his shoulder to Constance White.

'Her name is Sarah Taggart. She's the daughter of a widowed fisherman named Donald Taggart.'

'She has seen us together. She may even have heard us. She must be killed.'

Constance White stepped closer and looked down on Sarah with a strange expression on her face, an expression Sarah had never seen before—a very hard expression, a sneer of superiority and contempt.

'Shoot her if you must,' said Constance casually.

Sarah drew a deep breath and shut her eyes as the man cocked the hammer of his revolver.

'No. Wait,' interrupted Constance. 'Someone may hear the shot.'

'What can we do then?' asked the stranger.

'Leave her.'

'No, we can't leave her. That would be far too dangerous. She would talk.'

'Let her. She is only a child. No one would listen to her. No one would believe her. And if anyone did listen to her, it would be her word against mine.'

'What do we do then?'

'Let her go. She can do us no damage. I am considered to be the "wise woman" of the village. She cannot tell tales about me and be believed. It is perfectly safe to release her.'

'If you say so,' responded the stranger doubtfully. But as he spoke Sarah was relieved to see that he released the cocked hammer of his revolver, and put the weapon back into his coat pocket.

'Be off with you then!' he snarled viciously at Sarah. 'Clear off, or I will kill you—regardless of what Miss White says. And don't think I'm worried about a shot being heard—I could strangle you with my bare hands.'

Sarah struggled to her feet, brushed the loose dirt and leaves off her dress and began to run down the hill.

'Don't stop and don't look back!' shouted the man behind her. Sarah was terrified—she didn't stop, and she didn't look back.

All of these events I learned of only later, from Sarah Taggart herself. While they were going on we were sitting in pitch darkness on board the Bruce-Partington submarine, taking shallow breaths and keeping very still.

Every so often there would be some mysterious bubbling in the ballast tanks, and the ship would lurch to one side or the other.

Despite the cold I was surprised to find that I was sweating. I pulled my handkerchief out of my pocket and wiped my forehead. Then the ship lurched again, and the sounds around us changed—instead of occasional bubbles I could faintly hear the slap of waves on the hull.

'We've broken the surface!' shouted Captain Sullivan excitedly. I heard, rather than saw, him climb up the short, steel ladder and undo the levers that held the hatch fast. A moment later the hatch was thrown open and fresh air and daylight came streaming in. I breathed a sight of relief, and said a short prayer of thanks to God who had chosen to rescue us from an early death, rather than take us home to be with Him.

'We're not out of the woods yet,' Sullivan shouted down to us. 'The submarine is riding very low in the water—any decent wave would flood us in an instant. We need to bail out some of the water that's on board, so that we ride a little higher. Doctor, Jock keeps a bucket near the engines—see if you can find it.'

'Righto,' I replied, and started looking.

'Benton, while Dr Watson is doing that, you'd better see if you can get either of the engines going.'

'Yes, sir.'

I quickly found the bucket. Holmes and I took turns filling it and handing it up the ladder to Captain Sullivan, who emptied the water overboard and handed the empty bucket back down to us.

While this was going on Lieutenant Benton worked on the engines.

'The electric motor is hopeless,' he said after a few minutes. 'It's full of water. I'll give the steam engine a try.'

As Holmes and I continued working with Captain Sullivan to bail out the water in the ship I could hear Benton behind me clanking and banging away at machinery that we hoped would take us back to safety.

'If I can't get this thing going ...' muttered Benton as he worked.

'What's the problem?' I asked as I filled the bucket again. 'Now that we're on the surface, surely we're quite safe.'

'Not quite, doctor. This Loch is very treacherous. I've seen it as flat as a mill pond one minute, and filled with nine foot waves the next.'

'Why, a wave like that ...' I began.

'Would sent us to the bottom in an instant,' completed

Benton, as he went on with his work.

Sarah Taggart ran in through the front door of her father's cottage, her face flushed, and out of breath.

He father was sitting in an armchair in front of the fire. When she entered he looked up in alarm.

'What's wrong, lass? Whatever's happened to you?'

Sarah sank down onto a kitchen chair before replying, 'Ah, nothing. No, nothing at all. I've just been for a walk on the moor that's all.'

'Are you sure, girl? You look as though you'd seen the devil himself.'

'No, I'm fine. Don't worry about me, Pa.'

Meanwhile, out on Loch Ness the waves were rising, and more and more water was spraying back in through the hatchway, even as we were bailing it out as fast as we could.

As we worked I heard a sound behind me that was a delight to my ears—it was the ticking over of the small steam engine that drove the ship when it was on the surface.

'I've done it, sir,' called Benton. 'The steam engine is going at about half power. I'm going back to the helm, sir, to take us back to the castle jetty.'

'Good work, Benton,' said Sullivan. 'It looks as if we're going to make it.'

14

Three hours after our terrifying experience on the Loch, we were gathered around the big fireplace in the library of Forgill Castle. We had all had hot baths, put on dry clothes, and were drinking steaming hot coffee.

'That was rather a close shave you chaps had,' said the Duke of Forgill.

'You can say that again,' I responded.

'But I don't understand it at all,' complained Sir James Partington, co-inventor of the submarine. 'Does it make any sense to you?' he added, turning to his fellow designer.

'No, not at all. Complete mystery, I'm afraid,' said Professor Nigel Bruce. 'I mean to say—the two-way valve is the most original part of our whole design. The effectiveness of the ship as a weapons system is based on that valve.'

'Quite so,' agreed Partington. 'And we've refined it, and tested it, in every possible way. So I simply cannot imagine what can have gone wrong with it.'

'We'll know shortly, sir,' said Commander Lethbridge-Stewart. 'I have Jock Munro out there now stripping down the valve to discover the cause of the fault.'

'I think you will find, gentlemen,' said Sherlock Holmes, 'that your two-way valve is entirely blameless.'

'Are you suggesting human interference, Mr Holmes?' asked Lethbridge-Stewart.

'All the clues point in that direction,' Holmes replied.

'And you're quite right, Mr Holmes,' exclaimed Jock Munro, as he hurried into the room. 'Sorry for barging in like this—and I'm afraid I could na help overhearing the last part of your conversation. Mr Holmes has hit the nail right on the head.'

As he spoke Munro held up that elaborate brass valve, which was still dripping water over the Duke's expensive carpet.

'Well?' demanded Lethbridge-Stewart. 'Don't keep us in suspense man. What did you find?'

'Someone had attempted to remove the valve. They must have been interrupted in their work, because they never completed the removal of the device. However, they did succeed in loosening it in its casing—and that's why it flooded when the submarine submerged.'

'Well, I must say that's something of a relief,' said Partington with a sigh. 'If there was something wrong with the design of the valve we would have had to go back to the drawing board and start again. But if it was human interference, then our valve has not failed. Not that this is any comfort to you chaps who were on board—but it's a great relief to Bruce and me.'

'But who could have done it?' asked Lethbridge-Stewart. 'We've had someone on guard the whole time. Did any of you chaps see anything suspicious when you were on watch?'

'My watch was as quiet as the grave,' muttered Professor Bruce. 'Only chappie I saw was that coachman of yours ... what's his name?'

'Angus MacRanald,' offered the Duke.

'Yes, him. He came to ask if I would like a whisky to keep me warm. But he didn't get inside the submarine—I'd be prepared to swear to that.'

'And, of course,' added Partington, 'it would be necessary to be inside the ship to remove—or loosen—the two-way valve.'

At that moment the large double doors to the library swung open and the Duke of Forgill's sour faced butler announced, 'A gentleman from Scotland Yard to see you, your Grace.'

'Show him in, Campbell—show him in,' muttered the Duke irritably.

The butler stepped to one side, and there was our old friend Inspector Lestrade of Scotland Yard.

After the greetings and introductions were over Holmes asked, 'Well, what brings you up here, Lestrade?'

'Your brother Mycroft thought it might be best if I came in person, Mr Holmes—with the information you requested.'

'What information? I didn't know about this?' I said.

'I didn't mention it, Watson,' explained Holmes, 'but before leaving London I asked Mycroft to let me know the whereabouts of the leading foreign agents currently in this country.'

'Well, Mr Holmes—Mr Holmes said, that is to say, the *other* Mr Holmes said, that is ... your brother said, that there were only two men capable of taking on a task like the Bruce-Partington submarine, and their names were ...' at this point Lestrade consulted his note book, and then continued, 'Louis La Rothier and Adolph Meyer.'

'And you were supposed to find out the whereabouts of these two?' I asked.

'Exactly, Dr Watson. However, and this is the

embarrassing bit—both of them seem to have disappeared. At any rate neither man is in London.'

'In that case I think we can safely say that both of them are somewhere in this district,' remarked Holmes.

'Both of them, Holmes?' I queried. 'Surely not.'

'I believe so, Watson. It can't have escaped your attention that the events that have happened since we arrived at Loch Ness cannot be explained by the activities of any one spy or saboteur.'

'No, I can't say I had noticed, really.'

'What we are facing here are two ingenious criminals, working against each other, as well as against us.'

'That makes the situation almost impossible,' said Sir James Partington, throwing his hands in the air. 'One clever and ruthless villain—backed by all the resources of a major foreign power—you might have been able to counteract. But two such men? Not even Sherlock Holmes is equal to such a task.'

'Don't you be too sure of that, Sir James,' I said. 'Holmes has already defeated such master criminals as Professor Moriarty, Colonel Sebastian Moran, and Dr Grimsby Defoe. There is no criminal in the world who is his equal.'

'Thank you for your confidence, Watson.'

'But what are we going to do, Mr Holmes?' asked Lestrade.

'Our first step is find you accommodation at the village inn,' Holmes replied to the inspector.

'He's more than welcome to stay here at the castle,' volunteered the Duke.

'Thank you for your offer of hospitality, your Grace,' responded Holmes. 'But since Watson and I are here, Inspector Lestrade would be more useful as our eyes and ears in the village.'

'If you think so, Mr Holmes,' said Lestrade doubtfully. 'When do we get started for the village?'

'Right now,' said Holmes leaping out of his armchair with his old vigour, like a hound on the scent, eager to begin the chase.

15

Twenty minutes later Holmes, Lestrade and I were standing in the main room of the village inn booking a room for the Inspector.

While this was happening, Holmes said to the innkeeper, 'You have one other guest staying here at present, don't you?'

'That's right,' replied the innkeeper, a man named McGuffey. 'Mr Alfred Milton, the former Bishop of Madang, in New Guinea, has been with us for almost a month now.'

'I wonder if it would be possible to have a word with him?'

'I'll send the girl up to his room and see if he's there.'

As the innkeeper dispatched his daughter to inquire of Mr Milton, I remarked, 'Odd you should suggest that, Holmes. I thought I saw Milton in the corner of the room when we were at the front door, but he appears to have vanished. Perhaps I was mistaken.'

Inspector Lestrade completed booking his room, and then the girl returned to explain that Mr Milton was confined to his room with a headache.

'Well, perhaps another day then,' said Holmes.

'What's so dashed important about this Milton fellow?' asked Lestrade.

'That, I suspect, is something that you'll discover when you meet him, Inspector.'

'Why must you be so mysterious, Mr Holmes?'

'It's a weakness of mine. You must allow me to indulge in my taste for the dramatic.'

Leaving Lestrade to take his bags up to his rooms, Holmes and I strolled out into the village square. Standing on the other side of the square, staring at us, was young Sarah Taggart. She seemed to be having difficulty making up her mind about something.

At last an expression of firm resolution came over her face, and she walked across the pavement to where we were standing.

'Mr Holmes? Dr Watson? May I have a word with you, please?'

'Yes, of course. Shall we step back inside the inn?'

'I'd prefer to speak to you in private. Could you call into our cottage on your way back to the castle?'

'Certainly,' replied Holmes. 'We'll see you there within the hour.'

'Oh, thank you Mr Holmes, thank you.'

'What was that all about?' I asked as she ran off.

'Perhaps, nothing at all,' replied Holmes thoughtfully. 'Or perhaps the key to this whole mystery. We must not pass up a clue when it is offered to us, Watson.'

A short time later we left Inspector Lestrade to make his observations in the village, while Holmes and I set out on foot to return to the castle.

'What I need, Watson, is my violin,' said Holmes as we walked. 'I need to *think*–to apply my mind to all that has happened–to reason and deduce. And, as you know Watson, nothing aids my concentration so much as music.'

'Actually Holmes, I put your violin case into our bag just as we were leaving.'

'Good old Watson! How reliable you are. As soon as we are back at the castle I shall retire to my room, take up the violin, and play—play and think.'

Soon we had arrived at the Taggart's cottage, with its pretty front garden of highland flowers. We knocked at the door and were admitted by Sarah Taggart.

'Come in, gentlemen. I've put the kettle on, and I'll have a pot of tea for you in just a moment. My father is not here right now—he's out in his fishing boat.'

A few moments later we each had our cup of tea and Holmes asked, 'Now, what's this all about Miss Taggart?'

'It's about Constance White.'

'Oh, her! The village "witch"!' I snorted.

'I saw her today ... out on Tulloch Moor ... meeting with someone.'

'Did you indeed,' said Holmes, leaning forward eagerly in his chair. 'This sounds most promising—pray tell us more.'

Over the next half hour Sarah Taggart told the whole story of her adventures in vivid detail.

'What does it mean, Mr Holmes?' she asked when she had finished. 'Why was Constance White meeting with that stranger on the moor? And why did he threaten to kill me?'

'Good questions, Miss Taggart. And they deserve good answers, which, I'm very much afraid I can't give you just at the moment. At least, I can't give them to you in detail. However, I offer you this speculation—that Constance White has been paid by this stranger to spread rumours and fears about the so-called "creature" of the Loch.'

'Why, that's amazing Mr Holmes,' the teenager gasped.

'How did you know? Constance has been talking about nothing but the creature for more than two weeks now.'

'What sort of things has she been saying?'

'That the old monster has been disturbed and is restless. She keeps saying that it is angry and out for blood.'

'And no doubt,' commented Holmes, 'her utterances have achieved their desired effect.'

'And what is that, Holmes?' I asked.

'To frighten the locals, Watson. To make them restrict their movements on the Loch to a bare minimum. Especially to keep them off the Loch at night.'

'You're quite right, Mr Holmes,' said Sarah. 'That's exactly what everyone's doing at the moment. That's why my Pa is out clearing his nets now, instead of doing it after dark. It's all because of what Constance White has been saying.'

As we stood in the doorway of the cottage, thanking Miss Taggart for her help, and making our farewells, we heard a racket from further down the road.

'Now, what on earth can that be?' I asked.

I soon had my answer, for around the bend came a long line of circus carts, pulled by large draft horses. Some of the carts carried cages holding wild animals—we saw a sleeping lion, a restless, pacing tiger, and a sleek, black panther, among other beasts. Other brightly painted carts were sealed, and held, I presumed, the tents and other equipment the circus needed.

Riding on the carts were the strange and colourful circus folk. Although, I must say, they didn't look like a particularly friendly or happy crowd.

While Holmes and I were observing the circus carts, we were ourselves under observation—although we didn't know it at the time.

73

Inside one of the sealed carts was a thin, rat-faced man, with a black beard, wearing a thick tweed Norfolk jacket, stout boots, and brown leather leggings that reached almost to his knees. As he passed the cottage he was looking out of a small slot in the side of the cart.

'So, there you are Sherlock Holmes,' he muttered to himself. 'You have crossed my path once too often, Mr Holmes—and soon you must die!'

16

As soon as we returned to the castle, Holmes retired to his room and before long I could hear the mournful note of his violin—a sad and melancholy tune that he often played to aid his concentration.

I sat in the library and read the newspapers that were lying on the coffee table—*The Times* and *The Scotsman*—until I became restless. Then I pulled on my overcoat, and decided to take a brief walk around the castle grounds before dinner. Stepping out of the heavy, wooden gates of Forgill Castle I began walking slowly, with no particular destination in mind, towards the shores of the loch.

As I walked, I thought. What did Holmes mean when he said that the events we had experienced were the results not of one villain, but of two? How could he possibly know that? To the best of my knowledge, I had seen everything Holmes had seen, and heard everything he had heard. Nevertheless, he had deduced things I had missed.

Puzzling over this I continued walking until I was some distance from the castle. Looking back I saw a man—a short, stout man, dressed in a black overcoat—creeping around the outer wall of Forgill Castle as if he didn't want to be seen. Clearly, he had not seen me. The distance was too great for me to make out the man's face, so I started walking in his direction.

As I closed the distance between us, I noticed that he was standing on tiptoes as if trying to look into one of the windows of the castle. Which window was it? Ah, yes, then I remembered—he was at one of the windows of the servants' quarters. Why would he be spying at a window there?

Drawing nearer I called out in a loud voice, 'Hey! You there—what do you think you're up to?' At the sound of my voice the man turned and fled. He put on a burst of speed that quite surprised me, and although I ran after him, he quickly lost me.

But as we ran I thought I caught a glimpse of his face— and for a moment I thought it was the face of Alfred Milton. Later, as I walked back to the castle, puffed and trying to catch my breath, I decided I must have been mistaken. Why would the retired bishop of Madang in New Guinea be creeping around the castle walls?

That night as we sat down to dinner, I told the others around the table about the incident.

'I'll double the guards,' said Commander Lethbridge-Stewart in response, adding, 'you must have been mistaken about the man's identity. Alfred Milton is a harmless elderly man. It can't possibly have been him.'

'My thoughts entirely,' I agreed.

'To the contrary Watson,' said Sherlock Holmes. 'I'm certain your first impressions were quite correct, and what you describe is exactly the behaviour I would expect from Mr Alfred Milton.'

This remark caused much disagreement and provoked a conversation that went on for the next ten minutes. Holmes took no part in this conversation, but sat back and listened with a pleased and eager expression on his face, rather like a cat about to close in on a cornered mouse.

As the meal was ending that night, and people were starting to rise from the table, the duke's sour faced old butler entered the dining room looking agitated.

'Excuse me your grace, but the constable from Foyers village has just arrived and wishes to speak with you. He says it's urgent.'

'Well, show him in Campbell—show him in.'

A moment later a young, uniformed policeman entered the dining room and snapped to attention as he addressed the duke. 'Constable North, your grace, from the Foyers police station.'

'What can I do for you young man?'

'I was wondering if you could provide some men to assist with a hunt, your grace?'

'A hunt? At this time of night? Hunting for what? I take it you're not hunting for stag in the glens?'

'No, your grace. It's the panther.'

'Panther? What panther?'

'The panther belonging to the circus people, your grace. It appears to have escaped. Well, they reported to me that it has definitely escaped. And we're getting together a hunting party.'

'Right,' snapped the duke, leaping to his feet, 'I'll order Campbell to round up all the able bodied men among the servants, and I'll arm them from the gun room. What about you, Lethbridge-Stewart? Would the military care to join the hunt?'

'We'd be delighted to assist. I'll round up my men. Some of them are carrying arms, but the others will need weapons from your gun room.'

'We'll take care of that. Is that what you want, constable?' asked the duke, turning towards the young policeman.

'Thank you, sir,' was the reply. 'That's exactly the help we need.'

'Well, what do you say, Watson?' asked Holmes, turning towards me. 'Shall we join them for a little sport on the moors?'

'Certainly, Holmes,' I replied. 'Why not. Always happy to be of assistance wherever we can.'

An hour later a large party of us, under the command of the Duke of Forgill began the long trudge up the slope of Tulloch Moor. We were strung out in a long, straight line—two dozen men, each armed with a hunting rifle or shotgun from the duke's collection.

I won't tell you the whole story of that long night, of the cold that made our teeth chatter, of the strange, savage growls of the panther that we often heard ahead of us in the dark, of the even stranger crashing and thumping that we heard in the heather, and that made even the bravest of us feel nervous.

The hunt ended with a shout from the duke's game keeper, who was at the far end of our line, halfway up the slope of Dun Dearduil. He was one of a number of men who carried a lantern as well as a gun.

'Your grace!' he yelled. 'I think I've found it. And it's dead.'

We all hurried in the direction of his voice, and before long we were gathered in a large circle around a very strange corpse.

The creature before us had once been a huge and magnificent member of the cat family. It was around nine feet long, and, even in death, its body showed the ripples of heavy muscles. In life it had been a powerful and dangerous animal, with long, sharp, deadly claws.

The game keeper was kneeling by the body when we arrived.

'Something has attacked and killed it,' he announced. What sort of animal, I wondered to myself, would be capable of defeating the large, powerful, efficient killing machine which is a living panther?

'How did it die?' asked the duke.

'Crushed to death, your grace,' replied his game keeper. 'Something huge and heavy has crushed it to death.'

This announcement was greeted by a stunned silence. After a lengthy pause the silence was broken by a voice from the back of the crowd, one of the locals, who said, 'The beast—that's what did it.'

'Aye,' came another voice. 'It can only have been the beast from the loch.'

17

We slept deeply in our beds that night—exhausted by the hunt on the moors. But the sleep of many of us was disturbed by nightmares of the beast of the loch.

But while we slept other, less honest, folk were afoot. The events that happened while I slept I was able to reconstruct later.

The room being used by Jock Munro as a workshop was an old storeroom on the ground floor of the castle. Shortly after one o'clock in the morning the door of this workshop was unlocked, in slow and stealthy movements, by a tall, broad-shouldered man who hid himself in the shadows. Having turned the old brass key in the lock he pushed back the door very slowly in case it creaked.

Inside the room he struck a match and lit a stub of candle. This he placed on a work bench as he began to search. It didn't take him long to find what he was looking for. Wrapped up in an oilcloth was the Bruce-Partington two-way valve—the secret device that made their submarine such a powerful weapon.

The thief lifted up the heavy, brass valve and placed it in a cotton sack he was carrying. Then he blew out the candle and left the room, re-locking the door as he did so.

Ten minutes later he was outside the castle and making

his way down the dark road towards Forgill village.

The thief, was a big, solidly built man who took long strides. Soon he was passing the dark windows of cottages that housed the sleeping fishermen and their families, and it was not long before he was standing behind the rear wall of the village inn to keep his appointment.

The thief was startled to hear a low moan coming from somewhere quite close. For a moment he lit a flickering match to dispel the pitch blackness. In its dim light he discovered a drunken fisherman curled up against the back wall of the inn—sound asleep in a drunken stupor.

The thief nudged the sleeping man with the toe of his boot. The curled up body shifted slightly, mumbled something in a drunken slur, and then began to snore, deeply and regularly.

As the clock on the village church chimed 2 am the back door of the inn slowly opened.

'Are you there?' said the figure in the doorway, peering into the darkness.

'I'm here,' growled the thief, quietly, in reply.

'Do you have it?'

'Aye—I've got it. Do you have the money?'

'All of it.'

'Let me count it.'

'You'll have to strike a match to do that.'

'Then I'll strike a match,' growled the thief. 'But you're not getting it until I've counted the money.'

With these words he struck a match. By its dim, flickering light the sleeping fisherman, lying against the back wall of the inn, became visible. The man lurking in the doorway uttered a gasp of surprise.

'There's someone here,' he hissed.

'He's dead drunk,' shrugged the thief, continuing to count the money. 'Ignore him.'

'But what if ...'

'He's in a drunken stupor, I tell you! I checked! Now shut up while I finish counting.'

With that the two men returned to their transaction. Which was why they did not see the drunken fisherman open one eye, and then raise himself up on one arm. And it is why they were taken completely by surprise when the "fisherman" leaped to his feet, rushed at them, and clipped handcuffs on them—one steel bracelet on the thief's large wrist, and the other on the thinner wrist of his fellow criminal.

'Hey! What's this ...?'

'What's going on?' they cried.

'You are both under arrest,' said Sherlock Holmes, turning back the collar of the fisherman's jacket that had hidden his face. Taking a police whistle out of his pocket, Holmes blew a single, loud note. Two minutes later Inspector Lestrade was at his side, carrying a lantern and looking the two criminals up and down.

'Alfred Milton and Angus MacRanald—just as you said it would be, Mr Holmes. Remarkable—quite remarkable. How you do it, Mr Holmes, I'll never understand.'

MacRanald began flexing his huge muscles and looking around for a way of escape.

'I wouldn't attempt it, if I were you,' warned Holmes. 'In the first place you are handcuffed to a colleague in crime who would never be able to keep up with you if you ran. And, if you are thinking of trying to attack us, let me tell you that I have mastered *baritsu*—the Japanese system of wrestling—and despite the difference in our sizes I have no doubt that I could overpower you.'

As the big man's shoulders slumped it was obvious he had given up, and had accepted his defeat.

'Well, Mr MacRanald and Mr Milton—or should I say Adolph Meyers—I have arranged with the inn keeper to lock you in the cellar until the police van calls for you in the morning,' said Inspector Lestrade, jingling a set of keys in his hand. 'So, if you'd like to step inside the inn I'll take care of your temporary accommodation.'

Later that morning, as we stood in the pale, wintry sunshine outside the inn, I heard a full report of the night's events from Holmes and Lestrade.

'But how did you know, Holmes?' I asked.

'It was obvious from the first that "Alfred Milton", the retired bishop of Madang in New Guinea was a fraud,' he replied.

'It wasn't obvious to me,' I muttered.

'New Guinea is a German colony, not a British one,' continued Holmes, 'which is why I asked Milton, or Meyers as we must call him now, if he was a Lutheran bishop. His claim to have been a Church of England bishop in a German colony rang false. My suspicions were confirmed on the day we booked Lestrade into this inn.'

'In what way?'

'By his remarkable disappearance, Watson, as soon as Lestrade approached. Meyers, under the name of Milton, was afraid that he would be recognised by the professional policeman from Scotland Yard.'

'He needn't have worried,' added Lestrade, 'since my memory for faces is not as good as all that.'

'Given those suspicions,' Holmes continued, 'I was confident that Milton was Meyers, and your report of his behaviour confirmed this, and alerted me to the fact that his plot was about to reach a climax.'

'And what was his plot?' I asked.

'To steal the Bruce-Partington two-way valve,' Holmes explained. 'Since the attempt by Hugo Oberstein to steal the plans in London had failed, a certain foreign power employed Adolph Meyers to steal the thing itself. He had sufficient money to be able to corrupt one of the servants at the castle—the coachman Angus MacRanald—and that was how the thing was done.'

'I see. All quite simple, really, when you explain it.'

'In fact, elementary, Watson, quite elementary. It was MacRanald who loosened the valve, in his first, failed, attempt, to steal it. He thus, unintentionally, almost caused our deaths by drowning.'

'Unpleasant fellow,' I snorted.

'Undoubtedly, Watson. And now that he and Meyers are under lock and key, half of this puzzle has been solved.'

'Only half, Holmes?'

'That's right, Watson—only half.'

18

Something very old, and very large, was moving through thick beds of weeds at the very bottom of Loch Ness. In that inky blackness, never reached by the faintest gleam of sunlight, an ancient mind was deeply troubled. Its huge body trembled as it thought about the alien presence in the loch. In the darkest recesses of its dark, old mind, it was disturbed by the alien invasion of its home.

Within that ancient mind was a sense of territory. Loch Ness was its territory, and its family's territory, and had been for countless centuries. Now another large creature—a powerful, hunting creature—had entered its domain, making it restless and hostile.

Slowly, that ancient, primitive mind resolved to remove the alien thing, the hated, unwanted thing, from Loch Ness. And slowly the huge body began to move.

Sherlock Holmes, Inspector Lestrade and I ate our lunch that day at the village inn. As we finished a delicious meal of roast lamb I said, 'Now Holmes, you've kept us in suspense for long enough. What steps are to be taken to solve the second half of the puzzle? Where do we investigate next?'

'I suggest we go to the circus, Watson.'

'The circus, Holmes?'

'If we can rent a pony cart from the innkeeper, I suggest

that we travel down the road to the next township, where we shall find the circus about to give its afternoon performance, on the village green at Foyers.'

'But surely we can't afford to take the afternoon off, Holmes,' protested Lestrade. 'We have work to do.'

I, however, could see from the glint in Holmes' eye that the visit to the circus was no mere amusement—but rather, that something serious was afoot. So I nudged Lestrade in the ribs, and said playfully, 'Come along Inspector. You know the old saying—all work and no play makes Jack a dull boy.'

'That's all very well, but ...'

However, by then Holmes and I were gathering our hats and coats to leave. Lestrade shrugged his shoulders and joined us. He knew, as well as I did, that Holmes never suggested any step in an investigation, however seemingly trivial, without having a definite object in mind.

Which is why, two hours later, we were packed into a tent on the village green at the town of Foyers, along with some 200 other people, watching trapeze artists, clowns, jugglers, and tightrope walkers.

'I still can't see the point of all this ...' began Lestrade as the circus hands were pulling down the tightrope apparatus and setting up the cage for the lion taming act.

'Sshh,' interrupted Holmes. 'This is the act we've come to see.'

'Oh, it is, is it? Well, it still makes no sense to me,' grumbled the Inspector.

To an accompanying roll of drums several large, wild cats leaped out of their travelling boxes and into the large cage in the centre of the ring.

'And now, ladies and gentlemen,' bellowed the ringmaster, 'the Great Luigi will risk death by entering the cage behind me—a cage which holds savage killer animals from the jungles of Africa and India.'

To another roll of drums a man ran into the arena, and entered the animal cage. He was a thin, rat-faced man with a black beard. He was wearing a brightly coloured, spangled uniform—a typical circus costume.

I won't bother to describe his act, but it was clever enough, as he made two lions, a tiger and a leopard leap over hurdles, sit up on their hind legs, jump through rings, and, as a climax, leap through a flaming hoop.

As he left the arena Holmes rose from his seat saying, 'That's our man, let's follow him.'

Outside the big tent we saw the lion tamer heading towards one of the circus caravans.

'Monsieur La Rothier,' Holmes called out loudly. The lion tamer stopped in his tracks, and slowly turned around.

'Are you speaking to me, sir?' he asked. 'If so, you have the wrong name. It is Luigi, not ... whatever you said.'

'The game is up La Rothier,' said Holmes grimly. 'The very fact that you stopped and responded when I called your real name proves that my deductions are correct. Lestrade, I suggest you clap your handcuffs on this man.'

Lestrade moved forward quickly, but the lion tamer moved even faster, running towards the travelling cages that held the lions, the tiger and the leopard.

'Head him off, Watson—around the other way,' shouted Holmes as he ran in pursuit.

I did as Holmes said, and ran around the group of brightly painted caravans to cut off La Rothier's retreat. Inspector Lestrade was by my side as I ran. As we rounded the last in the row of caravans I saw Holmes and La Rothier grappling hand to hand in front of one of the circus carts.

For a moment the lion tamer managed to break free from

Holmes' grasp. As he did so he reached out and released a lock on the cart. This caused the side of the cart to fall open, and there, inches away from the struggling figures of Holmes and La Rothier was a growling, angry leopard.

As Holmes flung La Rothier to the ground the leopard sprang. In an instant I pulled my old army revolver from my coat pocket, and, without waiting to take aim, I fired. In mid stride the rippling muscles of the giant cat went limp, and it fell heavily to the ground.

Holmes lifted the still struggling spy from the ground, and led him over to Lestrade to be handcuffed.

'It's almost a pity to kill something as beautiful as that,' I muttered sadly, looking down on the carcass of the magnificent leopard. 'Still,' I continued, 'it was the leopard or you, Holmes. I didn't have a choice.'

'Good old reliable Watson,' said Holmes heartily. 'You were wonderful, Watson, simply wonderful.'

'I was? Oh, yes, I suppose I was.'

As the struggling La Rothier was led away, he turned around and hissed viciously, 'You will not escape. Your doom is sealed, Sherlock Holmes.'

'What an unpleasant fellow. I wonder what he meant by that, Holmes?'

'If it was anything more than an empty threat, then we shall find out. Yes, I'm sure of that. If La Rothier has left a trap waiting for us, we shall undoubtedly find out.'

19

That night Inspector Lestrade joined the rest of us for dinner at Forgill Castle.

'Now you must explain to us, Mr Holmes,' said the duke, 'why you suspected there were two spies operating in this district and not just one.'

'It was clear almost from the beginning,' replied Holmes, 'that this project was under two different attacks—one designed to steal its most important secret, and the other intended to destroy it and bring it to an end. It was also clear that these two separate attacks were unco-ordinated. If both attacks were being planned and executed by the same mind the order of events would have been different—the Bruce-Partington two-way valve would have been secured first, and then the ship attacked later. But since the first attack on the ship occurred before the valve had been stolen I deduced that two different agents were involved.'

'Yes, quite logical,' agreed Commander Lethbridge-Stewart.

'When Inspector Lestrade brought us the news that the two most dangerous foreign spies in London had both disappeared I had no doubt that both had come to this district, and both were active—in all probability with each being quite unaware of the other.'

'But the circus, Holmes—how did you know to look there?' asked Lestrade.

'Where else could a stranger hide in a district like this. The Loch Ness district is a place of villages and small towns, a place where everyone knows everyone else. A stranger cannot hide in such a place unless he either supplies himself with a false identity—which Adolph Meyer did—or else hides among a group of strangers, namely the circus folk.'

'Which La Rothier did,' I said.

'Precisely, Watson. When one of the big cats escaped from the circus I operated on the assumption that it had been released deliberately.'

'Deliberately?' asked Captain Harry Sullivan, his voice rising in alarm.

'Deliberately,' repeated Holmes, 'as a diversion. That directed my attention towards someone travelling with the circus who had charge over those wild cats. For that reason I addressed the lion tamer by the name of the spy Louis La Rothier. When he instinctively responded I knew we had found our man.'

'What about Constance White?' I asked. 'What role did she play in all of this?'

'I believe that further investigation will reveal that she was paid by one of those two agents—either Meyer or La Rothier—to spread rumours and alarm, to frighten people away from the loch, especially at night.'

'Which of them do you think it was, Holmes?'

'Almost certainly La Rothier, Watson. Meyer was the one seeking to obtain the two-way valve, while La Rothier had the task of bringing the tests to a complete halt. For that he needed access to the loch when no one else was about. It suited his plans to frighten others away from the loch.'

'Were they paid by two different foreign powers, Mr Holmes?' asked Commander Lethbridge-Stewart. 'Or were both hired by the same power to carry out these different tasks?'

'Unless one of them—or both of them—tell us, we shall probably never know.'

'I understand how Meyer was carrying out his task of stealing the secret of the submarine,' I said, 'but how did La Rothier manage his part of the affair? How did he inflict the damage on the submarine we saw on our first day here, Holmes? Those steel pipes that had been ripped off the outside of the submarine indicated an attack of great violence. How did La Rothier go about that?'

'You have put your finger on the one remaining question, Watson.'

'Oh, have I?' I said, feeling rather pleased with myself.

'Yes, Watson—you have pointed to the one part of the puzzle that remains to be solved.'

'Mind you,' suggested Lieutenant Benton, 'now the two spies have been rounded up and are under lock and key, the answer to that question probably doesn't really matter.'

'I think it matters a great deal,' said Sherlock Holmes in deadly earnest.

'What do you propose doing about it,?' Lethbridge-Stewart asked.

'Is the submarine ready to be taken out into the loch again?' responded Holmes.

'Yes, Jock has reinstalled the stolen valve, and checked the whole vessel from stem to stern. We were planning to take her out first thing in the morning.'

'With your permission, Commander,' said Holmes, 'I would like to be on board.'

'Why, Mr Holmes?'

'Because the solution to the last part of the puzzle lies out there,' Holmes replied, pointing to the tall windows that lined the dinning room, 'out there in the loch.'

'If you wish to, you may certainly be on board. Do you have any objections, Captain Sullivan?'

'No, sir. I'm more than happy to have Mr Holmes with us once again. I would quite like to show him that the disaster of his last voyage with us is not how the submarine normally behaves.'

'That's settled then. When do you intend taking the submarine out?'

'Just as soon as the sun is high enough in the sky—first thing tomorrow morning.'

The next morning on the jetty there was some resistance when I forcefully requested that I be allowed to accompany Holmes on the submarine's voyage.

Holmes, good old friend that he is, strongly supported my request. Captain Sullivan was doubtful.

'It's not that I don't want you on board, Dr Watson,' he explained. 'It's just that I had hoped to have Jock Munro with us to run some engineering tests.'

'Forget about me,' said Jock generously. 'We can run a second voyage later today, and I'll do the tests then. Mr Holmes and Dr Watson will be leaving Loch Ness soon—I would like them both to have a run on our ship and see how grand it really is.'

'Very well, Dr Watson,' said Sullivan. 'With Jock's support it looks as though you have a berth on this voyage under the loch.'

And so it was that half an hour later we were going through the now familiar routine of steaming out towards the middle of the loch with the top hatch open. Then

Captain Sullivan closed the hatch, transferred the motive power from the steam engine to the electric motor, and gave the order to dive.

As we sank beneath the inky waters of the loch, we didn't know it at the time, but we were about to meet a creature out of our darkest nightmares.

20

The first hint of a problem came after we had been cruising successfully under the water for some five minutes or so.

'This is how this ship is meant to work, gentlemen,' Captain Sullivan was saying proudly, as we cruised a hundred feet below the surface of the loch, silent except for the quiet whirr of the electric motor. Sullivan was turning around to face us as he spoke, and we could see him clearly in the dim, yellow glow of the incandescent lamp.

We also saw the look of shock and horror on his face when, with a loud thump, the submarine suddenly shifted sideways.

'Benton, what was that?' he shouted to his helmsman.

'I don't know, sir. Except that ...'

'Yes, I know ... except that this is exactly how it began last time.'

'How what began?' I asked.

'The strange disturbances when the vessel went out of control,' explained Sullivan, 'after the guidance mechanism had been tampered with.'

'But it can't be the same problem, sir,' called Benton, from his place at the helm. 'Jock checked and re-checked the guidance system. This time nothing has been sabotaged.'

Then it happened again—a solid thump, and sudden shifting of the submarine's position in the water.

'How does the helm feel, Benton?' asked Sullivan.

'Solid as a rock, sir. All the controls are still answering. So it can't be quite like ...'

He stopped abruptly as the nose of the submarine dipped sharply downwards, and there was a sudden sense of forward movement.

For the next minute all four of us sat in that narrow steel cylinder—cramped and smelling strongly of oil—waiting for what would happen next.

'Do you remember what you said to us after the last occasion, captain?' Holmes asked quietly.

'What did I say,' responded Sullivan absent mindedly, his eyes on the dials that showed the depth of our dive.

'You said that it was almost as if this vessel had been attacked by a giant sea creature.'

'Just a figure of speech,' explained Sullivan.

'Or possibly—the literal truth,' Holmes said grimly.

At this Sullivan turned away from his dials and stared at Holmes.

'I don't understand what you're suggesting ...' he began, and then stopped when the ship began to be pulled back and forth in a series of rapid movements.

'Benton!' he shouted. 'Pull up, man! Pull up!'

'The controls are not responding, sir,' replied Benton, his voice still calm. 'But it's not like last time. Last time all the controls went slack—because, as we now know, the control wires had been snapped. Well, this time the controls are frozen solid—I can't shift them. It's almost though something has been wrapped tightly around the rudder and dive fins, preventing them from moving.'

'Wrapped around?' said Holmes thoughtfully. 'Yes, that might explain it.'

Suddenly we were all thrown back in our seats as we felt the submarine being pulled through the water, as if by a giant fist.

'Benton! Cut the engines,' barked Captain Sullivan. 'We might as well conserve our limited battery power.'

'Engines off, sir,' responded the Lieutenant.

Sullivan glanced at the dials on the panel in front of him and then said, 'We're being pulled through the water at 12 knots—that's faster than our top speed, submerged, under our own power.'

For a moment the vessel seemed to stand still and then, gripped and shaken once more by the giant invisible hand that apparently gripped us, we shot off into deeper water.

'Will the plates hold, sir—at this depth?' asked Benton.

'The reason we're still alive,' replied Sullivan, 'is because this submarine has been so solidly built. It's protecting us from whatever the crushing forces are outside our hull.'

The speed through the water, as reported to us at intervals by Captain Sullivan, never decreased.

'Surely, Captain,' said Holmes, 'we must have traversed almost the entire width of the loch by now.'

'Yes, I was just starting to think the same thing, Mr Holmes. We must be about at the western shore of the loch by now.'

As our slim, steel vessel was shaken again the incandescent lamp flickered momentarily and threatened to go out, then it settled again and continued to produce its dim, yellow glow.

There were sounds outside the hull that we could hear clearly now—strange thumps and scrapes, and the bubbling whoosh of the deep, dark water that we were passing through.

After a while these sounds changed, our forward movement slowed, and the small ship was pulled and tugged back and forth in various directions. A bump, combined with a clanging noise, came first from one side and then from the other.

'We're being taken through some sort of underwater tunnel or cave,' said Holmes as he sat listening intently.

'By Jove, Holmes,' I exclaimed, 'I think you're right.'

'I'm quite certain Mr Holmes is right,' confirmed Captain Sullivan. 'The only way to account for these movements and sounds is if we are being dragged through a cave system—an underwater cave system.'

Quite suddenly, and without any warning, the submarine floated free—as if the giant fist that had held us had opened its fingers and let us go.

'We're rising, sir,' said Benton in a hushed tone as he glanced at one of his dials.

We all sat tensely, waiting for the bump and clang that would come when we struck the roof of the underwater cave. But it never came. Instead, all sense of movement ceased, and, in the silence that followed we could faintly hear the lapping of small waves against our hull.

'We've surfaced, sir!' cried Benton with delight.

'Impossible!' snapped Captain Sullivan. 'Look at that depth gauge.'

'I suggest, Captain,' said Holmes, 'that your depth gauge has been damaged by the recent shaking given to this vessel. Lieutenant Benton is quite correct—we are on the surface.'

Sullivan looked at Holmes doubtfully, but then he released his safety harness and climbed up the short steel ladder to the hatchway. Once there he began to slowly unfasten the levers that held the hatch in place and kept it waterproof. He moved slowly, as if fearful of water flooding through the hatch at any moment.

But this didn't happen. Instead, when the hatch was fully opened fresh air came in—air but no light. Somehow we were on the surface, but still in darkness.

Sullivan climbed out onto the narrow deck of the submarine.

'By George!' he called out to those of us below him. 'Come out here and look at this!'

One by one we followed him onto the deck. We were floating on a lake of water inside a vast cavern. High above our heads a faint gleam of sunlight could be seen where a small tunnel entered the cavern.

'That's where the fresh air is coming from,' said Holmes. 'Somewhere far above us, after many twistings and turnings, that tunnel reaches the surface.'

'How do we get out of here, Holmes?' I asked.

'That, Watson, presents us with a very interesting problem.'

21

'Lieutenant Benton,' said Sherlock Holmes. 'Is there a hurricane lamp on this submarine?'

'Yes, sir, I think there is.'

'Then it might be a good idea to fetch it and light it—to give us a clearer idea of where we are.'

'Yes, of course, Mr Holmes. I'll fetch it at once.' So saying Benton climbed back down into the submarine, to return two minutes later with the hurricane lamp and a box of matches in his hands. Benton lit the lamp and handed it to Holmes.

We all looked around as Holmes held the hurricane lamp high over his head. The cavern we were in was so vast that the light could not reach the roof, and reached the distant walls only faintly.

'Where are we, Holmes?' I asked.

'Underneath the steep hills that look down on Loch Ness, Watson. We are in the lair of whatever brought us here.'

'And what did bring us here, Mr Holmes?' asked Harry Sullivan. 'Was it the legendary creature of the loch?'

'I doubt it. If such a creature exists—as Dr Cameron believes it does—then it will dwell in the depths. No, I suspect that this is the trap laid for us by Louis La Rothier.'

As we took this in we all looked around—still trying to make sense of our surroundings. The Bruce-Partington submarine was bobbing in the middle of a small lake of inky black water, some distance away from the steep, rocky sides of the cavern.

'Captain Sullivan,' said Holmes, 'would it be possible to restart the engines and take this vessel over to that far side—there appears to be a rocky shelf there.'

'Ah, yes, I see where you mean. Yes, we can do that in a jiffy. Come along Benton, back down to the controls.'

Holmes and I remained on deck while the ship's electric motor resumed its quiet whirr, and the vessel was steered over towards a large, flat, rocky shelf at the far end of the cavern. As we approach the shelf, Holmes took a rope from the deck and leaped onto the rock. A moment later he had tied the ship up to a stony outcropping, and Sullivan, Benton and I followed him ashore.

We explored our surroundings and found ourselves on a flat sheet of rock surrounded on three sides by towering, cliff-like walls, and on the fourth by the freezing black water.

'I still don't understand how we came to be here, Holmes, or what has happened to us,' I complained.

'I am not certain myself,' he replied, 'but I can make an intelligent guess. I owe you a confession Watson.'

'A confession?'

'Precisely. For I have one piece of information that I have not shared with you. The night that Lestrade told us about Meyer and La Rothier I sent a telegram from the village to brother Mycroft in London, asking for whatever information he could provide about those two agents. Of Meyer he could tell me nothing, and of La Rothier he had only one piece of information—namely that the man has a reputation as a skilled animal trainer.'

'Animal trainer? So, that's why you expected to find him in the circus?'

'In addition to the reasons I have already given you—yes. La Rothier, it seems, is reputed to be able to train, or tame, or make use of, almost any animal, fish or bird, from the smallest to the largest. His associate, at one time, was Wilson, the notorious canary trainer.'

'But how does that explain our present situation?'

Holmes' explanation was interrupted by a noise behind us. We turned around to see the black water in which the submarine floated boiling and churning.

'What on earth ...?' began Sullivan. But before he could finish his question, the answer—the horrible, ghastly answer—became apparent.

A long, glistening body emerged from the churning waters. The body was some 18 yards long. At one end of this body were two fins, at the other end water dripped off a head surrounded by ten waving, threatening tentacles. Its arms, or tentacles, were twice as long as its body. It swam towards us through the boiling water, watching us with its enormous, staring green eyes. The monster's mouth was a horned beak, like a parrot's, that opened and shut vertically. Its tongue, a horned substance, furnished with several rows of pointed teeth, came out quivering from this veritable pair of shears.

Its spindle-like body formed a fleshy mass that must have weighed tons. The varying colour of this body changed with great rapidity, according to the irritation of the animal, passing successively from livid grey to reddish brown.

'Holmes, what is it?' I cried.

'A giant squid, especially trained by the evil La Rothier, and released into Loch Ness for the specific purpose of destroying the Bruce-Partington submarine.'

'So this is the monster that destroyed our guidance system last week?' Sullivan asked, in a quiet, trembling voice.

'Precisely, captain,' Holmes replied. 'This is also the creature that has dragged us here to its lair.'

'For what purpose?'

'I think you'll find the purpose is obvious, captain,' Holmes said calmly.

Just at that moment one of the giant tentacles lashed through the air and wrapped itself around Benton. The poor man screamed in agony as we rushed to his aid. Sullivan pulled out a pocket knife and began hacking at the quivering flesh of the tentacle. Holmes picked up a loose rock and began to pound at another tentacle that was creeping across the rock towards us. I pulled my army revolver out of my pocket and carefully aimed straight between the beast's horrible green eyes.

I fired off all six cartridges. I am prepared to swear that all six bullets found their mark. And yet the creature showed no reaction—it appeared not to feel the shots at all.

Benton was being dragged, kicking and screaming, towards the water's edge. Nothing we could do appeared to have any impact on that fierce and powerful beast. I was certain that all was lost, that Benton would be killed first and we would quickly follow him.

But I was wrong, for at that moment another head broke through the surface of the inky water.

This was no giant squid—this was something altogether different, altogether more ancient and strange. A huge, broad, flat, grey head rose out of the water. For a moment it towered over the giant squid, then it opened a large, cavernous mouth lined with row upon row of thick, flat, grinding teeth. In a flash this mouth swooped down and seized the squid. Instantly that creature released its hold on Benton and turned to face its new foe.

We hurriedly grabbed Benton and pulled him as far back from the water's edge as we could. And there we sat, our backs against the rock wall, witnessing a titanic struggle between the world's largest invertebrate and the strange survival from the Jurassic age.

The two twisted and turned, lashing and crashing against each other. But it was an unequal contest—the giant squid never stood a chance. Within minutes its huge body was inert and lifeless. Once it was certain that its foe was dead, the other gigantic, ancient creature turned and looked at us with its small, beady black eyes. Then it slowly submerged beneath the water and vanished from our sight.

Recovering from the shock, I found my voice and stuttered, 'What ... what was it?'

'Having seen the creature face to face,' replied Sherlock Holmes, 'I can tell you, Watson, that your medical friend, Dr Cameron, is quite correct—it is a plesiosaurus.'

'That is the beast of Loch Ness? The creature of legend?'

'It is indeed.'

'Why did it kill the squid?'

'Because it was a giant sea creature invading its domain— invading its territory. No doubt the plesiosaurus, like all animals, is strongly territorial. What matters for the moment, Watson, is that you examine Benton and do what you can to dress his wounds.'

'Yes ... yes, of course, Holmes. Straight away.'

I fetched a first aid kit from the submarine and did what I could for Benton. He had been gripped by the suckers on the giant squid's tentacles, and in the centre of each sucker— as I discovered when I examined the corpse—was a hooked claw. These had torn poor Benton's flesh. However, none of the wounds was very deep, and I was able to clean and dress them all with the materials in the first aid kit.

As I worked I heard Holmes and Sullivan speaking softly.

'Well, Sullivan,' asked Holmes, 'when it is safe to move Benton, do you think you will be able to get us out of here in the submarine?'

'I'd already thought about that Mr Holmes—and I'm quite certain I can. I'll have to run at half-speed so as not to damage the vessel against the rocks, but if I take it slowly I'm confident I can find the underwater tunnel that we were dragged in through by that ... that ... that horrible creature, and take us out the same way.'

And that, in fact, is what happened.

Much later that day, when we were packing our bag in preparation for leaving the castle, many questions started to occur to me.

'Holmes,' I asked, 'how did La Rothier get his giant squid into Loch Ness? There is no direct opening between the loch and the sea, so how did he do it?'

'It must have been brought up from the port at Inverness in a large tank.'

'But how could he have done that without anyone noticing?'

'If the tank was on a brightly painted cart, and was part of a parade of similar circus carts—who would notice?'

'Oh, yes. Yes, of course.'

Later still, as we sat in the duke's coach being driven to Inverness, where the Royal Navy cutter *HMS Drake* was waiting to take us back to London, I said, 'That ancient creature Holmes, that plesiosaurus thing—I find it hard to believe that any such thing ever did exist, let alone that one small colony of them still does exist, hidden at the bottom of Loch Ness.'

'You should not find any creature strange or unbelievable Watson. After all, it simply proves yet again the amazing variety and wonder of this creation, and of the Maker who designed it.'

'Yes, of course, Holmes. You're quite right, of course— quite right.'

'And not only has our Maker provided us with strange creatures, but also with delightful ones. Don't forget that fine, plump goose that brother Mycroft is bringing for our Christmas dinner!'

Afterword

The most common mistake made by authors who attempt to write new Sherlock Holmes stories is to give the great detective fairly ordinary, drawing room murders to solve. Holmes rarely tackled ordinary cases. (There are, of course, exceptions: "Silver Blaze" is a straightforward murder mystery, and an excellent one.)

On the whole, Holmes will always be seen at his best when confronted with a puzzle that is bizarre as well as mysterious, and well beyond the capacity of any other detective.

So, why did Conan Doyle not give Holmes and Watson a "Loch Ness monster" adventure?

In all probability, because that particular monster did not properly emerge into the consciousness of the public until after he had stopped writing. The modern spate of sightings began in the 1930s—towards the end of Conan Doyle's writing career—and the most energetic searches for "Nessie" have been relatively recent.

In 1960, a British aircraft engineer named Tim Dinsdale made a short film of a dark object moving through Loch Ness. Since then, investigations using sonar have found large moving bodies in the loch. In 1972 and 1975 American scientists took underwater photographs they claim show the creature—a claim others dispute.

By the way, in Billy Wilder's 1970 movie *The Private Life of Sherlock Holmes*, Loch Ness is the setting for the climax which features both a submarine and the "Loch Ness monster". Sadly, in that film the so-called "monster" turns out to be the submarine! Now that, in my view, is a cheat. In a story about the Loch Ness monster, there has to be a real, flesh and blood monster!

Perhaps the British authorities agree with me, because they have given "Nessie" a proper scientific classification (*Nessiteras rhombopteryx*) just in case it turns out to be there, and to be in need of protection from scientists and sightseers.

Finally, what do I think? Do I believe a monster is really there, lurking in those murky depths? I don't know. But if it does turn out to be there, I shall be inclined to agree with Holmes that it 'simply proves yet again the amazing variety and wonder of this creation, and of the mighty Creator God who made it.'

Footsteps
in the
Fog

Sherlock Holmes is not the only remarkable and unforgettable hero created by Sir Arthur Conan Doyle. There is also the astonishing (and often overwhelming) Professor Challenger. The only complaint it is possible to make is that Conan Doyle wrote too few Challenger stories. The following tale seeks to redress the balance, by introducing a slightly younger professor, and teaming him up with Holmes and Watson.

By the way, an old nemesis re-appears in this tale. No, not Professor Moriarty—he really did die at the Reichenbach Falls (regardless of what other revisionists may claim to the contrary). But there is some evidence that his lieutenant (the "second most dangerous man in London") Colonel Sebastian Moran was not hung, but sentenced to life imprisonment. And that opens up all sorts of possibilities ...

1

The prisoner in cell 13 was strangely calm. His powerful, yet sinister face showed intense concentration. Colonel Sebastian Moran had once been a big game hunter, before he became a man-hunter and was jailed for murder. He displayed the same steady nerves and calm focus he must have shown while waiting in a jungle hide for a man-eating tiger.

'That's Moran,' said Wilson, the chief warder to the new recruit, as they paused at the door of cell 13. 'He's in for life—for murder and attempted murder.'

Moran turned and faced the two warders standing on the other side of the bars that formed his cell door. He had a bald head surrounded by long, thick, grey hair, a weather-beaten face, and a thick, grey moustache.

'He looks harmless enough,' said the new recruit.

'Don't let his looks fool you, my lad,' replied Wilson. 'When he was second in command to the late Professor Moriarty, Scotland Yard regarded him as the second most dangerous man in London. After Moriarty's death, at the hands of Sherlock Holmes at the Reichenbach Falls, he moved to the top of the list.'

As they watched a purple flush coloured the face of the prisoner in cell 13, and he slowly fell forward onto his bunk.

'Sir! He's been taken ill.'

'Careful, my lad. Men like him have been known to fake sickness before. You stay here in the corridor, ready to call for help. I'm going in.'

With those words Wilson pulled out a huge key ring, found the key to cell 13, and unlocked the door. He hurried to the bunk, and knelt at the prisoner's side.

'He's not breathing. Fetch a stretcher and call for the doctor!'

As the young man ran off, Wilson loosened the collar of the prisoner's shirt, rolled him onto his back, and began to pump his chest.

There was the sound of running footsteps, and a moment later the cell was crowded. Two more warders had arrived carrying a stretcher. With them was the prison doctor, a middle-aged, bald headed man in a black suit with a stethoscope around his neck.

'He's still alive,' reported the doctor, after a quick examination, 'but his breathing is very shallow and his pulse

111

is weak. Take him to the prison infirmary at once.'

As Moran's limp body was lifted onto the stretcher and carried out of the cell, Wilson muttered, 'That's very strange. I've never seen anything like it before. And Moran has always seemed so fit and healthy.'

The prison infirmary was a small hospital ward with bars on the windows and the only door. The two warders carrying the stretcher laid the prisoner from cell 13 onto one of the beds. The other five beds in the room were all empty. The doctor arrived a moment later, puffed and out of breath, having half-run and half-walked down the long corridors of the prison.

He sat at the patient's bedside, and used his stethoscope to conduct another examination. 'Still breathing,' he muttered to himself. 'I can't understand what's happened to him.'

'Excuse me, sir,' said one of the warders who had carried the stretcher, 'do you need us any longer? Because we really should be getting back ...'

'Yes, of course,' the doctor replied. 'You can leave me here.'

'We'll have to lock you in with the prisoner, sir,' explained the warder. 'It's regulations. This prisoner here must be under lock and key at all times. He's regarded as highly dangerous.'

'Well, he's not dangerous now. As you can see, he's unconscious.'

With a curt wave of his hand the doctor dismissed the two warders. As they left they locked the barred door to the prison infirmary.

The doctor again checked the pulse of his patient, and then went to a bench at the far end of the room to prepare an injection. As soon as he left the bedside, the eyes of the prisoner on the bed snapped open. He glanced around the room, and then sat up—slowly and stealthily, careful not to make a sound. He eased his feet onto the floor and stood up.

Then he began moving towards the doctor, whose back was still towards him—moving as silently as a big game hunter stalking his prey. Suddenly he seized the doctor from behind and wrestled him to the floor.

'Don't make a sound!' hissed the prisoner, as he pressed his hand over the doctor's mouth. 'Do you promise to remain absolutely silent?'

The doctor nodded. The prisoner removed his hand, and, as he stood up, said, 'If you are cooperative I shall let you live. If you resist in the least, I shall have to kill you.'

As he spoke there was a cold, hard light in his eyes, and the doctor believed every word he said. 'Take off your suit, and then sit in this chair,' continued the prisoner, 'while I tie you up and gag you.'

'How did you do it?' asked the doctor, as he took off his suit coat and trousers.

'Oh, my "illness" you mean? A little trick I learned in India years ago,' replied the prisoner, as he bound the doctor with twisted sheets from one of the beds. 'There are yoga masters there who have the most remarkable control over their bodies. They can almost stop their heartbeat and breath at will. I spent these last two years in prison practising the technique ... while I planned my revenge on the man who put me here.'

These last words were muttered with a bitter, savage edge, and the doctor was glad he was not the man who was about to be hunted down by this cold-blooded killer.

Once the medical man was bound and gagged, Colonel Sebastian Moran went into the doctor's small office that opened off one end of the prison infirmary.

There he used a scalpel and cold tea from a teapot to shave off his own thick moustache, and to trim back his long, thick, grey hair. Then he dressed himself in the doctor's suit, put the doctor's black, felt hat on his head, being sure to pull down the wide brim to partially hide his face, and picked up the doctor's medical bag.

But before leaving the office he sat down at the desk and wrote a short note.

'You see,' explained the prisoner, as he walked back into the ward, 'my whole plan began when I noticed a remarkable resemblance in general appearance between ourselves, dear doctor. And, before I leave, if I am to play your part—then you must play mine.'

With these words he lifted the doctor's tightly bound and gagged body from the chair onto one of the beds, and pulled up the sheets so that they almost covered the face.

Then he walked to the door and called the guard. It was Wilson who came.

'How's the prisoner then?'

'Much better. He's sleeping now. It would be best if he were not disturbed until tomorrow.' Moran had spent months perfecting his impersonation of the doctor's voice.

'If you say so, doctor.'

An hour later, long after the 'doctor' had left the prison, Wilson decided to check up on the sick prisoner in the infirmary. But when he pulled back the sheets what he found was his own prison doctor—tightly bound and gagged.

As the alarm was being raised and the police alerted, Wilson found the note lying on the desk in the doctor's small office.

The note read: *Please inform Mr Sherlock Holmes that he has less than a week to live. I am the greatest hunter in the world—and he is the quarry I am hunting.* And the note was signed, *Colonel Sebastian Moran.*

2

Later that same night, John Ferguson was walking around St John's Hall, in Regent's Park, checking that all the outer doors were locked. Ferguson was the nightwatchman at St John's Hall, which stood on a curved roadway called the Inner Circle amidst the trees and bushes and rolling parkland of Regent's Park.

Ferguson had reached the back of the hall, and was checking the small wooden back door when something caught his eye. Glancing up into a cloudless sky, sprinkled with stars, he saw a streak of light.

'Shooting star,' he said to himself.

'Quite right,' replied a voice beside him.

Ferguson hadn't realised that he had spoken aloud, and, startled, he turned to the small man who was standing at his side. Seeing the questioning look, the small man introduced himself.

'Jabez Whitney is the name. Cab driving is the game. I'm just allowing my cab horse over there to have a nibble on your grass before I take 'im home for the night. I 'ope you don't mind. You don't seem to 'ave any shortage of grass,' he added, glancing around.

Ferguson just grunted in reply. He was paid to keep an eye on St John's Hall—not the grass. They returned their attention to the shooting star.

'You're quite right,' continued Whitney, 'that thing there is a shooting star. But do you know what a shooting star really is, sir? I read all about shooting stars in the *Daily Gazette* just the other day.'

Ferguson kept gazing, silently, at the night sky. Whitney took this as an invitation to continue. 'Meteors,' he said, 'that's what they are. Great lumps of rock that are hurtling through space. And when they enter our atmosphere, they burn up, like. And that's what makes them shooting stars. Only they're not really stars at all, you see—just meteors.'

'Well, this one's not burning up,' muttered Ferguson, his gaze directed at the long, thin, streak of light that now stretched across half the night sky.

'By golly, you're right!' exclaimed the cabman. 'What's more—I reckon it's gunna hit the earth. Not too far from here, either.'

The realisation that he was speaking the truth rendered both men silent. As they stood watching, the blazing white light grew brighter, and larger.

It was as though they were hypnotised, their feet cemented to the ground and unable to move. Soon, with the blaze filling the sky over their heads, they could hear it as well—a screaming whistle, like a tropical windstorm.

It was the little cabman who broke the spell. 'I think we'd better get outa here, chum,' he said, with a note of panic in his voice.

The two men turned and ran. They zigzagged across the grass, as if uncertain in which direction to find safety. Finally, Ferguson settled on a giant, ancient oak tree about a hundred yards beyond the edge of Regent's Park Lake. Jabez Whitney decided this oak would be as good as any other, and followed him.

As both men crouched behind the ancient oak Whitney

muttered, 'Amazing! Blooming amazing!'

Even the silent John Ferguson was moved to words, as the dark, moonless night was turned into noonday brightness by the blazing meteor in the sky. 'I've never seen anything like it,' he said.

'And never will again,' added the cabman.

Both men watched in silent wonder as the light filling Regent's Park glowed a brilliant blue-white and the noise of the plummeting meteor became an ear-bursting scream.

'Great Caesar's Ghost!' shouted the cabman over the noise, 'that thing's gunna land in Regent's Park!'

Both men threw themselves to the ground, and a moment later there was a hissing, crackling explosion, and the ground beneath them shuddered. Then all was silent.

They looked up, and found the blackness of the moonless night had returned.

'Where is it? Where did it land?' asked Whitney anxiously.

'I can't see a thing until my night vision returns,' replied Ferguson as he clambered to his feet. He stood still, and stared at the black, star sprinkled sky. Slowly his eyes recovered from the white blaze they had been subjected to, and he blinked and looked around.

'It's crashed in the lake,' he said at last, and started to walk across the grass. Jabez Whitney hurried to his side.

The two men strode across the intervening distance rapidly, and then came to an abrupt halt.

'Except that there isn't any lake any longer,' said Whitney, stating the obvious. Where the Regent's Park Lake should have been was an empty, muddy hole. In the middle of that hole, embedded in a crater of mud, was a rock about the size of a football.

'So—that's it,' murmured Ferguson.

'A little thing to cause such a big fuss,' added Whitney.

Just then the rock began to glow.

'Hello—it's doin' something,' said the little cabman.

The two men watched in silence as the meteor emitted a faint, green glow. Slowly the glow grew brighter, and then it began to pulse.

There were thin sheets of mist drifting between the men and the meteor—steam from the lake water that had evaporated when the burning hot meteor plunged into it. And the mist made it difficult to see clearly just what the strange visitor from outer space was doing.

But the one thing they couldn't doubt was that the meteor was glowing steadily brighter, and its light was pulsing faster.

'Meteors shouldn't do that,' said Jabez Whitney. 'At least, according to the *Daily Gazette* they shouldn't.'

John Ferguson began to clamber into the muddy hole that had once been the lake, and walk towards the strange, glowing, pulsing rock.

'I wouldn't do that, if I was you,' called out Whitney after him. But the nightwatchman paid no attention to the warning.

Just then, a cloud of mist brushed over the glowing rock, and as the tendrils of steam touched its surface they seemed to change. They seemed to take on the glowing, green appearance of the meteor itself. Then those tendrils of mist seemed to gather themselves up into a thick, pulsing, green cloud.

At this point Jabez Whitney's cab horse began to neigh and whinny, and rear and plunge. 'I can't stay,' he called out to Ferguson. 'I've got to see to my horse.'

And because he turned and hurried away, Whitney did

not see what happened next. He did not see the green, faintly pulsing cloud spread itself around John Ferguson. He did not see the cloud spread itself over Ferguson's face and mouth, and he did not see the nightwatchman collapse in the mud, screaming silently.

3

It was a foggy night on Baker Street, and Sherlock Holmes and I were glad of the blazing fire that warmed our rooms at number 221B.

Holmes was pasting newspaper cuttings in one of his index books—his enormous collection of crime reports that, added to his own uncanny memory, made him feared by all criminals, both great and small.

I poured myself a fresh cup of tea and went to stand in the bay window looking out into Baker Street.

'Foul night, Holmes,' I remarked.

'But good weather for crime, Watson,' Holmes responded. 'It is in the shadows of darkness, and under the cloak of fog, that the criminal likes to operate. On the whole the criminal mind is small, and tends towards the obvious. The great criminals are gone, Watson. Those great battles of intellect that I once engaged in against Professor Moriarty and Colonel Sebastian Moran—like a giant game of chess, with the whole of London as our chessboard—they are a thing of the past.'

'It sounds as though you miss them, Holmes.'

'I must have a challenge, Watson. Without a challenge I sink into unutterable boredom.'

At that moment a hansom cab pulled up at our front door.

'A visitor, Holmes,' I remarked. 'In fact, it's Inspector Lestrade of Scotland Yard. What can have brought him out on a night like this?'

A few moments later we discovered the reason for his errand. As Lestrade settled into the basket chair facing the fire I poured him a cup of tea.

'Ah, thank you, Dr Watson. Just what I need on a dreadful foggy night like this.'

'Well, Lestrade?' said Holmes. 'To what do we owe the pleasure of your company?'

'I've come with a warning, Mr Holmes,' replied the Scotland Yard man.

A look of keen interest came into Holmes' thin face. His hawk-like profile and sharp, grey eyes lit up.

'There has been an escape,' continued Lestrade, 'from one of Her Majesty's prisons. He was supposed to be kept under special and constant attention, in cell 13 of Dartmoor Prison, but he got away none the less. Devilishly clever scheme he devised to get himself out. I dare say only he could have thought of it, and only he could have pulled it off.'

'Who are you talking about, Lestrade—you haven't told us his name,' I complained.

'Oh, haven't I? Sorry. It's Moran—Colonel Sebastian Moran.'

'So, now the fun begins, Watson,' said Holmes grimly.

'You may call it fun, Mr Holmes,' Lestrade remarked, 'I certainly don't. He left this note behind. I thought you'd want to see it.'

Inspector Lestrade fished the note out of his overcoat pocket and handed it to Holmes. I looked over Holmes' shoulder as he read the short message: *Please inform Mr Sherlock Holmes that he has less than a week to live. I am the greatest hunter in the world—and he is the quarry I*

121

am hunting. And the note was signed, *Colonel Sebastian Moran.*

'Do you think he means it, Holmes?' I asked.

'He most certainly means it, Watson,' replied the great detective. 'Colonel Moran is in deadly earnest over this business.' As he spoke he turned around and fetched an index volume from a bookcase. The volume had a large "M" stamped on its spine.

'My collection of M's is a fine one,' said Holmes. 'The late lamented Professor Moriarty himself is enough to make any letter illustrious. And here is Morgan the poisoner, and Merridew of abominable memory, and Matthews, who knocked out my left canine tooth in the waiting room at Charing Cross, and, finally, here is our friend.'

He handed over the book and I read; '*Moran, Sebastian, Colonel.* Convict. Formerly 1st Bengal Pioneers. Born, London, 1840. Son of Sir Augustus Moran, C.B., once British Ambassador to Persia. Educated Eton and Oxford. Served in the Afghan Campaign (mentioned in dispatches). Author of *Heavy Game of the Western Himalayas*, 1881; and *Three Months in the Jungle*, 1884.'

On the margin was written in Holmes' precise hand: 'The second most dangerous man in London.'

'It was two years ago,' commented Lestrade, 'that he was convicted and sent to prison for the murder of Ronald Adair.'

'And the attempted murder of Sherlock Holmes,' I added.

'Indeed,' agreed Lestrade. 'And it was Holmes who caught him and sent him to trial. Clearly now he wants his revenge. May I propose, Mr Holmes, that I arrange for a constable to be stationed outside your front door at all times.'

'You may certainly propose, inspector,' Holmes replied, 'and it is very kind of you to do so. But I reject your offer. Let there be no guard. Let Colonel Moran come. This is a tussle between him and me. At the end only one of us will be left standing. Either Moran will be in handcuffs on his way back to prison, or I shall be dead.'

In vain did Inspector Lestrade attempt to change Holmes' mind, and eventually he left us, sadly shaking his head at the folly of the great detective.

As the Scotland Yard officer left our rooms, Holmes turned to me, rubbing his hands gleefully, and said, 'Well, Watson—the game's afoot!'

At that moment, in another part of Baker Street, an incident was occurring that I was to learn of only later, but which was to have a great effect on our lives.

On the corner of David Street and Baker Street, not far south of Regent's Park, Fred Duncan, a barman at the *Rose and Crown* public house, was making his way home. He was walking slowly because the fog was thick, and the gas lights that lined the street were almost invisible in that heavy, damp, choking atmosphere.

Fred Duncan came to a halt when he noticed that one patch of fog in front of him seemed to, somehow, be thicker than the rest. And it was a different colour too. Instead of the usual dirty grey colour of London fog, this was green—faintly glowing green. Fred took a cautious step closer to investigate. Whatever the pale light was in this fog, it seemed to pulse with a faint but regular pattern. Fred took off his hat and scratched his head.

This had him puzzled. He had seen many things in his time, but never anything like this.

'I wonder of it's dangerous,' he said to himself. 'Perhaps that funny colour means it's infected with some disease or other.' As this thought struck, Fred backed away. But the patch of thick, green fog followed him. In fact, it drifted closer and closer. No matter which way he moved, the green, glowing patch of fog moved with him.

Fred Duncan became alarmed, and was about to turn and run when, suddenly, the cloud of coloured fog rushed at him, settled on his chest, and then started crawling up towards his face.

He was too terrified to call out or scream. All he could do was to watch in horror as it crept up over his throat, and mouth, until it covered his face. And then he did scream. But it was too late. The scream was silent. Smothered.

4

The next development in this strange adventure occurred the following morning. I was not present, but I have compiled my report from the accounts of those who were.

It was one of those brilliant, sunny mornings that often follow heavy fog. In Regent's Park Professor Summerlee of the Royal Society was supervising a gang of workmen. He was a tall, thin, withered man with a bitter expression on his face.

'Come along, come along,' he urged the workmen laying planks across the mud, creating a temporary bridge to the meteor in its crater, 'we haven't got all day.'

'I dunno 'ow much time you got, professor,' replied one workman in blue overalls, 'we got as much time as it takes.' With those words he turned his back and returned to laying planks, slowly and carefully, across the broad expanse of mud that only the day before had been the Regent's Park Lake.

Professor Summerlee paced back and forth, and fretted and complained. It made no difference. The planking was laid at the workmen's own pace. But, eventually, it was finished. Summerlee walked out on the planking and squatted down on the edge of the crater.

'Remarkable,' he murmured to himself. 'Most remarkable.'

'And this lump of rock come from outer space, did it professor?' asked one of the workmen.

'It did,' replied Summerlee with an acid smile. 'And now we need it lifted into that cart over there, so that it can be taken into St John's Hall for closer investigation.'

'I'm your man then,' said the workman, rolling up his sleeves and spitting on his hands. 'I'm as strong as a bull I am. Not that it's gunna take much strength to lift that little thing.'

'Just be careful that's all. This meteor may be composed of completely unknown material.'

But the workman wasn't listening to this warning. He swaggered down the gentle slope of the mud crater, and bent over the football-sized piece of rock from the stars. A moment later there was a loud scream, and he leaped backwards.

'It burned me,' he called out, to anyone within earshot. 'That rotten thing burned me.'

'Odd,' muttered Summerlee to himself, 'it should not still be hot—not an object of that size—not after lying out here all night.'

'Talking to yourself again Summerlee?' boomed a raucous voice from over his shoulder. Summerlee turned and found himself facing a giant bear of a man. His size was overpowering, and his head was enormous. He had the face and beard of an Assyrian bull—the face was florid, and the beard, so black as to almost have a suspicion of blue, spade shaped and rippling down over his chest. The eyes were blue-grey under great, black tufts of eyebrows, very clear, very critical, and very masterful.

'Ah, Professor Challenger,' complained Summerlee, 'I should have expected you to turn up.'

'And if I had turned up a few minutes earlier I could have

saved you from making a damned fool of yourself.'

'No one could have known the meteor was still hot,' protested Professor Summerlee, in his whining, acid voice.

'I would have known,' boomed Challenger, 'because I would have had the wit to test it for temperature before allowing anyone to handle it.'

There was a heavy silence as both men stared at the strange object that had travelled countless millions of miles through the vacuum of space.

'How do you account for its temperature?' asked Summerlee at last.

'I don't,' boomed Challenger. 'I study first, I experiment, I take measurements—only then do I offer a theory.'

'So you don't have one of your hair-brained ideas to explain this phenomenon?'

'I knew it wouldn't take you long to become offensive, Summerlee,' growled Challenger.

At that moment the foreman of the work gang approached them, his cap in his hand.

'Professor Summerlee,' he said, apologetically, 'my men are refusing to touch that thing again. Because Jack got so badly burned, you see. He has great blisters coming up on both hands.'

'You tell those men from me ...' began Summerlee, in his high-handed manner.

'Hold your horses, Summerlee,' interrupted Challenger, 'let me handle this. Now then, Mr ...?'

'Jenkins,' said the foreman.

'Now then Mr Jenkins, let's tackle this with a bit of common sense. What say your men round up as many blankets as possible to use as insulation, and then we move the meteor?'

'Well, I don't know ...'

'And tell them,' boomed Challenger, in a voice that must have carried half way across Regent's Park, 'tell them that I'll take off my coat and work beside them.'

'Well, in that case,' Jenkins said, brightening up visibly, 'I'm sure they'd be happy to work.'

And so it was that half an hour later Professor Challenger, in shirtsleeves, and four workmen, in overalls, lifted the piece of rock out of the mud and onto a small cart standing nearby.

'By golly, that thing's heavy,' complained one of the men, as they released the rock and it tumbled into the cart.

'He's right,' confirmed Challenger. 'So there's your second unaccounted for fact, Summerlee—this meteor weighs far more than it should for its size. Now, what are your plans for this thing?'

'My intention is to move it no further than St John's Hall. Once there I intend to invite a suitable group of physicists, chemists, geologists and astronomers to examine it.'

'I have no quarrel with that procedure,' growled Challenger, as he put his coat back on.

'And at the same time,' continued Summerlee, 'I intend to open the hall to the public, and allow them to see the meteor.';

'No!' roared Challenger, like a wounded bull.

'Why ever not?'

'We don't know whether this thing is safe or not.'

'Safe? Of course it's safe.'

'You dunderheaded dimwit! We know almost nothing about these objects that wander between the planets—and you are prepared to expose the public to the unknown? I protest! I protest most vigorously, sir!'

'Protest noted,' said Summerlee in his most acid voice, 'and overruled.'

5

That night the fog settled again on Baker Street—this time, it seemed, thicker than ever.

Alexander Henderson, a clerk employed by the Capital and Counties Bank, was walking down Baker Street, his mind preoccupied by a lecture he had heard that evening at the Pastors' College, adjacent to the Metropolitan Tabernacle. In fact, so preoccupied was he with his thoughts that he suddenly looked up and realised he had no idea where he was.

In every direction, he could see nothing but dense, impenetrable fog. He turned around trying to find his bearings. This was a mistake, for after turning and looking in every direction several times, he was no longer certain in which direction he had been walking.

Then came the clop of horse's hooves and a shadow loomed out of the fog. Just in time Henderson leaped clear of the hansom cab.

'I have to find my way back to the footpath,' he said, as he picked himself up off the road, and dusted off his hands and knees. Moving cautiously, feeling forward through the fog with his hands and feet, he soon came to the gutter, and, just beyond that, a brick wall.

'At least,' he thought, 'I run no risk of being run over here.'

Henderson crept slowly forward through the fog, one hand on the wall. He had to find out exactly where he was, and recover his sense of direction. Soon he came to the yellow glow of a gas lamp—but this penetrated no more than a few feet into the dense, damp, clinging fog. Henderson left the comforting yellow glow behind and pressed on.

Soon the wall he was following changed from brick to stone, and he passed a set of stone steps leading up to a large, wooden door. A few paces further on he came to a corner, and there, fastened to the building, were street names. He struck a match and held it up to read the signs. One said "Baker Street" and the other "Adam Street".

'Then I'm still going in the right direction,' muttered Henderson. 'And this building must be the church— St Bede's on Baker Street.'

Just then, as his match flickered and went out, he saw another light no more than two yards ahead of him. But this time it wasn't the yellow glow of a gas lamp, or of another pedestrian carrying a candle or lamp—this time the light was a strange, glowing green.

It grew larger and nearer, and Henderson, filled with curiosity, stepped towards it.

'Hello?' he called out. 'Is anyone there?'

The smothering silence of the fog was the only reply. But the green light was brighter, and Henderson hurried towards it. Suddenly he stopped. There was something sickly, something unhealthy, about that light. He began to back away—but the green glow followed him.

Within a few steps he had backed up against the church wall. Green fingers of fog stole towards him. As he watched in silent terror, the green fingers wrapped themselves around his chest, and began to crawl, like some horrible spider, towards his face.

That's when he screamed. But his scream was choked,

smothered, by cold fingers of green fog. Henderson could feel it covering his face and creeping into his mouth and down his throat. And that was the last thing he ever felt.

'Is anyone there?' called a voice from the church door. It was the Reverend Henry Bunyan. He hurried down the stone steps, lantern in hand, and looked around.

Within a few seconds he had found the body of Alexander Henderson. He felt for a pulse. There was none, and he sadly dropped the lifeless arm back on to the young man's chest.

Then Bunyan took a close look at the victim's face—it was covered by what appeared to be green spider web. Bunyan held his lantern closer to get a better look, but as he did so, the spider web began to dissolve. Within a minute there was none left.

'How curious,' he muttered to himself. 'How very puzzling.'

The next morning Sherlock Holmes and I were in our sitting room warming ourselves in front of the fireplace. Our door opened and in walked our landlady, Mrs Hudson, carrying a tray containing two hot breakfasts—bacon, toast and eggs.

Behind her came a pretty girl carrying the teapot.

'New maid?' I asked, as I took my seat at the table.

'No, Dr Watson. This is my niece, Patience. She's staying with me for a short while. She's a country girl, and her parents wanted her to see a little of London.'

'Pleased to meet you m'dear,' I murmured, as I spread butter on a piece of hot toast. 'The important thing about London is not to get into any trouble. You listen to what Mrs Hudson here tells you and you'll be all right.'

'I'm certain I will, Dr Watson,' she said with a bright smile. Then she looked at her aunt and gave a nudge.

'Oh, yes,' Mrs Hudson said, as if she had forgotten something. 'Mr Holmes, this is my niece, Patience— Patience, this is Mr Sherlock Holmes.'

'How do you do?' said Holmes, with formal politeness.

'I'm terribly pleased to meet you, Mr Holmes,' gushed Patience, 'even in Devon we have heard of your amazing exploits, and everyone talks about you.'

Holmes said nothing, but I could tell that his vanity was pleased.

Mrs Hudson ushered her niece out of the room, and I picked up *The Times*.

'What's in the morning paper, Watson?' asked Holmes as he helped himself to more bacon.

'Let's see now. "Fog Murderer Claims Third Victim"— does that interest you?'

'Read the story, Watson, if you please.'

'Ah, well, it says: "The third mysterious death in as many days occurred last night, when the body of Alexander Henderson was found by Rev. Henry Bunyan on the steps of his church in Baker Street." Why, Holmes—that's our Mr Bunyan, our local minister.'

'Keep reading, please Watson.'

'Yes, of course. "All three deaths occurred on nights of exceptionally heavy fog, and in mysterious circumstances. Unconfirmed reports say that all the deaths resemble drownings, but all the victims were found well away from any substantial body of water. The first victim, nightwatchman John Ferguson, was found beside the lake in Regent's Park, but only after all the water in that lake had been evaporated by the meteor which struck there on Wednesday night (see report on page 3)." Oh, I shouldn't have read that last bit. Well, what do you think, Holmes? A homicidal maniac? A new Jack-the-Ripper who has found a bizarre way to kill his victims?'

'I don't have enough information yet, Watson. It is a capital error to theorise in advance of the facts. What else is there?'

'Well, the meteor is the big news story. And there's an amazing letter from a fellow named Challenger, claiming that the meteor is dangerous and warning members of the public to stay away from the exhibition of the meteor in St John's Hall. Bit of a crackpot, eh?'

'Not at all, Watson. Challenger has one of the best minds of our generation. He is one of the few men I would put on a par with myself.'

'How do you know him?'

'He has conducted some scientific inquiries for my brother Mycroft. A remarkable man, this Challenger.'

'What do you know about him?'

'Let me see now,' said Holmes, leaning back in his chair, placing the tips of his fingers together, and calling on his prodigious memory for the information. 'George Edward Challenger: born 1863; graduated from Edinburgh University 1891; British Museum Assistant Researcher 1892; Assistant Keeper of Comparative Anthropology 1893; resigned after acrimonious correspondence that same year; winner of the Craystone Medal for Zoological research; Ex-President of the Palaeontological Society ... and much more in the same vein. A brilliant, if erratic, man, Watson. In fact,' added Holmes, leaping from his chair at the breakfast table, 'he is living quite close by.'

'Is he, Holmes?' I muttered, my mouth full of eggs and toast, and not much interested in where the fellow might be living.

'Mycroft tells me that Challenger has a suite of rooms in Seymour Mansions, at the Wigmore Street end of Baker Street.'

'Very interesting, to be sure,' I replied, as I buttered another piece of toast.

'More than interesting, Watson—convenient. Since we are about to visit him.'

'Visit him? When? Why?'

'Now, old chap. Because I wish to know more about this meteor Challenger deems dangerous.'

Full of his old energy, Holmes pulled on his travelling cloak as his spoke, and threw my hat to me across the room. I abandoned my attempts to finish breakfast, pulled on my overcoat, and followed him out into Baker Street.

6

Although the sun was shining, it was a cold, bleak sun, and most of the fog had not yet cleared. Carriages, cabs and four-wheelers rumbled through the fog, looking like fleeting shadows looming out of the grey-white mist and then disappearing again.

The cold was biting, and seemed to soak through our very clothes. Sherlock Holmes wore his heavy Inverness Cape and deerstalker hat, while I had my thick old army greatcoat on, and a bowler hat to protect my head from the chill dampness. Despite these precautions we had to walk briskly to keep warm. The thick fog was damp and depressing. It seemed to cling to us at every stride.

'One day, Watson,' said Holmes as we walked, 'Challenger will make a major scientific discovery that will shake the world. You mark my words—he's that sort of chap.'

We were walking south along Baker Street, and every intersection was hazardous. We could neither see the approaching traffic, nor could they see us. We had crossed over both Crawford Street and Dorset Street safely when the incident happened. We paused on the corner of Blandford Street, and, being unable to see any approaching vehicles in the rolling blanket of fog, listened intently. We heard nothing and stepped from the curb.

Halfway across the road Holmes suddenly stiffened and became alert.

'Run, Watson!' he shouted, as he grabbed my arm and dragged me towards the footpath. As he did so a runaway cab brushed against my arm and knocked me to the ground. Holmes helped me to my feet and we scrambled to the safety of the sidewalk.

'Well done, Holmes ...' I said, gasping for breath. 'You've saved my life.'

He made no reply, but stood beside me silent and thoughtful, brushing the street dirt from the arms and knees of his cloak.

'I say,' I continued, 'why couldn't we hear that cab coming, Holmes?'

'Because the horses' hooves were muffled, old chap.'

'Muffled? But why on earth would anyone muffle their horses' shoes on a day like this?'

'So as to catch a pedestrian unawares, Watson.'

'Pedestrian? What pedestrian?'

'Me, old chap. I'm very much afraid that cab was meant for me. I'm sorry that you were the one who was knocked over. But at least you've suffered nothing worse than a bruising.'

'I still don't understand, Holmes.'

'You may think of that cab, Watson, as a first calling card from Colonel Sebastian Moran—the first but not the last.'

'So, he's already here in London, then? And already trying to kill you?'

'Precisely, Watson. That first attempt was a feeble one, but Moran will have known that. He may even have regarded it as nothing more than warning—letting me know the old battle of wits is on again.'

At this point a small child, a grubby street urchin, ran up and thrust a note into Holmes' hand. Having done so, he turned on his heels and disappeared into the fog. Holmes read the note and gave a mirthless chuckle.

'It's from him, Watson,' he remarked as he handed me the slip of paper. It read: *My spies are watching your every move. Prepare to meet your Maker.* And it was signed: *Colonel Sebastian Moran.*

'Why, the infernal cheek of the fellow.'

A grim expression came across Holmes' face as he said, 'The battle is joined, Watson—the battle is joined.'

While we were having this conversation a landlord was showing a new tenant the top floor flat at number 106 Baker Street, next door to Bedford College.

'There's one sitting room, one bedroom, and a shared bathroom down the hall,' said Albert Cartwright, the landlord. The new tenant, a tall man with a bald head and a weather-beaten face, looked over the rooms.

'Are they satisfactory, Mr ... I'm afraid I didn't catch your name?'

'Miller ... Samuel Miller.'

'Are the rooms to your liking, Mr Miller. They're a little small, I know, but ...'

'They'll do.'

'Fine. Then if you'd like to pay the first month in advance, I'll give you the key.'

This transaction completed, the landlord left the room.

Colonel Sebastian Moran, for it was he who had called himself 'Miller', sat down on the narrow bed, deep in thought. By now Holmes would have the note. By now he would know that he, Moran, was close by.

'This is a battle to the death, Sherlock Holmes,'

murmured Moran quietly. 'A battle to the death.'

His thoughts were interrupted by a knock at the door.

'Come in,' snapped Moran.

The newcomer was an ugly young man with a scar across his face. He had used many names in his short life. At the moment he was known as Sid Jones.

'How did it go?' demanded Moran.

'I missed him in the fog.'

'That was only to be expected. It was just meant to be a warning. In fact, if you had succeeded, it would almost have spoiled my fun—taken the pleasure out of the hunt.'

'I did knock over that mate of his, though,' said Jones with an ugly grin.

'Did you, indeed? That meddling medical idiot! I think while we're at it, we might as well kill Dr John H Watson, as well as Mr Sherlock Holmes.'

'What about my fee?'

'Oh, you'll be paid for today, never you fear. And your work is not done yet, my good Jones—not by a long chalk.'

'What ya got in mind, then?'

'You are to report back here tomorrow afternoon. In the meantime, I will do some careful planning. Sherlock Holmes is bound to become involved in the investigation into these "fog murders"—and when he does, that may well give us the chance we want. But before that happens, there are other assistants I need to recruit, and some rather specialised equipment I shall need.'

7

The rooms occupied by Professor and Mrs Challenger were on the first floor of Seymour Mansions on the corner of Baker and Wigmore Streets.

When we knocked at Challenger's door it was opened by an odd, swarthy, dried-up person of uncertain age, wearing a dark jacket and brown leather gaiters. I found out later that he was Challenger's coachman, who also filled the gap left by a succession of butlers who couldn't cope with the eccentric professor. He looked us up and down with a searching light blue eye.

'Expected?' he asked.

'Tell the professor that Mr Holmes is here to see him.'

'I'll try,' replied Austin, for that was the man's name, and he disappeared into the interior of the apartment, leaving us standing in the doorway.

'Unusual household,' I remarked to Holmes.

'Occasionally visitors to our rooms at 221B have been heard to make the same remark,' replied Sherlock Holmes with an impish look.

'Really? Oh, yes, I suppose they have.'

Suddenly a small woman was standing in front of us. She was a bright, vivacious, dark-eyed lady, more French than English in her type.

'May I ask if you have met my husband before?' she inquired.

'We have not had that pleasure,' I responded.

'Then I apologise to you in advance. I must tell you that he is a perfectly impossible person—absolutely impossible. If you are forewarned you will be the more ready to make allowances.'

'It is most considerate of you madam.'

With that she was gone again, and her place taken by the odd butler and coachman, Austin, who muttered, 'Follow me, gentlemen.'

He led us down a long passage, opened a door at the end of it, and stood aside, gesturing that we should enter.

The room was a large study, lined with books from floor to ceiling on three sides. Professor Challenger sat in a rotating chair at a broad table, which was covered with books, maps and diagrams. His appearance made me gasp. I was prepared for something strange—but not something quite as strange, and overpowering, as this. Indeed, it is only my long acquaintance with Sherlock Holmes, one of the most eccentric men in London, that allowed me to retain my composure.

Challenger's thick, black beard covered most of his face, and fell from the level of his broad shoulders to cover much of his barrel chest. His hands, at the moment holding a large map, were huge and covered with long, black hair.

As he looked up he said, in a voice that was part bellow, part roar, and part rumble, 'But you're not Mycroft—so who the deuce are you?'

'My name, professor, is Sherlock Holmes.'

'Sherlock! Sherlock!' cried Challenger, his demeanour changing at once, 'I am delighted. Your brother speaks so highly of you. And, of course, the wretched newspapers are full of your amazing exploits. And this must be Dr Watson. You are a fine writer, doctor, a fine writer. Your reports in *The Strand Magazine* make fascinating reading, fascinating reading indeed.'

As he spoke Challenger had leaped up and rushed around the table. He shook us both warmly by the hand. My hand, I noticed, almost disappeared in his giant one in the process.

'You are the only people I would consider welcoming to my study without an appointment. Let me order a pot of tea, and you can tell my why you've come.'

Ten minutes later, as Austin was pouring the tea, Holmes explained.

'It's about the meteor that crashed in Regent's Park, and your letter to *The Times* on the subject.'

'Wonderful! Wonderful!' cried Challenger. 'I should have known that you'd be intelligent enough to see my point at once. This thing comes from the dickens knows where, it is composed of material that we are yet to analyse, it may release particles or radiation into our atmosphere, and yet that idiot Summerlee insists on showing it to the public.'

'Who is Summerlee?' I asked.

'An asinine chemist, appointed by London University, clearly on one of its bad days, as a professor.'

'Also a fellow of the Royal Society,' said Holmes quietly.

'Well, yes, he is that too,' admitted Challenger grudgingly. 'He has done some good work in the past. But the fellow is such a blasted idiot when it comes to looking at the bigger picture.'

'And what do you see, Professor Challenger,' asked Holmes, leaning back in his chair and placing the tips of his fingers together, 'when you look at the bigger picture?'

Challenger took a moment to reply. For some seconds he looked back and forth between the two of us, and then he said, 'The fog murders—that's what I see.'

'I rather suspected you might,' Holmes remarked. 'Please carry on.'

'Well, I ask you,' bellowed Challenger, as he threw his huge weight back in his rotating chair, 'think about when that meteor crashed in Regent's Park—Wednesday night!' His huge fist thumped the desk on these words. 'And when did the so-called "fog murders" begin? Wednesday night!' Another thump. 'Where did the meteor land, and where was the first victim of these "fog murders"? In Regent's Park!' Another thump. 'And who was the first victim? A nightwatchman in the park who in all probability was an eyewitness to the meteor!' A fourth thump made the books on the desk jump. 'And where have the subsequent murders been? In Baker Street, starting at the Regent's Park end and working down the street!' A final thump, and he leaned back in his chair with a satisfied scowl on his face.

'Are you suggesting some connection between the meteor and the murders?' I asked.

'You catch on quickly, doctor,' said Challenger.

'But ... I fail to see how ...' I stuttered.

'I also fail to see how,' Challenger remarked, 'for the time being. But it's worth investigating, isn't it? And it's worth keeping the blasted public away from the meteor, just in case, isn't it?'

'Most certainly,' agreed Holmes. 'You have made a circumstantial case that is certainly worth following up. So, shall we adjourn to St John's Hall and take a look at this meteor?'

'At once,' cried Challenger, beaming all over his huge face, and then he added in a bellow, 'Austin!'

When the man appeared Challenger said, 'Kindly get the coach ready, Austin—my friends and I are about to begin a most unusual investigation.'

8

The fog was thinning when Austin brought the coach to the front door. And by the time it had made its way through the heavy traffic of Baker Street, and along the Inner Circle of Regent's Park, the sun had broken through and the fog was dissipating.

'Over here, gentleman,' boomed Challenger, leading the way across the rolling grass towards what had once been Regent's Park Lake. Halfway to his destination he was stopped by a police constable.

'I'm sorry, sir, but members of the public are not allowed any closer to the meteor site.'

'I'm not a member of the public you buffoon! I am Professor George Edward Challenger, and I demand that you let me pass.'

'I don't care if you're Charlie's aunt—my orders are to allow no one to pass. I'm sorry, sir, but orders is orders.'

'It's all right, constable,' said Sherlock Holmes. 'This man is with me.'

'Oh, I'm sorry, Mr Holmes, I didn't see you there. He's with you, you say? Well, in that case, there's no problem. You may proceed, gentlemen.'

I was once again struck by the respect, almost the veneration, in which Holmes was held by London's police service. Challenger said nothing, but grumbled into his beard as he followed Holmes and me to the edge of the area of mud that had once been the lake.

'Does it surprise you, professor,' asked Holmes, 'that this entire body of water was evaporated when the meteor struck?'

'Not at all. The descent through the atmosphere would have heated the meteor to something in the vicinity of 2,200 degrees Centigrade. Of course, it was very much larger when it first entered the atmosphere. Most of its bulk would have burned up in that heat. The relatively small rock that remains is only the remnant.'

All three of us walked out on the planking that was still in place and inspected the crater that the meteor had left in the mud.

'And where was the body of John Ferguson found, Watson?' asked Holmes.

'According to the newspaper reports, lying in this mud, about halfway between this crater and the edge of the grass. He was face down, as I recall, and it looked as though he was running towards the grass when he died.'

'Suggestive, most suggestive. It is a pity so many large Scotland Yard feet have trampled over this mud. The signs of what happened to Ferguson have been destroyed.'

'Don't blame Scotland Yard—most of this trampling was done by the workmen employed by Professor Summerlee,' growled Challenger with a snort.

'This place has nothing further to tell us, I believe,' Holmes responded.

'Right,' said Challenger decisively, 'let's find Summerlee and look at the meteor itself.'

We found Summerlee in St John's Hall. It was too early for members of the public to be admitted; consequently the hall was empty and echoed to the sound of our voices.

The meteor had been placed on a large, solid table in the centre of the hall, with an area some ten feet wider than the table roped off to prevent members of the public getting too close to the rock from outer space.

Standing over the meteor, scraping a sample of material from its surface, was the tall, gaunt, stringy figure of Professor Summerlee.

'Ah, Professor Challenger and friends,' he said in his dry, half-sarcastic, wholly unsympathetic manner, 'welcome, gentlemen, welcome. Step up closer and examine our strange visitor.'

I was surprised at how small it was—about the size of a football.

'Why is one side of the meteor deeply pitted and scarred, and the other smooth?' I asked.

'Atmospheric friction,' explained Challenger, in a voice loud enough to fill a lecture hall, 'caused pits on one side—the side facing downwards, as it were, absorbing most of the heat.'

Holmes took his lens out of his pocket and examined the surface of the object closely. After a few minutes he remarked, 'Chiefly composed of iron combined with nickel. Without having done a chemical analysis I would suggest there are also small amounts of cobalt, copper, phosphorus, carbon and sulphur.'

'Amazing,' said Summerlee, a new respect in his voice.

'Wonderful,' bellowed Challenger. 'You are as full of surprises as your brother promised you would be.'

'Chemistry is by way of being a hobby of mine,' responded Holmes. As he spoke he scraped a small amount of material from the side of the meteor, and collected these scrapings on a piece of paper. This he folded carefully and placed in a pocket of his cloak.

'More than a hobby, old chap,' I volunteered. 'Holmes has developed several new forensic processes ...'

But my remarks were interrupted by an altercation at the front door. The next moment a young man with red hair pushed his way past the guard on duty.

'McArdle is the name,' he announced in a thick Scottish accent, as he strode across the hall towards us, 'from the *Daily Gazette.*'

'The pestilential press!' exploded Challenger, his black beard bristling with anger. And then he seemed to have second thoughts. 'Although on this occasion,' he added, 'you may be of some use to us.'

'Glad to be of service,' said McArdle with a cheeky grin.

'The general public need to be warned not to come anywhere near this infernal object. Not until it has been properly investigated and declared safe,' growled Professor Challenger, like a lion in its wrath.

'Outrageous poppycock!' snorted Summerlee, in his high, acid voice.

And once again the battle was joined between these two fiery men of science. Both spoke at once, each trying to drown out the other's voice.

Eventually McArdle succeeded in sorting some sense out of the noise. In particular he noticed the claim that Challenger was making.

'You are saying, sir, that there is a connection between this meteor and the fog murders?' he asked.

'Clearly,' said Challenger, his gorilla hands clasped together, his beard bristling forward, and his big grey eyes, half covered by his drooping lids, fixed benignly upon the young reporter, 'clearly you are not entirely destitute of natural intelligence. But what I am saying is "might be"—

there might be a connection between the arrival of this object and those tragic events.'

'I say it again—outrageous poppycock,' retorted Summerlee in his dry, sarcastic tone.

'Perhaps, Professor Challenger,' suggested McArdle, 'I could interview you at your home upon this subject.'

'Yes, perhaps that would be best. Here is my address,' said Challenger, handing over his card. 'Be at my front door at exactly two o'clock this afternoon.'

With those words he strode out of St John's Hall. Holmes and I followed him to where Austin was waiting with the coach. The drive back down Baker Street was conducted in silence. Holmes' chin was sunk on his chest and he was clearly deep in thought. As for Challenger, he was reliving his altercation with Summerlee—his grey eyes were flashing with anger and he uttered an occasional short bark of frustration.

When Austin stopped the coach to let us out at number 221B, Challenger said, 'There is a book of mine that you may find helpful in this investigation, Mr Holmes. It is entitled *Comets, Asteroids and Meteors*. I will have a copy delivered to you as soon as possible.'

With that Austin whipped the horses, and the remarkable Professor Challenger disappeared into the traffic of Baker Street.

9

That night Sherlock Holmes worked at his acid-charred bench of chemicals—conducting tests on his scrapings from the meteor and consulting scientific charts. As Holmes worked I read McArdle's amusing account of the battle between Challenger and Summerlee in the afternoon edition of the *Daily Gazette.*

While we were thus occupied the so-called 'fog murders' were drawing ever closer to us. Morris Hopkins, a warehouse foreman, was walking down Baker Street, slightly the worse for drink. He knew that his wife would scold him when he finally arrived home, and he was trying out various excuses in his mind, when he noticed a change in the thick fog that surrounded him.

Just ahead was the dim glow of a light. But it was a strange cold, green light. Hopkins remembered the stories he had read in the newspaper about the fog murders and instantly feared the worst. He turned to run, but in his haste and confusion, tripped over his own feet.

Lying on the footpath he looked up to see a dense, green, cloud of fog hovering immediately above him. The eerie green glow in that cloud seemed to pulse and throb, as though it was a living thing. Hopkins started to claw his way back towards the steps of the building behind him, but the green fog followed him, step by step.

He glanced upwards and saw the number over the steps—221B. Even in his dazed state he remembered that 221B Baker Street was the address of Sherlock Holmes, the world's greatest detective.

'Yes!' thought Morris Hopkins. 'Sherlock Holmes can save me, if only I can summon him in time.'

Gathering all his strength he leaped to his feet, and began to pound on the door. But as his did so, the green fog moved. It wrapped itself around him, like a crushing python snake, and then slithered up his body. Hopkins screamed at the top of his lungs. His scream was short lived—and so was he.

At the sound of the pounding on our front door I had put down my paper. When the scream rang out Holmes laid aside his chemical apparatus and hurried down the stairs ahead of me. He flung open the door and sprinted into the street.

There, on the pavement, right before our own front door, we saw the body of Morris Hopkins. I ran back into the house, grabbed my medical bag, and then returned to the poor man's side. There was nothing I could do—he was already dead.

'Look at his face, Watson!' snapped Sherlock Holmes. 'Look at his face.'

The dead man's face seemed to be covered by a thick layer of green spider web—at least, that's what it appeared to be.

'Have you ever seen anything like it before, Watson?'

'Never, Holmes. Not in all my years of medical experience have I ever seen anything like this—not even during my time in India, and I saw many strange things there.'

I reached out to touch the thick mass of oddly coloured web-like material but Holmes snapped out a warning.

'Better not, old chap. It might be dangerous.'

Taking the warning seriously I pulled back my hand, and, instead, took a large, white handkerchief from my pocket and scooped up an amount of the sticky 'web' in that.

As I stood up, Holmes pulled an official police whistle out of his pocket—he was the only civilian in London allowed to carry one—and blew a long, loud note. Before long we heard running footsteps, and soon a uniformed constable was at our side.

'It's another fog murder,' explained Holmes. 'You'll need to inform Scotland Yard and summon a police surgeon to examine the body.'

As the constable hurried off to carry out these instructions, I attracted my friend's attention, 'Holmes! Look at the victim's face.'

As we watched the green 'spider web'—or whatever it was—slowly disappeared. Within a minute there was no trace of it left. I opened up my folded handkerchief in which I had preserved a sample—that too had vanished.

'That's astonishing, Holmes!'

'We're dealing with unknown forces here, Watson. That being so, we need to gather our data with great care and precision. I wonder if you would do me a favour, old chap?'

'Certainly, Holmes. What is it?'

'I want you to accompany the police surgeon back to the morgue, and to be present—as my eyes and ears—at the autopsy on this poor man.'

Dr Charles Clarke, the police surgeon who arrived shortly after this conversation, agreed at once to my joining him.

'To be frank,' he said, 'I'd be glad of a second opinion. I've seen all of these "fog murder" victims, and to be honest, Dr Watson, I'm entirely baffled.'

Consequently, later that night Dr Clarke and I stood side by side, both gowned and scrubbed, in the morgue attached to the Bow Street police station.

As he carried out the procedure, Dr Clarke dictated notes to his young assistant, who took them down in shorthand.

'The skin has a waxy appearance, and a blue-grey colour,' said Clarke. 'The lips and nails are pale, the body is warm to the touch, and no rigor mortis is detected. The victim has been dead for less than three hours.'

An hour later when the procedure was complete and we were removing our gowns and gloves, Clarke said, 'Well, Dr Watson—now you've seen what I've seen in all the "fog murder" victims: the lungs filled with that strange substance.'

'Rather like thick, green spider web,' I suggested.

'Exactly. An excellent description, Dr Watson. But that is only part of the story. Based on my experience of the previous victims I can tell you that if we re-examine the lungs in an hour or so there will be no trace of that stuff. It will have vanished completely.'

'Indeed, in that case, what Holmes and I witnessed immediately after the attack becomes even more significant.' I told Dr Clarke about the green spider web on the victim's face that also disappeared. Clarke was more than interested and took detailed notes.

'What is worse,' he commented as he laid aside his note book, 'is that I cannot give a certain cause of death for these victims. What they most closely resemble are the many victims of drownings I have seen over the years—except, of course, for the complete absence of water!'

Shaking my head in puzzlement I remarked, 'This is a case that no one except Sherlock Holmes could possibly solve.'

10

It was after nine that night when I returned to our rooms to find Sherlock Holmes eager to hear what Dr Clarke and I had found. After I had completed my report Holmes said nothing, but as he so often did when he wanted to concentrate, picked up his violin, and began to play. It was a strange, sad tune of his own composition.

I placed the kettle on our fireplace, which was still burning merrily, and made a fresh pot of tea. I offered a cup to Holmes, but he didn't seem to hear me, so deeply was he lost in profound concentration.

Holmes paced back and forth across the carpet, the melancholy tune from his violin filling the air. In order to keep out of his way I sat down at his desk to drink my cup of tea. There, in the centre of the desk, was a brown paper parcel. It hadn't been there when I left, so, clearly a late messenger had delivered it.

Moved by curiosity, I untied the string and unwrapped the brown paper. Inside was a book: *Comets, Asteroids and Meteors* by G E Challenger. The professor had certainly been prompt in keeping his promise. I was about to open the front cover of the book when a shouted warning from Holmes stopped me.

'Don't Watson! Whatever you do, don't open that book!'

'Why ever not, Holmes?'

'Move back from that desk, Watson,' commanded Holmes, in a voice that conveyed great urgency. At once I stood up and moved back several paces.

Holmes fetched a walking stick from a corner of the room. He cautiously approached the desk, and, using the walking stick flicked open the cover of the book.

To my astonishment the inside of the book had been hollowed out, and crawling out of that hollowed space was a large, black, hairy spider.

The horrid creature crawled out of the book and onto the surface of the desk. There it seemed to become aware of our presence as it reared up, lifting its front legs in a menacing form of attack. But before it could spring Holmes crushed it with the walking stick in one swift blow.

When he was certain it was dead, he picked up the spider's body with a pair of tweezers and carried it across to his workbench.

'As I suspected when I first saw it,' he said after a few moment's examination, 'this is an import from the colonies.

'What is it, Holmes?' I asked, peering over his shoulder.

'A Sydney funnel web—one of the deadliest spiders on earth.'

'How could it be here, in London?'

'Oh, small creatures like this are imported by specialist merchants—specialists in death. It would have been from one of them that Colonel Moran purchased it.'

'Colonel Moran?'

'Who else, Watson? We can expect each of his murder attempts to be more ingenious than the last.'

'But how can he have known that Professor Challenger had promised to send you this book?'

'If you recall, Watson, the professor made the promise at our front door, in his usual loud voice. Any spy employed by Colonel Moran to hang around our premises could not have failed to hear it. Moran immediately acted by purchasing a copy of the book, hollowing out the interior, and placing this unwelcome surprise inside.'

'But what made you suspect, Holmes?'

'Several things. The lateness of the delivery. I expect that the book from the professor will come during the hours of daylight. Of course, Moran could not wait that long—his delivery had to arrive before the genuine article. And then there was the weight of the book. Paper is heavier than most people realise, and it is impossible to remove a large amount of it from the centre of a book, without the weight becoming disproportionate compared to the size of the volume. For those reasons I suspected Colonel Moran's handiwork. Of course, I couldn't know what surprise he had inside the parcel for us—only that it would be an unpleasant one.'

'Oh, I see. Quite straightforward once you explain it, really.'

'It always is, Watson. Quite elementary, in fact.'

While Holmes and I were facing the latest murderous attack from Colonel Moran, Mrs Hudson and her niece were sleeping peacefully on the floor above—Mrs Hudson in her own bedroom, and Patience in a room that had formerly been occupied by one of the maids.

As a country girl she was in the habit of sleeping with one window open a few inches—even in the midst of winter. While Patience tossed and turned on her bed, a strange light appeared at her partly open window—a pale, sickly, green light.

It oozed over the windowsill and then gathered itself into

a thick, green cloud of fog, hovering in the air over the sleeping teenager. At that moment something—perhaps the faint, pulsing green light in the cloud—woke Patience.

At first she rubbed her eyes, dazed and still half-asleep. Then she saw the fog monster. She was frozen by terror, unable to scream, unable to make a sound. She watched the thing coil and writhe in the air above her, and then, to her unspeakable horror, it slowly settled on her bedspread.

Over the top of her sheets Patience watched it as it gathered itself together, and then began to crawl up the bed towards her—like some hideous, green slug. That's when she screamed—a loud, terrified scream. The green fog monster seemed to respond to her scream, for it raised itself up, and rushed upon her face.

Soon Patience found it impossible to breathe. She struggled and tried to push the thing away, but there was nothing to grasp hold of, just thick, damp fog—fog that was suffocating her, choking her.

As that moment the door to her bedroom flew open and Mrs Hudson hurried in, holding up a lamp.

'Patience, Patience—whatever's the matter?'

Mrs Hudson saw the fog monster wrapping itself over Patience's face and mouth. Concern for her niece gave her strength, and Mrs Hudson rushed towards the creature, swinging her lamp. As the light of the lamp came closer the fog seemed to fly away in thin streams or tendrils.

Mrs Hudson swung the lamp in wider and wider arcs, and soon the green fog was flowing out of the partly opened window. Our landlady rushed over and slammed the window shut behind it.

Patience was in tears, sobbing with the horror of the experience. She looked up, and through her tears she saw Holmes and me in the doorway.

'You'd better take a look at her, Watson, and see if she's been injured in any way,' said Holmes crisply.

'How are you feeling my dear?' I asked as I checked her pulse and her respiration.

A moment later I was able to announce, 'she has just had a nasty fright—she's going to be fine. I'll go and get you a sedative my dear, to settle your nerves.'

When I returned with a mild sedative from my medical bag Mrs Hudson was explaining to Holmes what she saw, and how the fog creature—for that is how we were now thinking of it—fled as she approached with the light.

'That's very interesting,' muttered Holmes thoughtfully, 'interesting and perhaps very important. Come along Watson, we're going to pay a call on Professor Challenger.'

'What? At this hour? But it's so late, Holmes.'

'If I know the professor he'll be awake and working. And he'll want to hear this news. Come along, Watson—there's not a moment to spare. We'll leave your niece in your capable hands, Mrs Hudson.'

11

'So, light makes it flee, does it?' said Professor Challenger. He was leaning back in the rotating chair behind his vast desk, his gigantic hands clasped behind his head. His two large grey eyes were half covered with insolent drooping eyelids. His big head sloped back, and his beard bristled forward. Then he repeated the words again, 'Light makes it flee—most interesting indeed. I should have predicted this. After all it comes from the permanent midnight of outer space, and all the attacks have been at night. I wonder where it goes during the daytime? Perhaps it has found some convenient sewer that shields it from the light of the sun.'

'Of course, you see the possibility this opens up,' said Sherlock Holmes, focussing on practical solutions, rather than scientific speculation.

'I do indeed,' agreed Challenger, nodding his vast head.

'Well, I'm afraid I don't,' I said. 'What possibility?'

I think I heard Professor Challenger mutter the word 'imbecile' under his breath, but I ignored this.

'The possibility,' explained Holmes, 'of either destroying or capturing the alien life form that escaped from the meteor and is now swarming through the fog on Baker Street.'

'Oh, I see.'

'We would need lanterns with shutters,' continued Holmes.

'There are a number of those in the attic,' volunteered Challenger, 'I'll have Austin fetch them. The problem is that there are only three of us.'

'Unless you include Austin,' Holmes suggested.

'I wouldn't ask him—his rheumatism would not survive exposure to the cold and damp of the fog.'

'Only three then.'

Just then the front door bell rang, and we heard Austin go to answer it. A moment later he showed McArdle into Challenger's study.

'You asked me to bring you a copy of the morning edition as soon as it came off the presses,' said the red headed young reporter, 'and here it is.'

'Wonder of wonders,' boomed Challenger, 'a newspaperman who keeps his word. Hand over that rag, and let me read the article you wrote.'

McArdle handed over a copy of the *Daily Gazette* and we all sat in silence while the professor read the article printed at the top of page three.

'Amazing!' he roared. 'You have actually succeeded in quoting me accurately. Truly we live in a day of miracles.'

'McArdle,' said Holmes, 'are you game for a little action and adventure—possibly for a little danger? Perhaps even more than a little?'

'If there's a good story in it, then I'm game for anything.'

'Then I think we have a fourth for our patrol,' Holmes remarked.

'Yes, of course. Good thinking, Holmes. Why don't you brief McArdle while Austin and I search out those lamps.'

Challenger stamped out of the room on those short, thick

legs of his, as Holmes explained the night's events to McArdle.

'So,' said the journalist at the end of this narrative, 'that's all very interesting. But I still don't understand what you and the professor are planning to do.'

'If we patrol the length of Baker Street,' explained Holmes, 'the four of us, strung out in a line across the street, there is an excellent chance that sooner or later we will encounter this ... thing, whatever it is.'

'And when we do?'

'Each of us will be carrying a shuttered lantern. When the green glow is seen and an attack seems imminent, we will raise the shutters on our lanterns while surrounding it on all sides.'

'What do you expect the result to be?'

'Either we will succeed in confining and containing it, or, more likely, exposure to that amount of light will bring an end to whatever life-force is driving it.'

'Either kill it or capture it, in other words?'

'Precisely.'

Challenger returned wearing a vast, black cape and a broadbrimmed black hat, and carrying four lanterns with shutters. We lit these and then made our way out into the street.

It was after midnight by the time our patrol began. Sherlock Holmes made one end of our line, on the right hand footpath, while Professor Challenger made the other, on the opposite pavement. McArdle and I were in between, covering the roadway. We would have made a strange spectacle to any passing pedestrian—Holmes in his Inverness Cape and deerstalker hat, I in my old army greatcoat and bowler hat, McArdle in a trench coat and soft felt hat and Challenger a vision in flowing black.

We slowly patrolled the entire length of Baker Street,

and then turned to make our way back.

'How long are we going to keep this up?' asked McArdle.

'At least two more sweeps before we abandon the patrol for the night,' roared Challenger, like a wounded lion. 'Don't tell me your feet are giving out on you, young McArdle?'

'I can go as long as you can, sir,' the reporter replied.

This won a loud grunt from the professor, and then the patrol continued in silence.

As we were passing Bedford College I thought I heard a faint noise somewhere away to my left. Then, without warning, Holmes threw himself at me as he leaped off the pavement. He was not a moment too soon—for as he jumped a huge piece of stone crashed onto the footpath, exactly where he had been standing a moment before.

'Good grief, Holmes!' I exclaimed.

'I heard it coming,' said Holmes, as he caught his breath. 'You know how acute my hearing is.'

We both walked over and examined the fallen masonry. Shortly McArdle and Challenger joined us.

'It comes from the parapet of that building,' muttered Challenger, pointing upwards. 'A most unfortunate accident.'

With those words he waved us back onto the road to resume our patrol. Holmes and I looked at each other—we knew it was no accident.

'Colonel Moran again?' I asked.

'Most assuredly,' replied Holmes quietly, not wishing to alarm the others.

'When are we going after him, Holmes?'

'My dear Watson, I intend to compel him to come to me—in person.'

12

On the next sweep of our patrol I spotted a light glowing faintly ahead, somewhere through the fog. At first I thought it may have been our elusive quarry, but it quickly became apparent that this was the yellow glow of a lantern, not the mysterious green light we were looking for.

Drawing closer I realised that we were in front of our parish church, St Bede's on Baker Street, and that the lantern was held by the minister, the Reverend Henry Bunyan—a descendant of the famous author of *The Pilgrim's Progress.*

'Mr Bunyan!' I called out. 'What are you doing out here at this time of night?'

'Who's that? Oh, it's you, Dr Watson. Well, ever since that poor young man was killed on the very doorstep of the church I have got into the habit of coming out here with a lantern before retiring to bed. Just to check up, you understand.'

'Come along you chaps,' bellowed Challenger. 'One more complete sweep.'

'What are you doing?' asked Bunyan, and I explained.

'Well,' he said upon hearing the reason for our patrol, 'this lantern has a shutter, why shouldn't I join you. One more pair of eyes can't go astray.'

'Excellent suggestion,' said Sherlock Holmes, joining us, 'but for now we really must catch up with the others.'

Percy Turner was an old tramp who often slept in the doorways on Baker Street. On cold foggy nights he tried to make his way to Great St Helen's church where he would be given hot soup and a warm bed for the night. But on that particular Friday he simply felt too cold to move. So he curled up in a sheltered corner of the entrance to Lower Berkeley Street.

He lined his old overcoat with sheets of newspaper, and managed to make himself warm enough to fall asleep.

He woke up in the early hours of the morning. Blinking around he knew that something had startled him out of his sleep, but he didn't know what. Then he saw it—the green cloud that pulsed with a dim, sickly light. He blinked at it foolishly and made no attempt to avoid its approach. It felt cold and clammy when it settled on his coat, and looked alarmingly like a giant insect as it oozed and climbed its way up his coat. The last thing he remembered was trying to breathe.

We found his body on our last patrol of the night.

'Poor old Percy,' said Henry Bunyan. 'He mustn't end up in a pauper's grave. St Bede's will pay for his funeral.'

'I wonder why the creature does it?' rumbled Challenger; his massive voice reduced to a murmur by our tragic discovery.

'The same thought had crossed my mind,' said Holmes crisply. 'I wonder if, in some way, it draws energy from those it kills.'

'In other words,' Challenger said, his voice growing louder, 'this thing is *feeding* on its victims?'

'This is only speculation, mind,' cautioned Holmes. 'And, indeed this thing may be so alien that we never really understand its actions.'

When Henry Bunyan offered to inform the police about Percy Turner, our patrol split up—after agreeing to attempt a similar patrol the following night.

Holmes and I were walking back to our rooms in silence, too tired, and our minds too full, for speech. As we passed Crawford Street, and were within a block of our front door, a young uniformed policeman suddenly emerged from the fog.

'Who's there?' he cried in alarm.

Holmes and I stepped forward into the circle of light cast by a gas lamp.

'Oh, it's you Mr Holmes, and Dr Watson. Something terrible has happened—can you help?'

'Yes, of course, old chap,' I said. 'We're happy to lend a hand, aren't we, Holmes? You just lead the way.'

'Exactly what has happened?' asked Holmes.

But the young constable, who was walking at a half-run towards the Crawford Street corner, appeared not to hear the question. At least, he offered no answer.

We followed him as quickly as we could. Halfway down Crawford Street he stopped and beckoned us to hurry up.

When we caught up with him, we found him standing at the opening to a narrow passageway.

'This leads to Dorset Mews West,' he said. 'That's where it is—it's just horrible—the bodies, the blood.'

'Come along, Holmes,' I said, as I set off down the passageway. I could see a dim light at the end where the passage opened into the mews.

As I neared that opening there was a sudden cry of pain from behind me. I turned around to discover Holmes leaning against the wall in apparent pain.

'What's happened, old chap?' I asked.

'I've tripped over something in the dark—I think I've twisted my ankle.'

'Step out into the mews. There's a bit of light there, and I'll be able to see the damage.'

The young constable was leaning over my shoulder also looking at Holmes' injury, when suddenly Holmes grabbed hold of the young policeman in his powerful arms and thrust him through the opening into Dorset Mews West.

As he emerged into the dim gas light of the mews there was a strange sound—part thud, part hiss—and the constable crumpled to the ground, clutching his chest. I turned to rush to his side, but Holmes' firm grip held me back.

'He's dead, Watson—killed by a soft-nosed revolver bullet fired from an airgun. And the man who pulled the trigger was Colonel Sebastian Moran. The air gun is his preferred weapon for assassinations. Moran has several of them, especially built for him by the blind German gunsmith Von Herder.'

'But ... the policeman ...'

'He's no policeman, Watson—another of Moran's henchman. Waste no tears on him—he lured us here tonight knowing that if we fell into his trap it would mean our deaths.'

'That cold-blooded devil,' I muttered.

'Like calls to like, Watson—and those are the henchmen that Colonel Moran gathers around himself.'

'But Moran himself, he must still be close by.'

'No, he will have realised his mistake and fled by now.'

'But we could pursue him, Holmes. If your ankle will stand up to it.'

'There's nothing wrong with my ankle, old chap. I had to somehow stop you rushing headlong into the trap. As for pursuing the colonel—in fog and darkness? I think not. No, Watson, we shall adhere to our original plan and compel Moran to come to us, in our rooms—that is where we shall trap him.'

13

The next morning, when Mrs Hudson came to serve breakfast I asked, 'How's young Patience today?'

'Much recovered, thank you, doctor. She suffered no physical injury—it was just, as you said yourself, a nasty fright. And that sedative of yours gave her a good night's sleep. She's still a little shaken, but in a day or so she'll be as right as rain.'

Sherlock Holmes and I were still eating breakfast when the lean and ferret-like face of Inspector Lestrade appeared in our doorway.

'Come in, Inspector,' said Holmes warmly. 'Have you eaten?'

'Yes, I've had breakfast, thank you, Mr Holmes.'

'Then pour yourself a cup of coffee, draw up a chair close to the fire, and tell us the reason for this visit.'

'It's these here "fog murders" that are troubling me, Mr Holmes.'

'I thought you were fully occupied hunting for the escaped convict—Colonel Sebastian Moran.'

'Well, so I am, Mr Holmes. That is the case officially assigned to me at the moment.'

'And how are you progressing, Lestrade. Are you about to snap the jaws of your trap closed on the missing Moran?'

'To tell the truth, every lead we've had so far has turned out to be a blind alley. I'm getting absolutely nowhere. And then I thought of the "fog murders".'

'Does that mean you have a theory?' asked Holmes, helping himself to more eggs and bacon, and pouring himself a second cup of coffee.

'That's exactly right—a theory. And my theory is that Colonel Sebastian Moran might be behind these here "fog murders".'

'Interesting,' murmured Holmes through a mouthful of toast. 'Why do you suggest that?'

'He's a killer, we know that—a convicted murderer. And these murders commenced on the same night that he escaped from prison. Furthermore, they are all in the vicinity of Baker Street, and we know this is where he would come, since his avowed intention is to kill you, Mr Holmes.'

'You know,' Holmes said, pushing his chair back from the breakfast table, 'that is one of the finest displays of reasoning you have ever given, Inspector.'

Lestrade beamed from ear to ear. 'Why, thank you, Mr Holmes,' he replied.

'It's such a pity that you are totally wrong.'

'Wrong?'

'You have a bulldog tenacity that I admire, Lestrade. Unfortunately, you are almost completely lacking in imagination.'

'But ... but ... my chain of reasoning ...'

'Has a few missing links, I'm sorry to say. Principally that of motive. What possible reason could Colonel Moran have for killing these people? His purpose, as we know, is revenge. His target—well, his target is me. He gains nothing by these pointless killings, and each exposes him to the risk of discovery and capture—before he has carried out his main project, namely, my demise. No, I'm very much afraid, Inspector, that these random killings would work against Moran's interests, and for that reason, if for no other, he cannot be considered a serious suspect.'

Inspector Lestrade sat back in his chair and shook his head sadly.

'Don't be too distressed, Lestrade,' I said. 'Holmes and Professor Challenger have a line on the fog murders.' No sooner had I uttered these words than Holmes scowled at me, and I realised I had spoken out of turn.

'Really,' replied the Scotland Yard man unenthusiastically. 'If it doesn't involve Colonel Moran I'm not really interested. I was hoping the fog murders might give me a lead on his whereabouts. The Commissioner doesn't like convicted murderers roaming loose around London. He called me into his office yesterday afternoon. Gave me a right talking to, he did. I've got to get a lead on that man soon, or my life won't be worth living.'

'Cheer up, Lestrade,' said Holmes, walking over to the police detective and patting him on the shoulder. 'Moran will have to show his hand sooner or later. When his agents let him down, and his other attempts on my life do not succeed, he will intervene personally. When that happens—we'll have him.'

'Or he'll have you. And if that happens the Commissioner will have my hide.'

Inspector Lestrade rose from the basket chair near the fire a tired and worried man. 'Thank you for the coffee, Mr Holmes, Dr Watson. I just hope I don't end up pounding a beat again, that's all—I'm too old for that.'

And on that glum note, he left us.

At the same time that Lestrade was visiting us

'Samuel Miller', alias Colonel Sebastian Moran, had a visitor in his rooms at 106 Baker Street.

'Twice last night!' Moran was saying viciously. 'Twice we failed!'

'It was a pity about young Harry Latimer,' agreed Sid Jones. 'He was a good operator. We could have made a lot of use of him in the future.'

'He was a bumbling idiot! If he weren't, he'd still be alive. I'm surrounded by incompetents and idiots.'

Sid Jones kept his mouth closed, because Colonel Moran paid well, but the expression on his face made it clear he had no love for his employer.

'Anyway—what do we do next?' was his only response.

'See here,' Moran said, holding up a sheaf of papers. 'I have devised six different plans to kill Sherlock Holmes— one of these is bound to work. In fact, I'll warrant that it will take far fewer that six plans before I have my revenge.'

'Oh, yeah?' said Jones, disbelievingly.

'You may sneer, Jones, but I know all the plans I have in hand, and you don't. I am prepared to wager that one of my next two plans will work, and that Sherlock Holmes will be dead within 48 hours.'

'So, when do we get started?'

'I have already started. Don't imagine that all of my plans involve you. In fact, my next assassination plan is underway right now—even as you and I speak, the wheels are turning in a deadly and ingenious scheme.'

14

During that Saturday morning a messenger delivered a copy of Professor Challenger's book *Comets, Asteroids and Meteors*—the real thing this time.

Sherlock Holmes curled up on a sofa close to the fire and spent the rest of the morning reading the book.

That left me rather at a loose end. I had already read the morning editions of *The Times* and the *Daily Gazette*, and I had read every article in the current issues of *The Strand Magazine* and *The Lancet*.

I went up to Mrs Hudson's rooms to check up on Patience, but found her to be a teenager glowing with good health and in no need of a doctor. She had fully recovered from her ordeal of the night before.

Then late in the morning a delivery cart pulled up at our front door, and a large, wooden crate was unloaded. On the side of the crate was stencilled the label *Sutherland & Dundas*. Since they were the usual suppliers of both the chemicals and the laboratory apparatus that Holmes required for his experiments I took receipt of the crate and signed the delivery docket.

Then I offered the two carters half a crown each to carry the wooden crate upstairs to our sitting room.

'Where do you want it, guv'nor?' puffed one of the

carters, as they staggered through our doorway.

'Over in that corner, underneath that acid-stained, deal topped table. Does that meet with your approval, Holmes?'

'Whatever you say, Watson,' he replied, without lifting his eyes from the pages of Challenger's book.

With many a thump and a grunt the crate was securely stowed under Holmes' workbench. I paid each man his half crown and they left, one of them saying over his shoulder as they did so, 'I don't know what you got in that crate, guv'nor, but it's deuced heavy.'

With the carters gone, once again I found myself at a loose end.

'I'm a little peckish, Holmes,' I remarked. 'What about you—could you eat something?'

'Undoubtedly, Watson, undoubtedly,' he replied, still fully absorbed in his reading.

I summoned Mrs Hudson and ordered a plate of sandwiches and pot of coffee. When they arrived I offered Holmes a roast beef sandwich and a cup of coffee. He declined both.

With a sandwich in my hand, and a hot cup of coffee by my side, I took out my old Webley .45 calibre army revolver, and began to clean and oil it.

This, you will understand, was not work that was mentally taxing, and my eyes often drifted around the room. Having just re-assembled the revolver I looked up and noticed something odd about the crate that had been delivered that morning. The lid of the crate looked somehow less secure than it had been when it first arrived. There was a clear, black slit between the top edge of one side and the lid.

Keeping very still, and trying to look as if I was not observing the crate, I watched closely for the next few minutes. There could be no doubt about it—with minute slowness and great caution, the lid of the crate was being lifted up *from within*. Keeping an impassive look on my face, I slowly loaded all the chambers of my revolver with bullets.

The minutes ticked by in nerve-racking silence. Then I saw that something else was happening to the lid of the crate—some small object was beginning to appear, being pushed out from inside the container. It looked like a tube of some sort, and soon a full inch of this object was in view. And what is more—it was pointed directly at Sherlock Holmes!

I leaped from my chair, grabbed the startled Holmes by the shoulders and pulled him backwards. As I did so, a sharp hissing sound was heard, and something embedded itself in the wall with a thud. Holmes' lightning reflexes recovered from the surprise instantly.

'That,' he said, indicating a small, feathered dart embedded in our wall, 'is a poisoned dart. Where is the blowpipe, Watson?'

'There!' I cried, pointing at the crate under his workbench. Holmes strode across the room, and slammed the lid down firmly on the crate. There was a cry of surprise and pain as he did so, and the protruding end of the blowpipe was snapped off.

'We have deprived him of his weapon now Watson, so it should be safe to open the box and see what we have got.'

Holmes threw back the lid. Inside was one of the most amazing people I have ever seen in my life—an African pygmy. The broken end of the blowpipe was still in his hand, and on his face was an expression of anger and sheer hatred. Holmes reached into the crate and lifted out its occupant. His only response was to bite Holmes savagely on the hand.

Holmes set the small African on the rug in front of the fireplace, and reached for a handkerchief to bind up his wounded hand. The pygmy stood perhaps four feet tall, had reddish-brown skin and tightly curled brown hair.

'Another employee of the ingenious Colonel Sebastian Moran—wouldn't you say, Watson?'

'I'm sure you're right, Holmes. But let me see to that hand. I must properly clean and dress the wound.'

While I was preoccupied doing this, the small would-be killer made a dash for the window of our room, threw open the sash, and leaped out.

'The roof, Watson,' cried Holmes. 'He'll head for the roof.'

I followed Holmes out of our door and up the narrow staircase that led to the roof of our building. Throwing open the door onto the roof Holmes stepped out onto the leads and looked around. Already the African assassin was gone.

Holmes spotted him a moment later three rooftops away and travelling at an amazing speed.

'He comes from the tropical rainforests of Africa,' said Holmes, when it was clear that pursuit was impossible. 'He can climb as well as you and I can walk.'

'What a devilish attack,' I said.

'You mustn't blame him,' returned Holmes. 'Blame his employer, the evil Colonel Moran.' Then as we turned to leave the roof and return to our sitting room, Holmes added, 'We have not heard the end of Colonel Moran, Watson—not by a long mark.'

15

The following morning, being Sunday, we took Mrs Hudson and Patience with us to St Bede's. That night our landlady announced her intention of taking her niece to Portland Chapel to hear F B Meyer speak on 'The Life of Saint Paul'.

'Would you like to come with us, doctor?' she said, as they were departing.

'My old bullet wound is playing up, Mrs Hudson,' I replied, 'and I'd rather not take it out into the cold night air more than I have to.'

'Very well then, sir. We'll be back around half past eight, and I'll make you some supper then.' With those words they departed.

Some ten minutes later I became aware that Sherlock Holmes was extremely restless.

'What's wrong, Holmes?' I asked. 'Something's troubling you.'

'It's those two—Mrs Hudson and her niece. I shouldn't have allowed them to go out.'

'Portland Chapel is only a short walk away. They can hardly run into danger walking to chapel and back.'

'But they can, Watson, that's the whole point—they can. This part of Baker Street is the exact vicinity in which that murderous green phenomenon is operating. That makes being on the street after dark extremely perilous.'

'I see what you mean. Why do you think this particular place has become infected with that thing?'

'I never speculate without data, Watson. The truth is—we don't know, and quite possibly, we shall never know. Whatever life form this is—a bacteria or a virus—it is so alien to this planet that we cannot begin to guess at why it operates as it does, or where it does.'

'Hhmm, I see. Well, Mrs Hudson and Patience have gone. Perhaps we should have stopped them, but we didn't. They'll be safely in the chapel by this. So, there's not much we can do.'

'There's one thing, old chap.'

'Oh, yes, what's that?'

'We can ensure their safe return. I propose that as the hour approaches eight thirty you and I, Watson, walk down Baker Street to intercept them on their return and escort them home.'

'That sounds sensible. By all means, let's do that.'

We filled in the next hour restlessly. Holmes returned to his experiments on the scrapings he had taken from the meteor, and I tried re-reading one of my favourite books: a history of the Fifth Northumberland Fusiliers—my old army regiment. But I was unable to concentrate, and ended up pacing the floor. I confess that Holmes' words had quite alarmed me.

At frequent intervals I checked my pocket watch. The time seemed to crawl by very slowly.

At last Holmes said, 'Let's be off, Watson. I find this waiting as intolerable as you do.'

I pulled on my old army greatcoat and bowler hat, while Holmes donned his heavy travelling cloak and deerstalker hat.

The fog was thick again on Baker Street—thick, cold and clammy. We walked briskly in the direction of the Portland Chapel, the exercise helping to keep out the cold. I flapped my arms against my sides as I walked, trying to keep my circulation going.

We had passed the corner of George Street, and were almost there when we saw them emerging from the crowd that was pouring out of the main doors of Portland Chapel.

'We've come to meet you, and walk you home,' I explained as we greeted them. 'How was your evening?'

'Oh, Mr Meyer is a most wonderful speaker,' gushed Patience with the enthusiasm typical of her age.

'And what did you think, Mrs Hudson?'

'Well, Dr Watson, I heard the great Mr Spurgeon speak when I was younger. Mr Meyer is not quite in that class, but he is certainly very good.'

'You're getting old and stuffy, Aunt Mary,' said Patience, good-naturedly. 'I can't believe anyone could have been better than Mr Meyer.'

Further conversation brought us almost to the door of 221B. With our front door in sight, Patience ran on ahead. As she did so, Holmes called upon her to stop and wait for us. She paid no heed.

A moment later the sound of her footsteps came to a halt, and she gave a startled cry, followed by a scream for help.

'Come along, Watson!' shouted Holmes as he ran in the direction of the scream.

We were by her side within a few seconds, and the sight that greeted our eyes was a truly horrible one—green, glowing fingers of fog had wrapped themselves around the teenager and appeared to be holding her firmly. Patience had squeezed her eyes tightly closed and was taking short, sharp breaths.

'Relax Miss Hudson,' said Holmes, 'we can drive this thing away.'

'Please be quick,' she pleaded, 'please make it go away.'

'Your lantern, please Watson,' snapped Holmes.

I handed over the hurricane lamp I was carrying. Holmes held it high and approached the coils of green, pulsating fog that were binding the helpless girl.

The 'fog creature' displayed no response. It did not retreat, and its grip on Patience did not diminish.

'It's not working, Holmes,' I said in despair.

The detective stepped even closer, and held the light within a foot of the pulsating mass that was wound around the arms and legs of Mrs Hudson's niece.

This time there was a reaction—but an aggressive one. Part of the green cloud detached itself, and shot towards Holmes like a spear thrust.

'Watch out, Holmes—don't let it get you too,' I warned.

'There must be someway ...' muttered Holmes desperately.

Then he raised the glass covering of the lamp and exposed the naked flame—this he thrust directly into the twisting, writhing mass of green cloud. The response was instantaneous—the green vapour withdrew rapidly, fleeing as fast as it could from the naked flame. Holmes swung the lamp, with its exposed flame, around Patience, and within seconds she was free.

She threw herself gratefully into Holmes' arms, and sobbed on his chest. Holmes handed the hurricane lamp to me, and looked decidedly uncomfortable. For all his genius Holmes was a cold fish, opposed to all displays of emotion.

Mrs Hudson came to his rescue.

'Go to your aunt, Miss Hudson,' said Holmes firmly,

taking her shoulders and gently thrusting her away from himself and towards our landlady. Mrs Hudson led the still sobbing teenage into our building. Holmes and I followed.

'Why did it not respond to the light?' I asked.

'We can only assume that it is getting stronger, Watson. It must, indeed, be absorbing some sort of energy from its victims—energy that is making it stronger and more powerful.'

16

Sherlock Holmes decided that it was imperative we share this new information with Professor Challenger immediately. So we hailed a cab and set off in the direction of Seymour Mansions.

As on the previous night we found the professor working late in his study.

'So, this strange, etheric biomass is now impervious to light. Hhmm, that makes us rethink our plans.'

Challenger raised his huge bulk from his rotating chair, and began to pace the carpet on those short legs as thick as tree stumps.

'The important thing to remember,' said Holmes, his tall, lanky figure leaning back in his armchair, 'is that naked flame appears to have a more dramatic effect on it than rays of light ever had.'

'Yes, yes, of course. Most important point,' muttered Challenger, as he kept on pacing.

'A practical suggestion,' said Holmes.

Challenger stopped pacing and turned to face him. 'Yes?'

'I propose we cancel tonight's scheduled patrol of Baker Street. We need to rethink our tactics and our weapons, before we resume our offensive.'

'You're quite right, of course. Indeed, I was going to

suggest something of the sort myself, but for an entirely different reason. I have been working on an apparatus that may be of use to us.'

So saying Challenger walked over to a side table and pulled back the sheet that was covering it. On the table was a strange instrument that resembled a ceramic cylinder, tightly wound with copper wire.

'I have been constructing an induction coil,' the professor explained, 'to use waves in the electromagnetic spectrum that would project a radiation to control this phenomenon— even more effectively than simple light rays. My plan was to use four of these. Each one would be attached to a wooden box that would contain a storage battery. And despite the changed behaviour pattern of the phenomenon I still believe these induction coils will work.'

'How many have you constructed?' asked Holmes.

'Only the one so far. But I can have all four ready by tomorrow night.'

'Then let's make our next patrol tomorrow—Monday night—instead of tonight.'

'Agreed.'

Professor Challenger turned a brass switch at the base of his demonstration induction coil and the device gave off a quiet hum.

'I can probably increase the power—and the range—of this device,' rumbled Challenger thoughtfully. 'And if we have four of them, operating at maximum power and maximum range ... yes, that should do it.'

He resumed his seat behind the huge table he used as a desk. 'The other thing,' continued Challenger, 'is what we are to make of the reaction to an exposed flame.'

Before he could say more there was a knock on the study door and Austin stepped in.

'Excuse me, sir,' he said, 'but Professor Summerlee is here. He asks to see you.'

'Summerlee! Summerlee!' yelped Challenger. 'What can he want?'

'There is one certain way of finding out,' said Holmes crisply.

'Yes, of course. Show him in, Austin. At once.'

A moment later we saw the gaunt figure and acid face of Professor Summerlee in the doorway.

'Good of you to see me, Challenger—at this time of night, and without an appointment.'

'That is a privilege I extend to very few,' boomed Challenger. 'Come in, Summerlee. Come in and take a seat. You know these gentlemen, I believe.'

Summerlee nodded towards us as he crossed the carpet. 'Good evening, Mr Holmes, Dr Watson,' he said in his dry voice.

'Well?' barked Challenger, like a huge hound defending his territory. 'You came here for a purpose—what is it?'

'It's the meteor,' replied Summerlee, with some hesitancy.

'What about the meteor?'

'It has begun ... well, not to put too fine a point on it ... it has begun to glow.'

'Glow?'

'That is what I said.'

'Indeed!' roared Challenger, a satisfied look on his face, like a lion that has just eaten a hearty meal. 'And what have you done about this strange behaviour.'

'I have closed the exhibition of the meteor to the public.'

'At last! I knew you would see reason eventually.'

'How long has the meteor been behaving in this fashion?' asked Holmes.

'Only this evening,' replied Summerlee, his usual arrogant manner once more in place.

'I wonder ...' began Holmes.

'You wonder what?' demanded Challenger, leaning forward across the desk, his huge, black beard bristling.

'The data is insufficient to draw a certain conclusion,' Holmes continued. 'Still I wonder whether there is a connection between the glowing of the meteor and the increased strength and power of the bio-mass infecting the fog.'

'Of course!' Challenger slapped his huge gorilla-like hand on the table. 'I should have seen it myself.'

'Seen what?' demanded Summerlee, acidly.

'The phenomenon that is infecting the fog and the meteor are still connected in some way.'

'Nonsense!' snapped Summerlee. 'What sort of connection could there possibly be?'

'Too early to say,' Challenger bellowed in reply, 'but I would speculate—some sort of etheric waves.'

'Stuff and nonsense,' sneered his scientific colleague.

'There is a way of putting this theory to the test,' suggested Holmes quietly.

'What way?' asked Summerlee.

'Yes, what way?' growled Challenger.

'Whatever is infesting the fog must be stopped before more lives are lost. With the help of Professor Challenger's new instruments, we will attempt to do that tomorrow night. I propose inviting Professor Summerlee to join us. If Challenger's theory is correct, when we extinguish the fog infection, the meteor should respond—most probably by ceasing its current glowing behaviour.'

Before either Summerlee or Challenger could respond

there was another knock at the study door.

This time Austin announced, 'Mr McArdle, sir. He has an appointment.'

The red headed reporter bounced cheerfully into the room. He caught sight of Professor Summerlee and picked up the icy atmosphere. Then he said, 'Come at an interesting moment, have I?'

In response to his question everyone spoke at once. Eventually order came out of the chaos. It was agreed that Challenger would build a number of additional induction coils, that our patrol of Baker Street would be postponed until tomorrow night, and that Professor Summerlee would join us on that patrol.

On that note the meeting broke up, and Holmes and I returned to number 221B.

17

The next morning Sherlock Holmes went out early, and I sat down to write up my notes dealing with our adventures at Loch Ness, including our encounter with the legendary Loch Ness monster.

I had been working for an hour when Patience Hudson knocked at the door and said there was a gentleman to see Mr Holmes.

'Tell him to come back later,' I said. 'Holmes is out, and has left no word as to when he will return.'

'The gentleman is most insistent, Dr Watson,' said Patience. 'He said if Mr Holmes is not here he would prefer to wait.'

'Oh, very well. Show him up then. I will deal with him.'

The visitor she brought up to our sitting room a few moments later was a white-haired, elderly clergyman.

'Boddington is the name,' he said. 'The Reverend Rufus Boddington.'

I shook the hand he held out and asked him to take a seat. He ignored my offer, and paced restlessly up and down our rug.

'I'm afraid I have no idea where Mr Holmes has gone, or when he will return,' I explained.

'Oh, dear me, dear me,' muttered the old gentleman,

'that is not good at all. I really do need to speak to him most urgently. I must return to my parish in Yorkshire by the afternoon train, and the matter on which I wish to consult Mr Holmes is a matter of life and death.'

'Perhaps I could be of assistance?'

He looked me up and down for a moment and then said, 'I doubt it. This is such a bizarre matter that I wish to engage the services of the world's first, and greatest, consulting detective.'

'Well, you're welcome to wait here if you wish,' I said reluctantly.

'That you, Dr Watson. That is most kind of you.'

'However, I'm afraid I won't be a very good host—I must get on with my work.'

'Certainly, certainly. I will be as quiet as a mouse. You do your work, I will sit here quietly and wait.'

Still grumbling under my breath about being stuck with this strange old man, I returned to my desk and to the notes I was writing up. Soon I was deeply engrossed in the task, remembering again the strange events that occurred on that particular journey into Scotland. I did not hear the visitor approach my chair from behind, and the first thing I was aware of was a cloth filled with chloroform being held over my mouth and nose. I struggled to free myself, but the more I struggled the more deeply I breathed, and I soon lost consciousness.

When I awoke I found myself bound hand and foot, by stout ropes, to our basket chair. The chair itself had been moved into the alcove formed by our bay window. In addition to the ropes, a thick gag had been tied around my mouth.

'Ah, you're conscious again, Dr Watson,' said the white-haired visitor in black clergyman's clothing—although I was certain by now he was not a real minister.

'I'm surprised at how long you slept. I must have given you a larger dose of chloroform than I realised.'

His voice was no longer quavering and elderly—it was younger, stronger, and darkly menacing.

Having caught the puzzled look in my eyes, he said, 'So, you still don't recognise me? Good, good. That reassures me that the disguise is effective. I am—Colonel Sebastian Moran, in person—come to bring an end to the life of Mr Sherlock Holmes.' With these words he gave a savage, mirthless laugh.

'The incompetent agents I have employed have failed. But I shall not fail. That clock on the mantelpiece is ticking away the life of Holmes. And after he has died—you shall be next, Watson. But first, you shall see your friend die at my hands.'

At that point there was a knock at our sitting room door. Moran hastily pulled the curtain across in front of the alcove in which I was sitting. But he didn't pull it all the way, and through the remaining gap I could see what was going on, as well as hear it.

It was Patience Hudson at the door. 'Oh, where is Dr Watson?' she asked.

'He just stepped out. Um, he asked me to wait here,' said Moran in his quavering old voice.

'Oh, I see. It's just that there is another visitor ...'

Before she could complete the sentence the Reverend Henry Bunyan, our minister, stepped into the room.

'Forgive the intrusion. I take it that both Holmes and Watson are out?'

'Quite correct,' said Moran, still playing his role as an elderly clergyman.

'Then I'm sure you won't mind if I wait until one of them turns up,' remarked Bunyan, putting the matter beyond discussion by taking a seat on the sofa in front of the fireplace.

Patience left, and the two clergymen—one real and one fake—fell into conversation.

'Where are you from, sir?' asked Bunyan.

'A village in Yorkshire.'

'And what denomination do you represent?'

'Um ... ah ... Congregationalist.'

'Really? How interesting. Which wing of the Congregationalist church do you belong to? Calvinist? Or Arminian?'

'Ah ... um ... I really wouldn't care to say. Although I have never been to Armenia in my life.'

'I see: "haven't been to Armenia". Well, in the light of that answer, sir—I denounce you as a fraud. You are no real clergyman. If you were, you would understand that Arminianism is a school of theology, and has nothing to do with the country of Armenia.'

As he spoke these words Bunyan leaped to his feet and angrily confronted the man I knew to be Moran. It was unfortunate that he did so. For a second later he found himself facing a deadly revolver.

'You are far too clever for your own good, Mr Bunyan. If you shout for help you will almost certainly bring about the death of the young woman, as well as your own demise. However, if you remain quiet and cooperative I will simply tie you up while I complete my business here.'

From my place behind the curtain in the alcove I saw Mr Bunyan bound and gagged as I was, and then led into Holmes' bedroom, where, undoubtedly, Moran tied him to a chair, just as I was tied.

Then we settled down to await the arrival of Sherlock Holmes, who could have no idea that he was walking into a death trap.

18

As I waited for Sherlock Holmes to arrive—and walk into the hands of Colonel Sebastian Moran—I struggled with my ropes, but to no avail. Moran had taken great care to fasten them most securely.

Eventually I heard the sound I had been dreading—the familiar sound of Holmes' footsteps on the stairs.

'Hello,' said Holmes as he entered, 'where's old Watson?'

'Ah, he had to step out for a moment,' said Moran, putting on his trembling, elderly voice.

'Did he, indeed? And who might you be, sir?'

'Boddington is the name,' said Moran. 'The Reverend Rufus Boddington.'

'And what is the nature of your business with this establishment?'

'I have come to consult you, Mr Holmes, in your capacity as a detective.'

'As a detective, eh? And why would Colonel Sebastian Moran need a detective?'

At these words Moran pulled a pistol out of his pocket and levelled it at Holmes.

'So, my disguise did not fool you?' he remarked in an

angry sneer. 'Never mind, I still have the upper hand.'

'Oh, your disguise is a very good one,' Holmes said calmly. 'Allow me to compliment you upon it.'

'Thank you, Holmes. I take that as a compliment from the master. But how then did you know that I was not who and what I claimed to be?'

'Because I know old Watson. And he is far too faithful to ever leave these rooms when an unknown visitor is here. Well, since you are the one holding the gun, perhaps you'll be kind enough to tell me what happens next.'

'Next—I kill you, Holmes. I have the pleasure of watching you die before my very eyes—a pleasure I have looked forward to these last two years. Everyday in my prison cell I thought of nothing except killing you.'

'How very single minded of you. You would have done better to focus on repentance and rehabilitation.'

'And you will not be the only one,' said Moran, ignoring Holmes' last remark. As he spoke he pulled back the curtain covering the alcove, and displayed me, helplessly bound and gagged.

'How are you, old chap?' asked Holmes, genuine concern in his voice. 'Are you all right?'

'He is fine. And your concern is wasted. My first bullet is for you—the second is for him.'

'I am your enemy, not Watson. Kill me if you must, but spare his life.'

'Enough of this idle talk! Prepare to die!'

'Now, I know you are a cruel fiend, Moran, but surely even you would not deny a last pipe before you pull the trigger?'

'Very well. Smoke one last pipe if you wish.'

Holmes reached up to the mantelpiece and picked up a

pipe I had not seen him use before. It was black with an unusually large bowl and a straight stem.

As he slowly filled the bowl with tobacco he said calmly, 'That pistol you're pointing at me—I take it that is one of Von Herder's famous air guns?'

'It is indeed. How perceptive of you.'

'And is the hand gun version as powerful as the rifle?'

'Every bit as powerful. And it also fires those large calibre soft-nose bullets that do so much damage to human flesh.'

'For a hunter such as yourself I would have thought that was rather a heavy gauge weapon for mere human beings.' As he spoke Holmes was tamping down the tobacco in the bowl with his thumb. The stem of the pipe was pointing directly as Moran while this was going on.

Suddenly there was a hiss and a thud, and the pistol flew out of Moran's now bleeding wrist. Holmes leaped onto Moran and for a moment there was a fierce struggle. But only for a moment—those slender hands of Holmes had a grip of iron. Within a minute he had fastened handcuffs around the wrists of Colonel Sebastian Moran, and was standing up, smoothing down his ruffled hair.

Once the would-be killer was secured Holmes' first step was to release me.

'How are you old chap?' he asked as he took off the gag and began untying my ropes.

'Completely unharmed,' I replied, 'but you must explain to me what just happened.'

'Colonel Moran is not the only one who can have air guns built to personal specifications. I ordered a rather special one some time ago from Straubenzee, the great gunsmiths of Switzerland. The Swiss are wonderful craftsmen, you know, Watson. However, unlike Moran, I had my air gun disguised as a pipe. It only holds one bullet, but it's a most effective weapon—as I'm sure you'll agree, having seen it in action. And now, Watson—I really think you should clean and bandage Moran's wound. We can't allow him to bleed on our carpet like that.'

'I'll do that while you release Mr Bunyan, Holmes.'

'Bunyan? Is he here too?'

'Bound and gagged in your bedroom,' I explained.

A few minutes later I had dressed Colonel Moran's wounded wrist, and Mr Bunyan had been released from his temporary imprisonment.

'And now,' said Holmes, 'I must send Billy the pageboy to summon a policeman. This is news that Inspector Lestrade, and all his colleagues at Scotland Yard, will want to hear—the recapture of that dangerous escaped convict, Colonel Moran.'

'I'll go,' offered Bunyan. 'It would be a pleasure to bring a policeman to apprehend that wretched villain.'

And so it was that an hour later Colonel Sebastian Moran was being escorted away under heavy guard, while Inspector Lestrade stood in front of our fireplace, beaming from ear to ear.

'I'll see to it that you get proper credit over the recapture of Moran,' said the inspector.

'That's very kind of you,' replied Holmes. 'But I won't accept any credit. I play the game for the game's own sake. The weapon with which I overpowered Moran is one that I had prepared many months ago—not especially for him, of course, but simply because this profession does entail certain risks, and it is best to always be thoroughly prepared.'

Lestrade declined to stay for coffee, and soon followed his prisoner to Scotland Yard.

'A good piece of work, Holmes,' I said, as I poured

myself a second cup from the coffeepot.

'But it will take a good deal more than a pistol, however ingenious, to solve our problems tonight, Watson.'

'Tonight, Holmes?'

'When we tackle the alien killer in the fog of Baker Street.'

19

That night after dark we all met in Professor Challenger's study at Seymour Mansions.

As well as Challenger, Holmes and myself, Professor Summerlee, McArdle the reporter, and Mr Bunyan were there.

'I've made five additional induction coils during the day,' Challenger explained. 'That's makes six in all—one for each of us.'

As this point Austin handed around the strange devices. I looked closely at the one Austin put into my hands. It was a plain wooden box, quite heavy because of the storage battery inside the box, with a brass switch on one side and, on top, a ceramic cylinder tightly wound with several layers of copper wire.

'Once you've turned it on,' continued the professor, 'don't touch the exposed wire—you'd get a nasty shock if you did.'

'What does this do?' asked Bunyan, turning the device in his hands over and over. 'How are we meant to use it.'

'Be patient!' roared the lion behind his desk. 'I'm coming to that. When we see this thing—the green glow, I mean, that gives away its presence—we are to surround it at a safe distance. Once it is surrounded we are all to turn on our induction coils, using the small switch on the side of the box. They must, under no circumstances, be turned on any earlier—the batteries will run down rapidly once the switch is operated. In fact, it's best if you wait until you hear my command. Then, if my calculations are correct, we will be able to close in on it quite safely. It should be rendered immobile and harmless.'

'And what then?' asked Professor Summerlee dryly. 'Do we explain that it's been badly behaved and ask it to do better in future?'

'Then,' bellowed Challenger, waving his huge, hairy hands over his head, 'then, you nincompoop, then we destroy it.'

'And how do you propose doing that?' Summerlee asked acidly.

'You'll see when I do it,' was all that Challenger would say in reply.

'If it comes off it'll make a great story,' chuckled McArdle.

'Which you will not write until I give you permission,' boomed Challenger.

'Certainly not, professor,' agreed the reporter, 'I wouldn't dream of it.'

'And if your plan doesn't work?' I asked. 'What do we do then?'

Challenger's great lion's head, with its rippling black mane, trembled as he replied, 'I would have expected more confidence from you, Dr Watson.'

'In other words,' said Summerlee, 'there is no alternative. If your plan fails, Challenger, we all flee—we shall have no other option.'

'That's enough! I shall listen to no more of this negativity. You have your equipment. We are all well rugged up against the cold and the fog. It is almost midnight. Let's get out onto Baker Street and commence our patrol.'

As on the previous occasion, Sherlock Holmes and Professor Challenger made the extreme ends of our line. Spaced out in between were Summerlee, McArdle, Bunyan and myself. The fog, if anything, seemed thicker, colder, and damper than ever before.

Having a line of six turned out to be much better than our previous line of four—it meant that we could just make out the next shadowy figure in the line on either side of us, and contact was not lost.

A clock in a distant tower struck midnight as we began our first sweep of the street. This passed without incident.

Halfway back down the street, now feeling the bitter cold seeping through our clothes—it happened.

It was the eagle eye of Sherlock Holmes that first caught sight of the phenomenon.

'There is a faint, green light about twenty yards ahead of us,' said Holmes crisply.

'You can't possibly see that far ahead,' complained Summerlee, 'not in this fog.' But a moment later he had to correct himself. 'Oh, I see what you mean now,' he said. 'Yes, there is something there.

'Holmes!' boomed Professor Challenger. 'You and I need to swing around to encircle it.'

The rest of us kept moving forward steadily. And then I caught my first clear sight of it. The sickly, green glow was pulsing like a faint heart beat in the fog just ahead of us. The thing seemed to have no definite shape—it was a twisting, whirling, writhing cloud.

As we drew nearer it seemed to settle down towards the ground, spreading out and assuming the shape of a gigantic, ugly insect.

'Holmes and I are behind it now, and moving in,' called out Challenger. 'Turn on your induction coils and hold them out ahead of you. Remember not to touch the exposed wire.'

I turned the brass switch on the side of the box I was carrying and heard the faint hum begin as power surged through the coil. Then I held it out at arm's length, in the direction of the green light, and advanced slowly forward.

The fog was now as thick as pea soup, and we had lost contact with each other. At Challenger's shouted suggestion we began calling out numbers around our line, so that our voices would give a guide as to direction and distance.

The light was larger and nearer now. It looked to me like the phosphorescent glow of a rotting carcass. In fact, I thought I had seen a similar evil glow once before. And then I remembered that I had. In the strange adventure of *The Hound of the Baskervilles* that awful hellhound had glowed in the dark just like that.

All seemed to be going well with Challenger's plan until a sudden cry from Bunyan alarmed us.

'Help! It's got hold of me!' he cried. 'It's wrapped itself around my ankles.'

We all ran in the direction of his voice. In a moment we were standing in a circle around Bunyan. The thing was indeed curled tightly around his ankles like a coil of rope that pulsed with a vicious gleam.

It was Sherlock Holmes who ran forward to rescue him.

'Hand me your induction coil,' called Holmes. Bunyan did as he was told. Holmes laid two induction coils, his own and Bunyan's, on the ground on either side of the pulsating, slug-like mass.

'That should hold it for a while,' he said. Then he stepped forward, grabbed Bunyan around the waist, and pulled him free from the thing's horrible grasp.

'Oh, thank you, thank you, Mr Holmes,' gasped a breathless Bunyan.

'What now,' said Holmes, turning towards Professor Challenger.

'Now, sadly, comes the execution,' said Challenger, as he took out of one of the huge pockets in his black cloak, a workman's blowtorch. 'This is a pity really. I would much rather study it. Unfortunately, it is much too dangerous.'

With those words he lit the torch, and a jet of hot flame shot out. Instantly Challenger rushed forward, moving surprisingly quickly for a man of his bulk, and thrust the brilliant red flame into the seething green mass. There was a momentary crackle, and then the whole thing flared up, as if it was a spray of paraffin. Like a blazing bonfire, or a giant firework, for a moment it lit up the whole street. Then it died to a wisp of smoke, and was gone.

The long silence that followed was broken by Summerlee's voice.

'Well, that appears to have been an effective form of execution, Challenger,' he said.

20

It was almost two o'clock in the morning, and Holmes, Challenger, Bunyan and I were gathered in our rooms at 221B Baker Street.

Our tired conversation was interrupted by the sound of footsteps on our stairs. A moment later Professor Summerlee opened the door of our sitting room.

'Any change in the meteor?' asked Sherlock Holmes.

'It was just as you predicted, Mr Holmes,' replied Summerlee. 'The meteor is now inactive. It is nothing more than an inert mass of iron and nickel.'

'With small amounts of cobalt, copper, phosphorus, carbon and sulphur,' said Holmes. 'I have now completed my chemical analysis, and my original estimate has turned out to be correct.'

'What was that thing in the fog, Professor Challenger?' asked Mr Bunyan. 'Can you explain it?'

'Explain it? No, not really. I doubt that anyone can. As to what it was—well, most probably a mass of microscopically small organic matter that somehow survived crossing millions of miles of the vacuum of space, and survived a temperature of 2,200 degrees Centigrade during the meteor's descent into our atmosphere.'

'Surviving all of that seems unlikely,' I remarked.

'Unlikely, but not impossible,' said Challenger, in what, for him, was a remarkable calm and tolerant tone of voice. 'But it was clearly connected to the meteor, and it *lived*—it was biological. I suppose it might not have travelled with the meteor. In might have been some sort of common local bacteria, or virus, that was infected and rapidly mutated by a chemical on the meteor or a radiation coming out of the meteor while it was hot. Personally I am inclined to doubt that sort of reaction could happen quite so quickly. Hence, I lean towards the theory that it was microscopic biological matter that was actually on or in, the meteor when it entered earth's atmosphere.'

'Yes,' said Summerlee, with a sober nod of his head. 'You are probably correct.'

'So life may not be restricted to this planet then?' I asked.

'So it would appear,' said Holmes, taking up the coffeepot, and pouring a fresh cup.

'What are the implications of that?' I asked. 'For instance, would the existence of life in space disprove the Bible?'

'Of course it would!' snapped Summerlee, his old arrogance re-asserting itself.

'What rot!' boomed Challenger. 'Why should the existence of life in space, or on some other planet, especially microscopic, bacterial life, disprove the Bible? If you believe that, Summerlee, you're a goose.'

'Evidence of life elsewhere—even minute bacteria—must spell victory for atheistic evolution and doom for the Bible,' drawled Summerlee, in his thin, acidic voice.

'You are not being logical, Professor Summerlee,' said Sherlock Holmes crisply.

'Logical?'

'Precisely. Life is the product of intelligent design. All life is based on information. If the Great Designer, in his abundant, wisdom and generosity, should choose to plant life elsewhere in addition to this planet, that doesn't eliminate the Designer—it simply tells us a little more about his design. And since we already know the fine tuning of the universe is so precise that it has clearly been designed to support life, why should we be surprised to find a little more of it in a place we hadn't thought to look before?'

Summerlee scowled in silence, but Bunyan remarked, 'Well said, Mr Holmes! As for the Bible, it concerns itself with God's huge, cosmic, life-transforming plans for us—the human race. If God has special plans that involve bacteria in outer space, or on Mars, or anywhere else, there is no reason to suppose that he would need to tell us about those plans. And the Bible is only about what we need to know to relate to God and make sense of life.'

'Well, I'm convinced,' I said. 'That answers my question. A loving, expansive, generous God might choose to make life all over the place—and all that would prove is that he is a loving, expansive, generous God. Anyone who thinks it disproves the Bible, is just showing their ignorance of what the Bible actually says.'

'Indeed,' remarked Holmes, as he leaned back in his armchair and stretched out his long legs, 'what you say is true. However, the more I think about it, the less I am convinced that what we were dealing with was bacteria from space. There is too little data for certainty, but I suspect some local, earthly organism, changed by its contact with the meteor. And I say that only because I know how narrow and specialised are the conditions under which life can arise. But either way—bacteria from space or changed bacteria from earth—it makes no real difference. Neither of those possibilities disproves the Bible or advances atheism. There is a constant temptation to try to make science do work it cannot do.'

Just then the pounding of feet on the stairs and the dramatic flinging open of our sitting room door interrupted our debate. It was McArdle, the reporter.

'He threw it back at me!' he cried, waving a sheaf of papers in the air. 'The editor threw my story back at me. The biggest scoop I've ever had! He said he didn't believe a word of it. It was all fantasy he said, and I should offer it to the fiction editor.'

'It just proves what I've always said,' boomed Challenger, 'never trust newspapers.'

'Sit down, young fellow,' said Sherlock Holmes, 'and have a cup of coffee. There's plenty more left in the pot.'

Afterword

In bringing together Sherlock Holmes and Professor Challenger my biggest problem was to do with timing, since the Challenger stories are set in a later period than the Holmes stories.

I solved the problem by imagining that Challenger probably changed very little during his lifetime, and even as a young man (with a broad, black beard!) he would have behaved like the short-tempered, middle-aged man Conan Doyle described in *The Lost World* (the original, not the Michael Crichton/Steven Speilberg one). For the same reason I was able to keep Professor Summerlee much as he is in that story.

However, I had to discard Malone, the journalist who narrates most of the Challenger stories, since he would have been a schoolboy at the time when *Footsteps in the Fog* is set. I replaced him with McArdle—who is Malone's editor at the *Daily Gazette* in Conan Doyle's stories, and is (as you have discovered) a young, energetic reporter in this tale. (By the way, McArdle returns in *The Wolfman of Dartmoor*, and I might bring him back in later stories in this series.)

The idea for the "alien life" element in this story was triggered off by contemporary newspaper hysteria about the possibility of bacterial life being found on Mars. One popular science commentator leaped into print declaring any such discovery to be "the death of Christianity". Anyone who can write that sort of nonsense may know a lot about science, but clearly knows almost nothing about Christianity.

There is nothing in Biblical Christianity that denies the existence of life elsewhere in the universe, particularly simple, single-celled bacterial life. The Bible is about *this planet*, and about us (and how we relate to the Creator God who made us). But I don't think I need to repeat the message here. Challenger has already made my point for me, and (as he would be the first to point out) he is much smarter than I am.

Wolfman
of
Dartmoor

This following tale presents Sherlock Holmes and Dr Watson with a difficult and dangerous challenge. It also presents you, dear reader, with a challenge—possibly even a difficult one (although certainly not a dangerous one).

To intrigue and entertain good Sherlockians everywhere I have built into the following tale as many cross-references as I could to "the canon" (that is, to Sir Arthur Conan Doyle's original stories). Your challenge, should you choose to accept it, is to identify as many of these cross-references as you can while you read.

At the end of the story I will identify the most prominent cross-references (but not necessarily all of them!). You have been challenged, now, read on ...

1

On the waterlogged, misty, high granite plateau which is Dartmoor stands the small village of Little Meldon—a dozen cottages, a church, a post office, and an inn.

A bleak sun broke through heavy clouds as a small boy, some seven years of age, ran out of the inn followed by a yelping terrier.

'Come on Blackie,' called the boy. 'Come for a run.'

As the two ran down the single street of the village the boy's older sister appeared at the inn door.

'Teddy!' she called. The boy paused and looked back. 'You be back in time for supper.'

The boy nodded and ran on.

The Scots terrier, with his young owner in close pursuit, ran out of the village and through clumps of stunted trees that had been twisted into strange and eerie shapes by the wild winds. Soon they were out on the open spaces, the wild wastes, of Dartmoor. In the distance could be seen the dark shapes of the high tors.

The boy and dog ran on, being careful to avoid the deep bogs and mires that filled the moor with dangerous traps for the unwary. All afternoon the two played together. For some time they chased each other around the weather-beaten slabs of granite that had once been a stone-age hut. Then the boy began searching for ancient flint arrowheads he knew could be found close by. The dog, meanwhile, ran off joyfully to chase nesting water birds.

After an hour swirling mists began to close in, the sun disappeared behind dark clouds, and an eerie, purple twilight settled over the moors.

Young Edward Grey filled his pockets with the flints he had collected and looked around for his dog. The Scots terrier was nowhere to be seen.

'Blackie! Blackie!' called the boy.

He walked towards the small stream of icy water where he had last seen his pet.

'Blackie! Blackie! Where are you boy? Here boy. Here boy.'

No cheerful yapping could be heard, and there was no sign of the dog. The boy began to worry, and ran up on to a low mound, looking in every direction as he called as loudly as he could, 'Blackie! Here boy. Here boy.'

Edward Grey kept walking and calling for half an hour, his hands deep in his pockets to keep them warm. When a light, misty rain began falling he looked around and realised that he had wandered off the narrow, worn track he had been following, and didn't know how to get back to the village. He was lost.

Arthur Grey, the publican of Chequers Inn, at Little Meldon village, became worried about his son when he noticed how dark it was getting outside.

'Alice! Alice!' he called out to his daughter. 'Where's Teddy?'

'Isn't he here?' she responded, walking into the front parlour of the inn.

'When did you see him last?'

'Taking Blackie for a run, a hour or two past,' replied the young woman.

'Well, I just hope he's back from the moors—that weather looks bad.'

The two of them searched the inn from cellar to attic without finding the boy.

'Teddy! Blackie!' called Alice as she searched.

Eventually they had to admit that the boy was missing.

Arthur Grey hurried around the village and roused up his neighbours to form a search party. The men of Little Meldon rugged up in heavy coats, boots and scarves and set out for the moor carrying lanterns.

As they made their way through the twisted trees and around the treacherous bogs and mires their voices could be heard, calling across the moor, 'Teddy! Teddy! Can you hear me? Call out if you can hear me, son.'

'Don't worry, Arthur, I'm sure we'll find him,' said the Reverend Mr Dobson, the minister of Little Meldon village church, encouragingly, as they searched.

'I pray that we shall, Mr Dobson,' murmured Arthur Grey, 'I pray that we shall. Ever since my Martha died three years back, I have felt the responsibility of those children like a special burden.'

'Surely Alice is not such a burden, Arthur? She is now ... what? Twenty-one years of age?'

'That's true. And she is a great help around the inn. But Martha's special concern was for young Teddy. There's such a big gap in age between Alice and Teddy. Of course, there had been Beryl in between them, who died of the influenza. But Teddy was Martha's baby, and on her death bed she made me swear I would take special care of him. Oh, if anything has happened to him, Mr Dobson, if anything has happened ...'

At that moment a voice called from a hundred yards away, 'He's here! I've found him!'

The boy was huddled under the shelter of a stone-age burial mound, curled up tightly, soaking wet, shivering and blue with the cold. Arthur Grey ran to him and lifted him up in his arms.

'Oh, my Teddy,' cried the publican, sweeping the small boy up. 'Can you hear me, Teddy? Are you all right?'

A faint voice, little more than a whisper, replied, 'I'm cold, Poppa.'

As the men were gathered together and turned back towards the village, the boy asked in a small voice, 'Where's Blackie? Where's my dog?'

It was the question he kept on asking that night as he was given a hot bath and tucked up in bed. He was still asking the question after the doctor had come, pronounced him cold but healthy, and left again.

'We'll look for Blackie in the morning,' his father promised, 'as soon as the weather clears. But I expect he will turn up of his own accord before long.'

The next day the rain was heavy and bitterly cold. The

dog did not return. The rain continued all night and all the next day. In fact, it was three days before the boy and his father could go out on the moor and look for the missing terrier.

They carefully retraced the path taken by Teddy and Blackie on the day they had both vanished. All the time young Edward Grey called his dog's name and looked around hopefully.

It was Arthur Grey who found the animal in the end —lying in a ditch, with its throat savagely torn out, as if it had been attacked by a giant, powerful vicious beast.

2

Rain was thundering against the window panes of number 221B Baker Street, as I turned to Sherlock Holmes and said, 'I doubt if our visitor will come in this weather.'

Holmes put down the violin he had been playing and said, 'There I disagree with you, my dear Watson. Read the note again—you will see that she is desperate. This rain will not deter her.'

I picked up the note that was lying on Holmes' desk and read it again: *If it is convenient I will call upon you tonight at seven. My sanity—and my father's sanity—lie in your hands.* And it was signed, *Edith Doppler.*

'Yes, I see what you mean, Holmes,' I remarked.

Despite the blazing heap of coals in our fireplace it was a bitterly cold night and Holmes was wearing his mouse-coloured dressing gown, over the top of his tweed suit, for warmth. The great detective had thrown himself in an armchair, his long legs stretched out towards the fire, when we heard the bell downstairs.

At the sound of footsteps on the stairs I opened the door to our sitting room.

'A visitor for you,' announced Mrs Hudson, our landlady.

'Edith Doppler, I believe?' I said as I stood back and

invited her to enter. 'I am Dr Watson, and this is my friend, Mr Sherlock Holmes.'

'I am sorry for intruding upon you, gentlemen. But if I don't talk to someone about what is happening I think I shall go mad. Perhaps I am already mad.'

Edith Doppler was a lovely young woman, with shoulder length dark hair, and deep, soft brown eyes set in a pale and worried face.

'This matter is very delicate, Mr Holmes,' she said, casting a shy glance in my direction. 'I can hardly justify myself if I speak before any third person.'

'Have no fear, Miss Doppler. Dr Watson is the very soul of discretion.'

She blushed slightly and accepted the seat on our sofa near the fire that I offered her. Then she continued.

'In that case,' she said, 'I had better tell you my story. My father is Professor Orville Doppler ...'

'The renowned archaeologist?' suggested Holmes.

'You've heard of him then. Just at the moment we are living in a rented cottage on the outskirts of the village of Little Meldon at Dartmoor. My father moved there to commence excavation of a stone-age burial mound at High Barrow. I must swear you to absolute secrecy when I tell you that father has found not a stone-age burial site, but a Viking one.'

'I had no idea the Vikings had ever occupied that part of the country,' I remarked.

'Nor had anyone else, Dr Watson,' replied Miss Doppler. 'Hence, you can well imagine my father's excitement. His discovery will turn the world of ancient history on its ear. He became like a young man again. He had seemed to age since my mother's death five years ago, but the sheer excitement of his unexpected find has brought back to him all his old youthful vigour.'

At this point she stopped, looked down at her gloved hands, and her blush deepened.

'Carry on, Miss Doppler,' urged Holmes.

'This is the difficult part,' she said slowly. 'With his renewed vigour and interest in life, my father began to court a young woman in the village. Her name is Alice Grey and she is the daughter of the proprietor of the village inn, Chequers. You will understand that there is quite an age difference. My father is fifty one years of age, while Alice is only two years older than myself—she is just twenty one.'

'How did she react to your father's attentions, Miss Doppler?' I asked.

'Well, she seemed to quite like my father, despite his eccentricities, and despite the age difference. Of course, there were one or two young men of the village she had walked out with. But my father was so infatuated, and so determined to win her approval, that she found him hard to resist.'

'How did Miss Grey's father, the publican, respond to all this?' asked Holmes.

'The truth is, Mr Holmes, that my father is quite a wealthy man, and Mr Grey raised no objections. At length, Alice agreed to become engaged to my father. And it was not long after this event that our real troubles began. I myself had become engaged just a short time earlier—to Trevor Franklin, father's assistant. Trevor lives at the house with us, and he has noticed the same disturbing things I have.'

Here she paused and asked if she might have a drink of water. I offered her coffee, but she insisted that a glass of water would do. Once she had taken a few sips, she resumed her story.

'Around this time a mystery clouded the routine of my father's life. He did what he had never done before. He left home and gave no indication where he was going. He was away a fortnight, and returned looking rather travel-worn. He made no allusion to where he had been, although he is usually the frankest of men. It chanced, however, that Mr Franklin, my fiance, received a letter from a fellow archaeology student in Prague, who said he was glad to have seen Professor Doppler there although he had not been able to talk to him. Only in this way did I, his own daughter, learn where he had been.'

Miss Doppler took another dainty sip of water and then resumed her tale.

'From that time onwards a curious change came over my father. He became furtive and sly. Those of us close to him—Mr Franklin and myself—have the feeling that he is not the man we had once known, but that he has come under some shadow that has darkened his life. His intellect is not affected. His mind remains as brilliant as ever. But there is something new, something sinister and unexpected. I attempted again and again to penetrate the mask he seemed to have put on—but all was in vain.'

For a moment, she was silent, and then she cried out, 'Mr Holmes, why has my father's dog twice attacked him?' and began to sob uncontrollably.

3

I fetched a glass of brandy for our guest and insisted that she drank some. She sipped a little and coughed, and then she began to regain her composure.

'If you are feeling up to it, Miss Doppler,' said Sherlock Holmes, 'we shall resume.'

She nodded in response.

'Now, you say that your father's dog twice attacked him?'

'Hardly terribly significant, surely?' I remarked.

'The same old Watson!' said Holmes with a chuckle. 'You never learn that the gravest issues may depend upon the smallest things. What do you make of these attacks upon Professor Doppler by his own dog?'

'Perhaps the animal is ill,' I suggested.

'But he has attacked no one else, Dr Watson,' said Edith Doppler, 'nor does he attack my father, except on very special occasions.'

'Perhaps it would be best,' proposed Holmes, 'if you resumed your story, Miss Doppler, at the point you had already reached.'

'Yes, of course,' she said, and then went on. 'You have to understand that my father had no secrets from me. I worked in my father's study, beside himself and Mr Franklin. I was his secretary, handling every paper which came to him, and in addition, I opened and organised his letters. Shortly after his return all this was changed. He told me that certain letters might come to him from London which would be marked by a cross under the stamp. These were to be set aside for his eyes only. I may say that several of these did pass through my hands, that they had the EC postmark, and were in a rough handwriting. If he answered them at all the answers did not pass through my hands.'

She paused for a long time, took another sip of brandy, and then resumed.

'And then there was the box,' she said very quietly.

'The box?' I asked.

'Yes, Dr Watson. My father brought back a little wooden box from his travels. It was the one thing which suggested a Continental tour, for it was one of those quaint, carved things which one associates with Germany. This he placed in a cupboard in his study. One day, when looking for a fresh bottle of ink, I picked up the box. To my surprise he was very angry, and reproved me in savage words for my curiosity. Oh, Mr Holmes, Dr Watson, relations between us had been so affectionate until then. Following the death of my mother we had grown very close, and had come to depend upon each other. It was the first time such a thing had happened, and I was deeply hurt. I tried to explain that it was a mere accident that I had touched the box, but all that evening I was conscious that he looked at me harshly.'

Miss Doppler dabbed at her eyes with her very damp handkerchief and then continued.

'It was that very same evening that Blaze attacked my father, as he came from his study into the hall.'

'Blaze, I take it, is the dog?'

'Precisely, Mr Holmes. He was named after a famous

race horse, but you've probably never heard of him. Blaze is an Irish wolfhound, a breed noted for its gentleness. And despite Blaze's size and powerful build he has always been a dear affectionate animal.'

'Singular! Most singular!' murmured Holmes.

'There was another scene of the same sort nine days later. We have had to banish Blaze to the stables. Mr Franklin and I agreed that this is not a case in which we can consult the police, and yet we are utterly at our wits' end as to what to do, and we feel in some strange way that we are drifting towards disaster. We cannot wait passively any longer.'

'It is certainly a very curious and suggestive case. What do you think, Watson?'

'Speaking as a medical man, I suspect an illness of some sort.'

'But my father was never in better health,' protested Miss Doppler. 'In fact, he is stronger than I have known him for years. But there are times when he has no recollection of what he does. He lives as in a strange dream. It is no longer my father with whom I live. His outward shell is there, but it is not really he. Is he going mad? Am I going mad? Is there some terrible disease that runs in our family? Or is he the victim of some diabolical plot? Mr Holmes can you do nothing to help us?'

'I have hopes, Miss Doppler, but the case is obscure. Dr Watson and I shall come at once to Little Meldon. You may expect to see us there by tomorrow afternoon at the latest.'

There were other important events in the case which occurred on that same day at Professor Doppler's archaeological site at High Barrow, of which I learned only later.

The professor himself, and his assistant Trevor Franklin, were in the trench that had been dug into the burial mound, while two local workman who had been hired as diggers were moving piles of soil. Suddenly Doppler looked up to see a strange face peering down at him over the rim of the trench.

It was the face of a woman of uncertain age, with a mop of black hair, and fiery black eyes.

'Have you found them yet?' she asked with a strange cackle.

'Who the dickens are you?' demanded Doppler.

'I am Mina, and I am in touch with the spirits.'

'What the blue blazes are you talking about?' demanded Doppler irritably. 'What spirits?'

'The spirits of those who are buried here. And of the things that were buried with them. Ancient things. Occult things. Things of great power. Have you found them yet?'

'You clear off!' shouted Doppler, now quite angry. 'You come from that gipsy camp don't you? I know your lot. Thieves the lot of you. Now clear off!'

The woman pulled a shawl more closely around her shoulders and said, 'But I shall return,' and somehow those innocent words sounded very threatening.

'What do you think she wanted, sir?' asked Trevor Franklin.

'Thieves, the lot of them!' repeated Doppler. 'There will be treasure in this burial mound, Franklin, you mark my words. Many Viking objects were made from gold and silver.'

'But we haven't told anyone this is a Viking burial site yet.'

'The gipsies can sniff out gold and silver. I want you to pay a local man to stand guard here at night from now on.

And talk to that idiot police constable in the village, what's his name?'

'Constable Potter, sir.'

'Potter, that's right. Talk to him, and make sure he comes out here regularly on his rounds. We must stop those gipsies,' hissed Doppler, with a wild light in his eyes, 'from stealing our treasure.'

4

The next morning Holmes and I caught an early train to Okehampton. From there we paid a man with a pony cart to take us to Little Meldon on the edge of Dartmoor.

The pony trap set us, and our bags, down in front of Chequers Inn in Little Meldon just before lunchtime. Over the door of the inn was a sign reading: 'Arthur Grey, proprietor, licensed to sell spirituous liquors'. As I carried the bags inside Holmes went in search of Mr Grey.

We finally found the publican in the snug parlour of the inn, before a blazing fire. Informed that we wanted rooms, he asked our names.

'I am Sherlock Holmes, and this is Dr John H Watson.'

'Sherlock Holmes? *The* Sherlock Holmes?'

'I know of only one,' replied Holmes quietly, although his vanity was always flattered when his name was recognised.

'There is only one Sherlock Holmes,' I assured Mr Grey. 'And this is he—the world's first, and greatest, consulting detective.'

'You embarrass me, Watson,' said Holmes.

'We are greatly honoured to have you in our establishment, Mr Holmes. You too, Dr Watson. Now, have you two gentlemen had lunch? No? Well, my daughter Alice can serve you a nice, hot mutton stew, if you care to take a seat at the table here. I'll take your bags up to your rooms in the meantime.'

Alice Grey herself served our meals. She was a tall, red-headed girl with eyes of the true cat green.

'What has the weather been like lately?' I asked, trying to engage her in conversation.

'The weather is like it always is,' she replied. 'You know what they say about Dartmoor—we get nine months of winter followed by three months of bad weather.'

And with that she left the room.

A few minutes later her father returned, carrying a huge pot of tea. 'I thought you might like something to wash down your lunch with,' he remarked, and then took a spare chair and sat down to talk to us.

'And what brings you gentlemen to Little Meldon?' he asked. 'It's the ghost wolf, isn't it?'

'Ghost wolf?' I responded, almost choking on my mutton stew.

'Aye, that's what folks is callin' it. Although for myself I can't make up my mind whether it really is a flesh and blood wolf, or a ghost of a wolf, or a ghost of something else. It's all quite puzzling really.'

'It can't possibly be a wolf,' I objected. 'At least, not a real flesh and blood wolf. There have been no wolves in England for hundreds of years.'

'Is that what they say, is it?' asked Grey.

'It's a scientific fact, Mr Grey,' I replied.

'Ah well, maybe there's more things in this world than them scientist chaps knows about.'

'You interest me strangely,' said Holmes. 'Tell me more.'

'Well, sir, it began back in July, and now being

September that makes it three months it's been going on, more or less.'

'What, exactly, has been going on?' I asked.

'The sheep killings, sir,' said Grey. 'I reckon that by now it must be hundreds of sheep have been killed. It's hard enough for moorland farmers to make a living without having their livestock killed by who knows what in the middle of the night.'

'Describe these killings, if you please,' said Holmes as he poured himself a second cup of tea.

'It varies a bit. It's always a flock that's up on the moor, well away from any farm house, that's attacked. So no one has ever seen anything or heard anything. All the farmer finds are the remains, afterward. And an unpleasant sight it is too. Most of them have had their throats torn out, you see. Whatever did it had huge fangs, you can see that. And razor sharp teeth. There's no other way to explain it. Some of the sheep are cut up completely—like they've been torn about and half eaten. Nothing but bits of carcasses left.'

While he was talking a small boy, aged about seven, I would have guessed, had slipped quietly into the room and stood just inside the doorway listening to Mr Grey finish his tale. When he did the boy spoke up.

'It killed my dog,' he said.

'Hello,' said Holmes, turning around, 'and who might you be?'

'Edward John Grey is my name, sir,' said the child, puffing out his chest.

'That's my son Teddy,' explained the innkeeper. 'You run off and play now, Teddy. I'm talking to these gentlemen.'

'But I want to tell them about Blackie.'

'And I'd like to hear what the child has to say,' said

Holmes, in a kindly way. 'I take it Blackie was your dog, is that right?'

'Yes, sir. Blackie was my Scots terrier. And the thing on the moor got him. Poppa and I found him after the rain stopped.'

'You run along now Teddy,' insisted Grey. 'I'll tell the gentlemen what happened to Blackie.'

As the boy ran out of the room his father said quietly, 'The poor dog's throat was just ripped out. A single swipe from some powerful claw, that's what it looked like to me.'

'Has anyone ever seen this "ghost wolf" on the moor?' I asked.

'Not seen it, Dr Watson,' replied Grey. 'No, not seen it. But they've heard it. Lots of folks have heard it. I heard it once myself.'

'What did you hear?'

The innkeeper leaned closer and said in a hushed voice, 'Howling! The most horrible, blood-curdling howling you could ever imagine.'

'And did this howling coincide with attacks on sheep?' asked Holmes.

'Aye, Mr Holmes. That it did. It was the howling as much as the savage attacks that make folk talk about a wolf. But because no one's ever seen it, they call it the "ghost wolf" you understand. Constable Potter, he won't have that it's no wolf. He says it's a dog that's attacking the sheep. He's been going around warning all dog owners to keep their animals locked up at nights. But it's not a dog, Mr Holmes—I've seen the wounds. No ordinary dog can do that sort of damage, not unless it has teeth like knives and claws like talons.'

5

Constable Bert Potter rode his bicycle along the narrow track that crossed the moor. Ahead of him the horizon was broken by the jagged lines of the dark granite hills called tors. Around him was open grazing land, dotted with the hardy, thick-coated sheep run by the moorland farmers.

The track he was riding on wove back and forth in broad arcs, avoiding the deadly bogs and mires that were scattered across the moor.

Light misty rain began to fall and then cleared again. Constable Potter's thick, woollen uniform kept him dry and warm. Since being posted to Little Meldon he had learned to ignore the weather—if he didn't he would never get his work done.

The policeman pedalled on through swirling mist until he reached the gipsy campsite, under the shadow of Vixen Tor.

As he got off his bike, and took his bicycle clips off the legs of his trousers, he could see only one person in front of the lone caravan—a wild haired, wild eyed woman of uncertain age seated at the camp fire.

'Good afternoon,' said the policeman.

'Ah, bad luck's arrived,' cackled the woman.

'Is your husband about, madam?'

'Hugo!' screeched the woman. In response, a heavily built, unshaven man came out of the caravan.

'What do you want?' he snarled at the constable.

'I've come to ask if you own a dog, sir,' replied Potter, restraining his own irritation at these people.

'Yes, we do. What of it?'

'Where is it now, sir?'

'Our son Robbie has taken it for a walk. Why do you want to know?'

'What breed of dog is it, sir?'

'It's a German Shepherd—not that it's any of your business.'

'A number of sheep have been mauled on the moorland farms, sir. Some of them have been killed. I believe these to have been the result of dog attacks. Has your dog been loose after dark at any time, sir?'

'And what if it has?'

'If there is any reason to suspect your dog might be involved in these attacks I will have to obtain an order from the magistrate to have the animal put down.'

'You're not killing our Hannibal!' shrieked the woman at the camp fire.

'Quiet mother. It won't come to that,' said the man. 'Now look here, constable. You have nothing to worry about, I can assure you of that. Our dog is always securely tied up at night. We always see to that, don't we mother?'

The woman just cackled, and then got up and lurched into the caravan.

'May I have your name please, sir?' asked Constable Potter, taking a small notebook out of his top pocket.

'Zak is the name—Hugo Zak.'

'And your wife's name?'

'Mina.'

'Do you have permission to camp on this land, sir?'

'You know as well as I do this is common land, constable, and unless the law has changed I am perfectly entitled to camp here.'

'How long do you plan to stay, sir?'

'Haven't decided.'

'So, how many of you are there, altogether?'

'Three of us—Mina, our son Robbie, and myself. Oh, and Hannibal the dog makes four, and I suppose we should include the dog, since he is what this fuss is all about. Will that be all, constable?'

'There is one other thing, sir.'

'Something's missing, and we've been blamed? Is that what it is? When anything goes missing, blame the gippos— that's the usual story. Well, let me tell you, constable—we are not thieves.

'Nothing has gone missing, sir—yet.'

'What do you mean "yet"?'

'I've had a complaint from Professor Orville Doppler that one or more persons from this camp have been seen in the vicinity of his dig on High Barrow. He tells me he expects valuable archaeological materials from the stone-age to be recovered from that dig, and he is concerned about the safety of the site.'

'It's the same thing, isn't it? Blame the gippos every time.'

'All I'm saying, sir, is that I'm placing High Barrow off limits. No one from this caravan is to visit the site. Is that clear?'

'Perfectly,' replied Zak, spitting out the word.

At that moment a dark young man in his twenties arrived with a large German Shepherd dog trotting by his side.

'Ah, this is my son, Robbie—and Hannibal the dog. Do

you want to explain to them everything you've just said to me?' sneered Hugo Zak.

'That won't be necessary, thank you, sir,' replied Constable Potter with studied politeness. 'I'll leave it to you to pass on the message.'

With those words he snapped his bicycle clips back onto the legs of his trousers, mounted his bicycle and pedalled away.

All of these things were reported to me later by Constable Potter. While they were happening Holmes and I were preparing to leave the snug parlour of Chequers Inn, and set out on foot for Professor Doppler's cottage.

Our table had been cleared by the innkeeper, and we were finishing a last cup of hot tea before departing, when a clergyman entered and asked, 'Is one of you gentlemen Sherlock Holmes?'

'I am,' replied Holmes.

'Please allow me to introduce myself. My name is Roderick Dobson, and I am the minister of this parish.'

'What can I do for you Mr Dobson?'

'Is it true you have come here to investigate the so-called "ghost wolf" of Dartmoor?'

'Quite untrue. We are here for other reasons entirely.'

'Oh, I am so pleased,' muttered the clergyman, sinking into one of the armchairs. 'It is my people I am worried about,' he explained. 'Some of them at least, are inclined to be somewhat, well ... superstitious.'

'I see. Perhaps you'd like to tell me exactly what rumours have been circulating,' said Holmes, his keen grey eyes lighting up with interest.

'In public they will talk about a "ghost wolf", but in their own parlours, late at night, they talk about—a werewolf.'

'Werewolf?' I remarked. 'I don't believe I'm familiar with the word.'

'According to legend, a werewolf, old chap,' explained Holmes, 'is a person who changes into a wolf. The word comes from an Old English term meaning *man-wolf.* Werewolves appear in many old stories. The technical term for a werewolf is, I believe, *lycanthrope.*'

'Quite right, Mr Holmes,' said Dobson. 'Folk around here are sometimes even afraid to say the word. Instead they'll talk about "shape-changers"—but they mean werewolves. The old remedies against werewolves are being talked of once again.'

'And what are they?' I asked.

'Saying the werewolf's real name, or hitting the werewolf three times across the forehead. Sometimes they propose trying to wound the werewolf, and then looking for a human being with the same wound. These legends and superstitions are unhealthy, Mr Homes, and I don't want to see them encouraged. There are enough real sorrows in the world, and enough real help in the Bible, without these simple folk haunting themselves with unnecessary fears.'

'I quite agree,' said Holmes, 'and you may be assured that our visit will do nothing to encourage such nonsense. Watson and I stand flat-footed upon the ground, and there we must remain. The world is big enough. No werewolves need apply.'

'Thank you, Mr Holmes,' said Dobson, rising and shaking him warmly by the hand. 'You don't know how much you've relieved my mind.'

6

Holmes and I walked down the one street of Little Meldon. A strong breeze blew fallen leaves around us in a whirl and made my overcoat, and Holmes' travelling cloak, flap against our legs. All the cottages—and the church, the post office and the inn—were built from the local granite. The stone blocks of these grey buildings were damp and dripping from the constant rain and mist, giving the whole place a rather gloomy air.

At the far end of the street we came to a high stone fence, with heavy iron gates. The gates were open so we entered and walked down a tree-lined drive to the door of a house of charming design—although built of the same grey stone as the rest of the village. It was surrounded by lawns and covered by purple wisteria. Judging from the size of the cottage—the largest in the village—Professor Doppler was surrounded with every sign not only of comfort, but of luxury.

Even as we knocked a grizzled head appeared at the front window, and we were aware of a pair of keen eyes from under shaggy brows which surveyed us through large, horn-rimmed glasses. A maid opened the front door, and a moment later we were actually in his sanctum, with the mysterious scientist, whose vagaries had brought us from London, standing before us.

There was certainly no sign of eccentricity either in his manner or appearance, for he was a portly, large-featured man, grave, tall and frock-coated, with the dignity of bearing which a scientist needs. His eyes were his most remarkable feature, keen, observant, and clever to the verge of cunning.

He looked at the visiting card in his hand, upon which was the name *Sherlock Holmes.*

'Pray sit down, gentlemen. What can I do for you?'

'Since Dr Watson and I are visiting the village of Little Meldon it seemed only polite that we should call upon the most famous resident of the village, the distinguished Professor Doppler.'

Doppler scowled at us, as a shadow of deep suspicion flickered across his features.

'What is the purpose of your coming to such a remote and out of the way place as Little Meldon?' he asked.

'The matter that calls us here is a delicate and confidential one.'

'Oh, indeed!' It seemed to me there was a malicious sparkle in the professor's intense grey eyes. 'Then you refuse to tell me?'

'It would be improper for me to answer questions upon the subject,' said Holmes, choosing his words carefully and gauging their effect upon the archaeologist.

'You have been hired to spy upon me haven't you?' At this point my heart leaped into my mouth. Had he somehow discovered his daughter's visit to our rooms? But his next remark made it clear that his thoughts were running in another direction entirely. 'Who has hired you? Was it Anstruther? Yes, of course, it must have been Anstruther. That dithering old fool has been my rival for many years. He resents every discovery I make. You might as well confess—you have been hired by Professor Anstruther to spy on my work here, haven't you?'

'I can honestly say that we have not,' replied Holmes calmly.

'Do you take me for a fool?' screamed the professor, suddenly hysterical. 'Do you imagine that I don't know I am surrounded by enemies. No one wants me to succeed—no one.'

'Please be assured, Professor Doppler, that it was not Professor Anstruther who hired our services.'

'Then who? Tell me that! You won't, will you? No, of course not!' With these words Doppler leaped from his chair and began to pace back and forth in a rapid and energetic motion. 'Who is selling my secrets to you? Is it someone from this household?'

Before either Holmes or myself could reply he walked across the room and rang a bell. The call was answered by a young man—tall, handsome, about thirty. He was well dressed and elegant, but with something in his bearing which suggested the shyness of the student rather than the self-possession of the man of the world.

'Gentleman,' said Doppler, a distinct sneer in his voice, 'this is my assistant, Mr Trevor Franklin—but undoubtedly you already know each other.'

'No, I can't say we do,' I responded. 'Never had the pleasure. How do you do, Mr Franklin?'

'Liars!' shrieked Doppler. 'You have been in touch with these detectives, haven't you Franklin? You might as well admit it. You are selling my secrets to the world. I swore you to secrecy over our find at High Barrow and you have broken your oath—tell me the truth now!'

'I swear professor that I have done nothing of the sort,' said the young man anxiously.

'We have had no contact with Mr Franklin whatsoever,'

said Holmes, rising from his seat. 'And if you are a gentleman, you will accept our word on that.'

'Hhmm,' grumbled Doppler. 'If I must, then I must.'

'I can only say that we have made a needless intrusion upon your time, Professor Doppler,' said Holmes. 'Come, Watson, we must be off.'

'Hardly enough, Mr Holmes!' the old man cried, in a high screaming voice, with extraordinary malignancy upon his face. He got between us and the door as he spoke, and he shook his two hands at us with furious passion. 'You can hardly get out of it as easily as that.'

His face was convulsed and he grinned and gibbered at us in his senseless rage. I am convinced that we should have had to fight our way out of the room if Franklin had not intervened.

'My dear Professor,' he cried, 'consider your position! Consider the scandal! Mr Holmes is a well-known man. You cannot possibly treat him with such discourtesy.'

Sulkily our host—if I may so call him—cleared the path to the door. We were glad to find ourselves outside the house, and in the quiet of the tree-lined drive. Holmes seemed greatly amused by the episode.

'Our learned friend's nerves are somewhat out of order,' said he. 'Perhaps our intrusion was a little crude, and yet we have gained that personal contact which I desired.'

'A classic case of paranoid symptoms, if you ask me,' I remarked.

'Listen, Watson! He is surely at our heels. The villain still pursues us.'

The sounds of running feet behind us, detected by Holmes' sharp ears, turned out, to my relief, not to be the formidable Professor, but his assistant, Trevor Franklin. He appeared around the curve of the drive and came panting up to us.

'I am very sorry, Mr Holmes. I wish to apologise.'

'My dear sir, there is no need. It is all in the way of professional experience.'

'I have never seen him in a more dangerous mood. He daily grows more sinister. You can understand now why Edith and I are alarmed.'

'Quite understandable, old chap,' I said.

'There has been a further development. The most extraordinary and alarming event occurred to Edith last night. With your permission she will call upon you at the inn this evening and tell you about it herself.'

7

Constable Bert Potter cycled down the slope from Vixen Tor and headed across the wild waste of Dartmoor. A thin, drizzling rain was falling, and the wind was blowing in strong gusts.

Potter had to ride slowly to avoid the pools of rain water that lay across the narrow path. It was twilight when he left the gipsies, and before he was half way back to the village, night had fallen. The policeman stopped to light the small lamp attached to the front handlebars of his bicycle, and then continued.

As he pedalled through the darkness—with only the faint, yellow glow of his lamp to light the way—the constable began to be haunted by pictures in his mind.

He remembered the horror of the dead sheep he had seen—savaged and mangled. He remembered the dark, lonely places on the moor where creatures might live never seen by human eyes. He remembered the dark, threatening looks of the gipsy, Hugo Zak. And as these pictures flickered through his mind, he wished he was back in the warmth of his own cottage, in front of his own fireplace, with his wife serving him a bowl of her wonderful ox tail soup.

These thoughts were interrupted by a strange sound that

attracted Constable Potter's attention. The sound came from somewhere behind him. He came to a halt and looked around. He could see nothing—just inky blackness in every direction, except for the small, yellow beam of light shining from his lamp onto the path ahead.

He resumed pedalling, but now his ears were alert for the slightest noise that might be out of the ordinary. He pedalled hard for another quarter of a mile, and then heard it again. He stopped and listened. He could hear the sighing of the chill wind, he could hear the faint dripping of rain water from wet bushes and rocks. But there was something else. Something he couldn't quite put his finger on.

Then he looked around and saw it. It was standing on a low mound of jumbled rocks a hundred yards away. And it was looking straight at him. It was a dog. A huge dog. No, not a dog, thought Constable Potter—that must be a wolf!

But how could he see it in the darkness? And then he realised—the creature was glowing with a strange, green, phosphorescent light. Terrified, the constable leaped on his bicycle and pedalled as hard as he could for the village. He was careful not to look over his shoulder in case a luminous, green, glowing wolf was following him.

While this was happening, Alice Grey was serving a hot curry to Holmes and me for our supper in the front parlour of Chequers Inn. Just as we were finishing the meal Edith Doppler arrived to speak to us.

The three of us sat in armchairs around the fireplace while she told her story.

'I crept away while father was occupied,' she said. 'If he knew I was here talking to you he would never forgive me.'

'Mr Franklin told us there was an incident last night, after you returned home from your visit to us,' prompted Holmes, 'is that correct?'

'Quite correct, Mr Holmes. I was awakened in the night by the dog barking most furiously. Poor Blaze, he is chained now near the stable. I may say that I always sleep with my door locked; for, as Trevor—Mr Franklin—can tell you, we all have a feeling of impending danger. My room is on the second floor. It happened that the blind was up in my window, and, at the moment when I was awoken by the dog, the clouds had cleared and there was bright moonlight outside. As I lay with my eyes fixed upon the square of light, listening to the frenzied barkings of the dog, I was amazed to see my father's face looking in at me.'

Miss Doppler's face had gone horribly pale as, in the re-telling, she re-lived the incident. I made her a hot cup of sweet tea and insisted that she drink some. After a time she was able to resume her tale.

'Oh, Mr Holmes, Dr Watson, I nearly died of surprise and horror. There it was, pressed against the window-pane, and one hand seemed to be raised as if to push up the window. If that window had opened, I think I should have gone mad. It was no delusion, Mr Holmes. Don't deceive yourself by thinking so.'

'You mustn't alarm yourself, my dear,' I said, patting her hand. 'Holmes and I believe your story absolutely.'

She swallowed some more tea, and then went on, 'I dare say it was twenty seconds or so that I lay paralysed and watched the face—my father's face, strangely twisted and pressed against the window of my second floor bedroom! Then it vanished, but I did not—I could not—spring out of bed and look out after it. I lay cold and shivering until this morning.'

'Did either you or your father make any reference to this incident this morning?' asked Holmes.

'No. Of course not. How could I?' said Miss Doppler

with a sob. 'And father no longer talks to me as he used to. At breakfast he was sharp and fierce in his manner and made no allusion to the adventure of the night.'

Then she broke down and began to sob uncontrollably. After some time she recovered, and Holmes and I offered to walk her back to her house. But at that moment Trevor Franklin appeared, and he provided safe escort for Miss Doppler back to the Professor's cottage.

Sherlock Holmes and I made our way into the crowded tap room of the inn, where the men of the village were laughing, talking, playing darts, and drinking Arthur Grey's nut-brown October ale. We had been there only a few minutes when the front door burst open, and a dishevelled Constable Potter burst into the room.

A hush fell and conversation ceased as Potter, struggling for breath, cried out, 'I've seen it! I've seen it! The ghost wolf!'

8

The hush was broken by a din of voices asking the constable a dozen questions at once.

'What did it look like, Bert?'

'Where did you see it?'

'Did it chase you?'

'Are you sure it was a real wolf?'

'Where is it now?'

'Is it heading towards the village?'

'What should we do about it?'

This confused noise was brought to an end by the booming voice of the innkeeper, Arthur Grey. Producing a twelve-gauge, double-barrelled shotgun from underneath the bar, Grey said, 'I don't know about the rest of you, but I intend to go and hunt down that monster while he's out there—and before he disappears again.'

This met with loud shouts of approval, and quickly the tap room emptied as the men hurried back to their cottages to fetch weapons. Twenty minutes later a large crowd was assembled at the inn, and was being organised by Constable Potter, who had, by now, recovered his composure.

'Now,' he announced, 'we need to organise this properly, otherwise we'll blunder about and end up shooting each other. We'll work across the moor in a line, starting from this village and moving, generally, in an easterly direction. Once you've been given your place in the line, don't move out of it. Everyone should carry a lantern, that will enable us to keep an eye on each other. The first person to see the wolf is to let up a cry, and the rest of us will move in that direction.'

The constable himself was armed now, for someone had lent him a Lee Enfield .303 rifle.

'Shall we join them, Watson?' asked Holmes.

'It seems like the neighbourly thing to do,' I replied.

'Yes, I'm sure it is. However, I was thinking rather more along the lines that it might be quite instructive.'

'Oh, I see. Well, I have my old Webley army revolver upstairs in my bag, so I'll go and fetch it.'

'And while you're about it, Watson, you might fetch my Ely .32 pistol. It's in my suitcase.'

Ten minutes later we were all assembled under the grove of trees on the edge of town. The innkeeper had welcomed Holmes and me as part of the hunting group, and had provided us with hurricane lamps. Potter and Grey between them sorted the shooters out into a long, straight line, with each man some ten yards away from the next. After a further reminder to keep our places in the line, and watch out for the deep bogs, we set off.

It was a bitterly cold night, and we were only kept from freezing by the fact that we were walking briskly the whole time. My neighbours to the right and left, local villagers, kept an eye on me, and shouted out if I wandered too close to a treacherous bog or mire. Holmes was at the other end of the line, and I didn't see him again until much later—when we all reassembled at the inn.

We had not walked far when a distant sound brought us

to a sudden halt. Faintly echoing across the dark moors came the sound of a wild, howling cry! It was a sound to chill the blood and make the stoutest heart miss a beat. After less than a minute, the sound ceased.

The villager next to me in the line whispered, 'It's out there.' With those words we resumed our hunt, trudging across the moor.

While we were conducting our 'wolf hunt' a significant event was happening at Moorgate farm—an event I was to learn of the next day.

A family called Bennett worked Moorgate farm, and they had all retired to bed for the night, when they heard strange noises in the farm yard. At the insistence of his wife, Mr Bennett got out of bed, lit a candle, pulled on his dressing gown, and went downstairs.

'Your gun,' called out his wife after him. 'Don't go outside without your gun.'

'Of course I won't, woman, do I look that silly?'

Bennet fetched down an ancient rifle from on top of a kitchen cupboard, pulled on his boots, and unbolted the back door.

All the time the sounds had been continuing in the yard. The Bennett's dog, which was chained up, was barking hysterically, there were loud squawks coming from the hen house, and strange thumps and bumps could be heard as well.

As Mr Bennett was about to open his back door he suddenly felt nervous. A cold chill ran down his spine. He was unsure what he would find when he opened that door.

'Well, go on then,' called out his wife, who was standing on the stairs behind him.

'I'm going, I'm going,' he said.

Holding his flickering candle up high, he swung open the door and stepped outside.

On the other side of the yard a large shadow was moving across the ground. It was crouching and skipping across the yard. There was no moon, and the candle gave little light, but Bennett could see that whatever it was, it was too large to be an ordinary dog. For a moment the shadow seem to crouch frog-like and then it ran across the ground on all fours.

'Don't just stand there, you fool—shoot it!' shouted Mrs Bennett, from the doorway behind her husband. He turned around and handed his wife the candle, and then raised the butt of the rifle to his shoulder.

'Stop,' he called out, 'stop or I'll shoot.'

'It can't understand you—it's an animal,' said Mrs Bennett scornfully.

But as if to contradict her words, at that moment the shadow stood up on its hind legs and ran towards an ancient oak tree that overhung the yard. As the Bennetts watched, open-mouthed, the creature began, with incredible agility, to ascend the tree. From branch to branch it sprang, sure of foot, and firm of grasp. When it paused it looked like some huge bat, glued to the trunk of the tree. Then it dropped to the ground and began creeping along again, once more on all fours.

Bennett pulled the trigger of his old rifle. The shot spun wildly into the air, and the echoes rang around the farm buildings. The creature in the yard, little more than a dark shadow in the darkness, suddenly stood up and sprinted over the fence and away across the moor—running as a man might run.

'I missed him,' said Bennett.

'Of course you missed him,' said his wife. 'You should

have given me the rifle—I'm a much better shot than you.'

After settling down the dog, and checking out the hens, the two of them, still grumbling, went back inside their farm house and locked and bolted the kitchen door.

As the farmer put the rifle back in its place on top of the cupboard he asked his wife, 'What do you think it was?'

There was a long pause before she finally replied, 'A shape-changer.'

9

We 'wolf hunters' were tired, cold and wet by the time we reassembled at the village inn.

'Did anyone see anything?' asked Constable Potter, in a depressed voice.

'Not a blessed thing.'

'Not even a rabbit—certainly not a wolf!'

'If it was out there it didn't come anywhere near me.'

These remarks were followed by a chorus of complaints about the cold and the damp.

'Are you sure you really saw it, Bert? You didn't imagine it?' asked one man.

'I saw it all right,' snapped the constable. 'You know I didn't believe in the wolf until I saw it. All along I thought it was a dog attacking the sheep. Now would I come telling you I saw a wolf, and dragging you all out onto the moor, unless I really saw it?'

Everyone agreed this was reasonable, and, one by one, they straggled off home to their own warm beds. Eventually, only Holmes, myself, the innkeeper and the policeman were left.

'You believe me, don't you, Mr Holmes?' asked Potter.

'I am quite certain you saw something on the moor

earlier this evening, constable,' said Holmes, choosing his words carefully.

'Thank you for your confidence, sir. Well, I'd better get back to my cottage. I'll have to be up first thing in the morning—and that's not all that far away.'

Those words were truer than Constable Potter realised, because at first light Mr Bennett from Moorgate farm was pounding on his front door, reporting the appearance of a 'shape-changer' in his farm yard in the early hours of the morning. After this report, Potter was able to say to the men of the village, 'Well, that's why we couldn't catch it on the moor—it was out at Moorgate farm, that's why.'

When the constable left the inn it was almost four o'clock in the morning, and Arthur Grey announced, 'I'm off to bed. How about you gentlemen?'

'There is one small thing I would like to check before I retire,' said Holmes. 'I wonder if I could borrow a hurricane lamp?'

'Why, of course.'

'And if you wouldn't mind leaving the front door on the latch until I return?'

'Certainly. Well, I'll see you in the morning gentlemen.'

'Where are we going, Holmes?' I asked, as Grey made his way upstairs.

'To Professor Doppler's cottage, Watson. Keep your revolver in your pocket and come with me.'

The deserted street of Little Meldon seemed strange in the early hours of the morning. A cold river of wind blew between the houses and in the distance an owl hooted.

When we reached the big iron gates at the Doppler house Sherlock Holmes dropped down onto his knees and began examining the driveway by the light of his hurricane lamp.

After several minutes he said, 'It is as I thought, Watson.'

'What have you found, Holmes?'

'Fresh footprints in the driveway. You see these older footprints have been filled with water from the rain earlier tonight. But these marks here have no water in them. They are fresh. Someone has been up and down this drive since midnight.'

'Do the footprints tell you anything else, Holmes?'

'Most interestingly they tell me that whoever made them was not walking, but running—see how the toe impression is much deeper than the heel impression. Striking, very striking indeed. Well, I think that's all we can learn for the time being. Let's get back to the inn, and try to get some sleep in what is left of the night.'

Both Holmes and I rose late the next morning, but Alice Grey still had a hot breakfast of bacon and eggs, toast and kidneys waiting for us when we came downstairs.

'Miss Grey?' said Holmes as she was laying the table.

'May I ask you one or two questions?'

'What about?'

'About your fiance—Professor Doppler.'

'What do you want to know?'

'Have you seen much of him lately?'

'Not lately, no. He has been very busy with his work. But I understand that.'

'I'm sure you do. What about the date for the wedding, has that been set yet?'

'Not yet. And I hope you won't take it amiss, Mr Holmes, when I tell you that none of this is any of your business.' And with that she left the room, closing the door as she went.

'Instructive,' said Holmes. 'Most instructive.' And with

those words conversation came to a halt for a time, while we each ate a large breakfast.

'What is the order of action for today, Holmes?' I asked, as we drank our coffee after breakfast.

'We return once more to the Doppler cottage, Watson.'

'Is that wise, Holmes? The Professor made it pretty clear that we are unwelcome there.'

'It is not the inside of the cottage I wish to see, Watson, but the outside.'

A few minutes later Holmes and I rugged up warmly, he in his Inverness cape and deerstalker cap, and I in my army greatcoat and bowler hat, and we set off once more for the Doppler cottage.

We stood for a moment at the great iron gates, and then proceeded cautiously down the curved drive. Before we came into sight of the house, Holmes broke off and led the way into the bushes. In this way we circumnavigated the house and the outbuildings, while Holmes scrutinised every door and window with his eagle eye.

Near the stable at the back of the house we found Professor Doppler's Irish wolf-hound, still chained up. It gave a few yelps when we first appeared, but settled down when Holmes walked over to it, and spoke to it gently. Soon he was scratching its head, and it was nuzzling affectionately into his hand.

'So, this gentle animal has attacked the Professor, eh Watson?' said Holmes, his hawk-like profile alert as he looked around the stable yard and the back of the cottage. Just then Edith Doppler emerged from the back door and Holmes beckoned her over.

'Is it wise for you to be here, Mr Holmes?' she asked.

'If I am to investigate this case, then my presence here cannot be avoided.'

'I suppose not. Is there anything I can do?'

'Three things. The first is to show me your bedroom window.'

'Come this way,' she said, leading us around the house, through the shrubbery, until we had a view of the side of the house.'

'It is there. The second on the left.'

'Dear me, it seems hardly accessible. And yet you will observe that there is a creeper below and water-pipe above which give some foothold.'

'I could not climb it myself,' I said.

'Very likely, Watson. It would certainly be a dangerous exploit for any normal man.'

'I must be getting back to my father soon,' interrupted Miss Doppler. 'You said there were three things, Mr Holmes. What are the other two?'

'First, do you think you could obtain the address of the man in London to whom the Professor writes?'

'Perhaps, I will certainly try.'

'Second, the dates on which your father's behaviour changes interest me greatly. Is there any way of identifying those dates?'

'I keep a diary. They will all be recorded there.'

'Excellent! If you could bring your diary to the inn at some time today that would be great help.'

'I shall do so, Mr Holmes. I promise you I shall.'

10

Around the middle of the morning a pale sun appeared from behind grey clouds, and we saw sunlight in Little Meldon for the first time since we had been there.

Sherlock Holmes was sitting on a bench, in the sun, in front of Chequers Inn. His long legs were stretched out, and the tips of his fingers were resting lightly together. His piercing grey eyes seemed to be staring at some point in the far distance. I had seen Holmes in this sort of mood before, and, knowing he was concentrating deeply, I was careful not to disturb him.

However, he *was* disturbed, not by me but by an angry bellow that rang down the street of the tiny village.

'Potter!' boomed the voice. 'Where is that man?'

The voice belonged to Professor Orville Doppler. He was standing in front of the policeman's cottage, pounding on the front door and shouting.

'Potter! Where are you?'

Faces began to appear at cottage windows as people looked out to see what the noise was all about. Fortunately at that moment Constable Potter cycled into the village street from whatever outlying farm he had been visiting.

'Ah, Potter! At last!' bellowed Doppler. 'There have been thieves up at the dig, at Upper Barrow. What are you going to do about it, man?'

'If you'd care to step into my cottage, Professor, I'll take down the details,' replied the policeman politely. With this the two men disappeared into Potter's house.

'Well, Holmes,' I said, 'what do you make of that?'

'As of yet, nothing, since there is insufficient data. However, I shall have a talk to the good Potter later in the day to see whether this information can carry our inquiries any further.'

At that moment Edith Doppler appeared between two of the cottages and hurried in our direction.

'Mr Homes, Dr Watson—father is out of the house at the moment, and that gave me the opportunity to come and see you with some information.'

'Excellent,' cried Holmes. 'I suggest we step inside the inn where we will not be seen should your father emerge from Constable Potter's cottage.'

A minute later the three of us were seated around a table in the front parlour of Chequers Inn.

'Firstly,' said Miss Doppler, 'I have obtained the address of the man in London to whom father writes. He seems to have written this morning and I got it from his blotting-paper. It is an ignoble thing for a trusted daughter to do, but perhaps it is all for the best. It is his interests I am considering.'

'Perfectly correct, Miss Doppler,' said Holmes encouragingly, as he glanced at the piece of paper that she handed over to him.

'Hhmm—Washington Sprague, a curious name. He should not be too difficult to locate, I imagine. Well, it is an important link in the chain.'

'Secondly, here is my diary, Mr Holmes. It contains the secrets of my heart. I trust it to your care, knowing that you are fully trustworthy. But do take great care of it, Mr Holmes.'

'I promise I shall, Miss Doppler.'

A moment later Edith Doppler was hurrying back to her cottage before her father should return and discover her absence.

'What are you going to do with the diary, Holmes?' I asked.

'I intend to make a close study of the dates on which the Professor behaved strangely. I would not be surprised to see a pattern emerge.'

'Oh, I see. And what about the name of the London correspondent—what do you propose doing about that?'

'Nothing, Watson.'

'Nothing?'

'You shall do something instead.'

'Me? Certainly, Holmes, if you wish. What did you have in mind?'

'I want you to take the afternoon train back to London, old chap, and track down this Washington Sprague for me.'

'What do I have to go on?'

'Only his name—admittedly an unusual one, so that should help—and the postal district EC. I suggest you might do worse than starting with our young journalistic friend McArdle at the *Daily Gazette*.'

'I'll throw a few things in a bag and be on my way at once.'

Half an hour later one of the villagers was driving me to Okehampton railway station in his cart. The train was a slow one and got me into London quite late. I surprised Mrs Hudson by turning up at Baker Street, and then I had the pleasure of getting a good night's sleep in my own bed, intending to begin my search for Mr Washington Sprague first thing in the morning.

However, while I was in London, strange things kept happening at Little Meldon.

Shortly after midnight, while the whole village slept, two dark figures crept in through the big iron gates at the entrance to Professor Doppler's house. The first move the intruders made was to scout around the house and find where the dog was tied up near the stables.

Blaze, the wolf-hound, began barking as soon as he became aware of the presence of the intruders, but the thieves threw the dog a large piece of fresh meat covered with laudanum, a powerful sleeping drug. Soon the animal was sound asleep, and the intruders could go about their business secure in the knowledge that there would be no barking dog to wake the sleeping inhabitants of the cottage.

Returning to the front of the house they searched for an unlocked window, and found one that opened into the Professor's study. Once inside they lit a candle and began searching for the valuable items they believed had been recovered from the dig on High Barrow.

From the drawers of the Professor's desk they took a number of items of Viking silver. These they placed in a small, canvas sack, and then made their escape.

Some two hours later a farmer near Willsworthy was woken by dogs barking in his yard. When he put his head out of his bedroom window to investigate, he heard other sounds—sheep on a hill above the farm, bleating in terror, and then a strange and horrible howling sound.

He got dressed, took a gun and a lantern, and set out across the moor to the hillside. When he arrived he found six of his sheep dead—their throats torn out by powerful, savage claws.

11

Early the next morning Henry Halifax, employed by Professor Doppler as a coachman and general assistant, descended from his bedroom above the stables to find Blaze still sound asleep. More disturbing was the fact that Blaze's chain was unfastened, and dried blood was smeared around the wolf hound's mouth.

When Halifax went into the house to pass on this news, the first person he found was Edith Doppler. She hurried out into the yard to see Blaze, closely followed by Trevor Franklin.

She lifted up the dog's head and said, in a relieved tone, 'Well, at least he's still alive.'

'Just take a look at all that dried blood around his mouth, Miss,' said Halifax. 'The strange thing is, I can't find a wound anywhere—and I looked real careful like.'

'That's because it's not his blood,' boomed Professor Doppler. Edith and Trevor turned around to find the Professor standing behind them.

'What do you mean, sir?' asked Franklin.

'Pretty obvious, isn't it? This dog has been killing sheep. Perhaps I should tell that oaf Potter so he can have it put down.'

'Father! Don't say that! Don't even think it. I can never

believe that Blaze has been responsible for mauling sheep. There must be some other explanation. Promise me you won't tell Constable Potter about this. Not until we've worked out what's really happened to poor Blaze.'

'Very well,' said the Professor reluctantly. 'Just put the chain back on and keep it on. I don't want farmers suing me because of that blasted dog. Better still—lock him up in the stables all day.'

With those words Doppler turned on his heels and stalked back into the house.

'There's no need to lock him up,' said Edith. 'Just make sure he's kept on his chain, please Halifax.'

'If you say so, Miss.'

'And we'll clear your name, Blaze,' said the girl, as she rubbed the dog's ears affectionately. 'I promise you we will.'

'Something strange is happening around here, Edith,' said Franklin quietly once Halifax was out of earshot. 'It's not just your father—there's more to it than that.'

While this was going on I was calling at the offices of the *Daily Gazette* in Fleet Street. I found James McArdle, the red-headed Scottish reporter seated at his desk.

'Dr Watson! It's great to see you again, mon!' he cried enthusiastically when he lifted his eyes from his paperwork and saw me standing before him. 'What brings you here?'

'Holmes has sent me back to London to trace a man,' I explained.

'Back from where?'

'Dartmoor.'

'This sounds interesting—tell me more.'

'Afraid I can't do that McArdle—client confidentiality, and all that.'

'Of course not, doctor, of course not. And I would never

255

press you to break client confidentiality—you may be assured of that. So, tell me—who is this man you want to trace.'

'His name is Washington Sprague.'

'What else do you know about him?'

'Nothing really. Except that he lives in the EC postal district.'

'Hhmm—not much to go on,' murmured the reporter, scratching his chin. 'Of course, it is an unusual name, and that's something.'

'What do you suggest?'

'One of my colleagues who sells advertising space is bound to have a commercial directory—we could start there if you wish?'

'Let's do it then, young fellow.'

McArdle led me down a flight of stairs and into another department on the great daily newspaper for which he worked.

'This is Stanley Horner—Stanley, this is Dr Watson.'

'Watson? Watson? Not the chappie whose stories about Sherlock Holmes are published in *The Strand Magazine*?'

'The very one,' said McArdle.

'I'm delighted to meet you, Dr Watson. You are a wonderful writer. Now tell me, sir, and I'm sure everyone asks you this, but—what is Sherlock Holmes *really* like?'

'Exactly as I describe him in my reports,' I said, a little stiffly.

'Fascinating, fascinating. And how may I be of service to you, Dr Watson?' asked Horner, clearly eager to please.

McArdle explained the nature of our mission, and Horner produced a large commercial directory from his desk. We searched through this for some minutes, but in vain. There was no listing for Washington Sprague.

'Hang on! I've just remembered! I've seen that name somewhere, if only I could remember where ... now where was it?'

McArdle and I looked on in breathless silence while Horner closed his eyes and concentrated. After a minute his eyes snapped open and he said, 'If my information is useful, will I end up in one of your stories?'

'Almost certainly,' I replied, as encouragingly as I could.

Horner once again closed his eyes and tapped his forehead with his finger, 'Where, where, where?' he muttered.

A long minute passed and then he shouted triumphantly, 'I've got it!' Several other people in the large office turned around and told him to hush. Speaking excitedly, but more quietly, Horner continued, 'I used to visit my grandmother in Stepney, and the omnibus I took ran down Commercial Road. I remember seeing the man's name on his shop, and I remembered it because it was such an unusual name. The Whitechapel end of Commercial Road—that's where you'll find him.'

'Thanks Horner,' called our McArdle as he dragged me away. 'Come along, doctor, let's go and find Mr Washington Sprague.'

In Fleet Street we hailed a hansom cab, and before long we were standing in Commercial Road, in front of a store with a faded sign reading, *Washington Sprague—General Goods.*

'Now we've found him, what do we do, doctor?'

'Get a look at him, and see what he's like. That's all. If he's to be approached, Holmes will do so.'

McArdle and I entered Sprague's shop and found it to be a large, but dingy and over-crowded place. The customers seemed to be mainly the less well off citizens of the surrounding Whitechapel area.

'Excuse me,' I said, stopping one shop assistant wearing a leather apron, 'is Mr Sprague here?'

'Sure, that's Sprague over there,' the young man replied, before hurrying about his business.

The person he indicated was an elderly man with a heavy build and a round face.

'So, that's Washington Sprague ... hhmm.'

'What now?' asked McArdle.

'Now, I take the next train back to Okehampton to report to Holmes,' I said.

'There won't be a train until this afternoon—why don't you let me buy you lunch, Dr Watson?'

I readily agreed to this proposal, and shortly afterwards the two us were in Ricoletti's enjoying their famous grill.

Now, it was a very pleasant and relaxed lunch, and, to be perfectly honest, I can't remember all the conversation that took place. However, in the light of later developments it is possible that I revealed a little too much to McArdle about our current investigation. It is true that McArdle asked many questions, although I can't remember him asking directly about the Dartmoor case. And it is true that I found him to be an excellent listener. So, I must have let something slip. At least, that's what later developments suggested.

My return journey was uneventful, and I found myself back at the Chequers Inn, at Little Meldon, by eight pm.

'Evening, Grey,' I said as I walked in the front door. 'Is Holmes upstairs?'

'Good evening, doctor. No, to be honest, I have no idea where he is.'

'No idea. What do you mean?'

'Only that he left the inn shortly after you did yesterday, and hasn't been back since. Sherlock Holmes has disappeared.'

12

Upon hearing this alarming news from the innkeeper I went straight to Holmes' room. When I found no note or message waiting for me there, I hurried around to Constable Potter's cottage.

'Disappeared, you say?' responded Potter, when I broke the news to him.

'Mr Grey says that Holmes left the inn yesterday afternoon and hasn't been seen since.'

'Well, I've seen him since.'

'Really, when?'

'Last night—at supper time. He called in to ask about the thefts the Professor had reported. In fact, he accepted my invitation to stay to supper with my wife and myself.'

'Did he say anything about his plans?'

'Not a word—but he was warmly dressed against the cold night air, so perhaps he planned a walk.'

'When he left here, did you see in which direction he went?'

'Yes indeed—he turned up the street, towards Professor Doppler's house.'

I didn't reply as I silently thought about the strange Professor, his violent manner, and the possibility that

Holmes had been attacked at the Doppler cottage.

'Are you certain that he's really missing?' asked the policeman, breaking into my thoughts.

'Well, his bed wasn't slept in last night, that's quite clear. On top of which, the folk at the inn haven't see him all day, and he left no note for me. You may take it from me, Constable Potter—Sherlock Holmes has vanished.'

'Do you suspect foul play, Dr Watson? Or is it possible that he is simply pursuing some clue?'

'Well ... I have to admit it's not totally impossible that he is chasing some line of inquiry,' I confessed.

'In other words,' said Potter, 'Mr Holmes has done this sort of thing before?'

'Ah ... well ... yes, on occasions he disappears for days at a time from our rooms in Baker Street.'

'In that case, Dr Watson, I suggest that you are becoming alarmed a little too quickly. Let's give it another twenty-four hours and see whether or not Mr Holmes turns up.'

'I suppose that would reasonable,' I said doubtfully. 'The question is—where would Holmes have gone? Where did he spend the night?'

'That's two questions,' responded the constable, who did not appear to me to be taking this disappearance seriously. Something of my concern must have shown itself because Potter placed a friendly hand on my shoulder and said, 'Look, Dr Watson, Sherlock Holmes is the world's greatest detective, he is a man of great abilities and well able to take care of himself. If you have heard nothing from him by this time tomorrow, then I will officially list him as missing and inform my superiors in the district police office.'

'Yes,' I replied, 'perhaps that is for the best.'

When I arrived back at the inn I found the place in uproar. The maids were rushing about, young Teddy was crying, and I could hear Mr Grey shouting something out in the kitchen.

'What is going on?' I asked one of the villagers in the tap room.

'They're all upset about the disappearance,' he replied. This astonished me, because when I had left to go to Constable Potter's house Arthur Grey had seemed quite unconcerned about the fact that Holmes had vanished.

'Well, I'm glad I'm not the only one worried about Holmes,' I muttered.

'What has Mr Holmes to do with this?' said the villager. 'Everyone here is in turmoil because Alice Grey is gone.'

'Alice Grey?'

'Aye. Who did you think they were worried about?'

'Hhmm ... never mind. So, Alice Grey has disappeared, eh? How long has she been gone.'

'Can't say for sure. But she was only missed about fifteen minutes ago—just after you walked out the door, in fact.'

'Did she leave a note or message?'

'I couldn't say. You'll have to ask poor old Arthur about that.'

At that moment the innkeeper charged into the tap room. His face was red and his hair dishevelled. I had never seen him so upset.

'Well, I've asked them,' he said, addressing everyone in the room, 'the maids, and Teddy and everyone. It appears no one has seen Alice since the middle of the afternoon. She set the scullery maid peeling potatoes, and that was the last anyone saw of her.'

'Has she gone of her own free will? Did she leave a note?' I asked.

'A note!' cried Grey. 'Yes, by Jove, there might be a note.

I'll take a look in her room.'

He ran from the room only to return disconsolate two minutes later shaking his head sadly and saying, 'There is no note or letter in her room. She wouldn't have gone off like this without warning me. Not Alice. She wouldn't have done it. Someone must have taken her—forced her to leave.'

'Are any of her things missing? Any of her clothes or personal possessions?' I asked.

'I'm not sure, Dr Watson,' replied the innkeeper in a flat depressed voice. 'I don't know if I could rightly tell. I could look in her wardrobe, but I don't think I'd know if anything was missing.' Then he seemed to come to life, and the colour returned to his face as he added, 'We must search for her. We should organise a search party. She may be out on the moor somewhere in need of help.'

'Aye, that's quite right, Arthur,' said a chorus of voices around the tap room. 'We'll help you search. Come along lads, let's get organised and help Arthur find his daughter.'

'I'll run and fetch Constable Potter,' said one of them as he darted out the door.

Soon Potter was amongst us, and, once again, organising us to patrol across the moor. Of course, I volunteered to join the search party, and so, for the second time in three days I found myself tramping across the moor at night, buffeted by bitterly cold winds, and chilled by damp mists.

Our starting place was the same as before—the clump of twisted trees on the edge of the village. This time most of us were unarmed, although one or two of the men, fearing trouble, carried shotguns.

Once again Constable Potter had set us in a straight line and started us tramping across the wild wastes. I had a second reason for taking part—in addition to a desire to help my neighbours—in that I thought such a search might turn up a trace of Sherlock Holmes.

While everyone else was just searching for Alice Grey, I was looking for the young woman, and, at the same time, for some sign of Holmes. As the night wore on the line of searchers seemed to spread out, and, apart from the sound of distant voices crying out, 'Alice! Alice!' I seemed to lose contact with those around me.

After stumbling on in this way for some minutes, through blinding mists, I reach a pile of stones—a cairn these things are called—erected in Neolithic times. I sat down on this and pulled a handkerchief from my pocket to wipe the clinging, cold moisture from my face.

As I was doing so I caught a glimpse of movement off to my right. I stood up and peered into the gloom. And then I saw it—a huge dog, so big it could have been a wolf, I suppose, loping across the ground fifty yards away. It was just as Constable Potter had described it—gleaming through the darkness with a strange, luminescent glow.

echoing savage sound that seemed to be baying for blood. I lay rigid in bed listening, until the howling faded into silence. It was yet another puzzle that seemed to have no solution.

I finally fell asleep trying to work out what might have happened to Alice Grey; where Sherlock Holmes had disappeared to; what strange creature was howling across Dartmoor; and whether I had seen a 'ghost wolf' on the moor in reality or only in imagination.

As I slept I dreamed of Professor Doppler running wild, killing sheep with a butcher's axe while Alice Grey and Mr Washington Sprague looked on. Then, in my dream, they were all killed by a gigantic, phosphorescent wolf, whose footprints were being tracked by Sherlock Holmes using a large magnifying glass.

I awoke after a restless night's sleep feeling as disturbed as when I lay down, and more concerned than ever over the whereabouts of Holmes.

After breakfast, feeling somewhat lost in the absence of my friend, I decided to take a walk down the single street of Little Meldon. Rugged up in overcoat and hat I set off.

I walked with little thought to my destination, and paying little heed as to where I was heading. And so it was with some surprise that I found myself at the Doppler house, standing in front of the two great iron gates. As I stood there, a cart came rumbling down the drive.

'Out of my way there!' shouted the driver. 'Stand clear! Don't block the driveway.'

I must have been slow to respond, for the cart had to come to a halt, just as I was moving back to clear the gateway. The driver of the cart was Professor Doppler.

'Oh, it's you, Dr Watson. I didn't recognise you,' he growled. 'I trust you are not coming to pay a visit.'

'I'm just going a for a walk,' I said defensively.

'Good! Because you would not be welcome, and, any way, I am just on my way to High Barrow.' I noticed that in the back of the cart were two of the local village men employed as diggers.

'Good morning, doctor,' sneered Doppler, as he whipped up his horse, and rumbled off down the road. However, while we were talking I had made a most remarkable observation. As a doctor I tend to notice people's symptoms, and in the case of the Professor I noticed his knuckles. They were thick and horny, and showed signs of heavy wear. Very curious knuckles indeed, which, at the time, I was quite unable to explain.

With Doppler out of the way I felt safe calling at the cottage, which I did.

A maid admitted me at the front door, and took me into the parlour, where I found Edith Doppler and Trevor Franklin deep in conversation.

After we had exchanged greetings Franklin said, 'I had a rather grim experience last night, doctor.'

'Please tell me all about it,' I replied, taking a seat close to the fire.

'I was lying awake in my bed at about two o'clock this morning when I was aware of a dull, muffled sound coming from the passage. I got out of bed, opened my bedroom door, and peeped out.'

The young man stopped to gather his thoughts and then continued.

'I should perhaps explain that Professor Doppler's bedroom is at the end of the passage, and that he has to pass my door in order to reach the staircase. It was a really terrifying experience, Dr Watson. I think that I am as strong-nerved as most men, but I was shaken by what I saw.

Looking out of my bedroom door I found the passage dark, save that one window half-way along it threw a beam of silver moonlight over part of the corridor. I could see that something was coming along the passage, something dark and crouching. Then it suddenly emerged into the light, and I saw that it was—the Professor! He was crawling, Dr Watson, crawling!'

As he paused Edith Doppler reached out and took one of his hands in both of hers to encourage him to continue.

'He was not quite on his hands and knees,' Franklin went on. 'I should rather say on his hands and feet, with his face sunk down between his hands. Yet he seemed to move with ease. I was so paralysed by the sight that it was not until he had reached my door that I was able to step forward and ask if I could assist him. His answer was extraordinary. He sprang up, spat out some atrocious word, and hurried on past me, and down the staircase. I waited for about an hour, but he did not come back. It must have been daylight before he regained his room.'

'Could he have been suffering from lumbago, perhaps?' I asked. 'I have known a severe attack make a man walk in just such a way, and nothing would be more trying to the temper.'

'Hardly, doctor,' responded Franklin, 'since he was able to stand erect the moment I spoke to him.'

'And my father has never been in better health,' added Edith Doppler. 'In fact, he is stronger than I have known him for years.'

'In that case, I find the Professor's behaviour totally baffling.'

'Clearly some embarrassment resulted from last night's encounter,' Franklin continued, 'for this morning he told me he did not want me at the dig site, but left me here to classify some specimens.'

'Well, Dr Watson, that is our grim news,' Edith said, 'have you any news for us?'

'Not good news, I'm afraid—Sherlock Holmes has vanished.'

14

Rapidly I explained the situation to Edith Doppler and Trevor Franklin.

'But where can he be?' asked Miss Doppler. 'Whatever can have happened to him?'

'I confess I don't know,' I replied. 'However, I have made up my mind that if he has not returned by midday I shall search for him on the moor. I was out last night, as part of the search for Alice Grey, and I kept my eyes open for any sign of Holmes—without success. However, I am confident that a search by daylight will be much more fruitful.'

Then I was bombarded with questions, and I had to explain about the disappearance of Alice Grey. It appeared that as the Doppler house was on the outskirts of the village they had completely missed the uproar of the previous night.

'Upon reflection,' said Edith, 'it is strange that my father was not informed, as Alice's fiance.'

'Yes, as you say,' I replied thoughtfully, 'strange indeed.'

I stayed on to have morning tea with Miss Doppler and Mr Franklin, and then returned to Chequers Inn. There I put my plans into action. I asked the kitchen maid to prepare a packet of sandwiches for me, then went up to my room and changed into my thickest tweed Norfolk jacket and put on a stout pair of walking boots.

An hour later I set out, with my old army revolver in one pocket, and a packet of sandwiches in the other.

Before long I was out amidst the wild, rugged scenery of Dartmoor. As I walked I occupied my mind—and drove out fears that something awful might have happened to Sherlock Holmes—by remembering the history of the place. If I recalled my schoolboy history correctly, the castle, manor and forest of Dartmoor had been granted by King Henry III to his brother Richard, Earl of Cornwall, in 1337. As a result, Dartmoor itself remains part of the duchy of Cornwall.

Around me were wide open spaces, and in the distance were high granite tors. The sky was filled with dark, threatening clouds and swirling mists came and went as I walked. I had learned from the villagers to stick to the well-trodden paths in order to avoid the deep bogs and treacherous mires.

I passed what is called locally a "standing stone", although I understand the technical name for these things is "menhirs"—they are tall, solid granite stones that have been set upright by primitive peoples at some time in the distant past, for what reason it is now impossible to tell.

As I continued walking, scanning the horizon constantly, I wondered whether these upright stones had been ancient burial sites, or, perhaps, if they had once been used for pagan rituals. The boggy ground I was walking across was divided by low stone mounds called "reaves". These, I had once been told, dated back to the Bronze Age, and were used in those primitive times for dividing the land between different tribes.

There was not another living soul within sight—I was

alone, and I might as well have been back in the Bronze Age, surrounded by savage pagans who hid themselves in the landscape. That wild waste had not changed in countless centuries, and, somehow, it would not have surprised me to have found a stone-age man, wrapped in wild animal skins, greeting me around the next corner.

The black thunder clouds caused the night to close in quite early, and it soon became apparent that I would be out on the moor, many miles from the village of Little Meldon, when it was fully dark. Once I realised that this would be my fate I calmly accepted it, and determined to continue the search for Holmes.

After a time I stopped at an outcropping of rock, where I sat down and ate my sandwiches. Then I continued.

The ground around me was rising now, climbing in a broad spiral sweep towards one of the high tors. My path had been curving towards the south as well as the east, and I knew that somewhere in that direction, across the wind-swept, mist-filled moor was the grim, dark building known as Dartmoor Prison. Many a murderer had escaped from that stronghold only to lose his life in the mires of the moor.

It was dark now, with just occasional patches of starlight showing through gaps in the clouds, and I was almost feeling my way forward up the rising slope of the tor. Suddenly, through the chill night air, came that howling sound again. This time it was louder and closer. The echoes made the source uncertain, but it could have been coming from somewhere not far behind me, or, perhaps, ahead of me. The long, savage howl ended in a kind of hysterical, cackling laughter that was almost human. That awful sound reminded me of the superstitious villagers and their beliefs concerning werewolves, that they called 'shape-changers'. I stood frozen to the spot for a long time. Around me now there was silence. When it was clear that the howling was over, I resumed my journey.

My path continued to curve around with a large wall of granite on one side and a steep drop on the other. Suddenly I stopped. Ahead of me was some sort of stealthy, sinister sound. It was an animal sound.

I heard a distinct scratching noise, as of clawed feet walking over rock, and then a heavy, animal panting. Cautiously I crept forward. Rounding a final corner, I saw it on the path ahead of me.

It glowed with a strange, luminescent light of a lime green colour. No sooner had I seen it, than it saw me. A low growl came from its huge throat, and it opened its slavering mouth to display a fearsome row of fangs. As it prepared to spring I dropped back a pace and struggled to get my revolver out of my pocket.

My Webley was in my hand but the hammer was not yet fully cocked when the creature sprang at my throat. I was certain my final moment had come when a sharp crack rang out, and the beast fell dead at my feet. A moment later Sherlock Holmes stepped out from behind a boulder, his Ely .32 pistol in his hand with a trail of blue smoke rising from its barrel.

'Holmes!' I cried out. 'I was never more pleased to see you.'

'Nor I you, old chap.'

'But where ... how ... I don't understand?'

'All in good time, Watson, all in good time. I have a flask of brandy here, and it looks to me as though you need some—for medicinal purposes.'

15

Sherlock Holmes took me back to the place where he had camped for the past two nights. There, sheltered from the winds by the circle of stones that had once been the walls of a stone-age hut, was a flickering fire.

'Here,' said Holmes, handing me the flask of brandy. 'Have a swallow of that—you'll feel much better.'

'Was it a wolf, Holmes?' I asked as I felt the brandy warming my blood.

'No, just the huge German Shepherd dog owned by the gipsies—the one they called Hannibal. Of course it was tricked up with phosphorescent paint, in much as same way as John Stapledon tricked up the "hound of the Baskervilles".'

'But why, Holmes?'

'It suited Hugo Zak to play upon the superstitions of the local villagers. When he heard their talk of a "ghost wolf" he decided to give them one—to direct their attentions away from his other activities.'

'What activities?'

'I'll tell you about those shortly. We have other business to attend to first.'

'I say Holmes,' I said as I took another sip of the brandy, 'you saved my life.'

'Had to, old chap,' replied Holmes with a smile, 'I couldn't lose my Watson. Now, if you're feeling recovered, we have a journey to make.'

As I stood to my feet I was surprised at how well I felt—tramping across the moor was clearly excellent exercise.

'Where are we off to, Holmes?'

'To witness a pagan ceremony at an old Druidic temple.'

I said nothing but my eyebrows must have expressed my surprise.

'It's not far across the moor,' Holmes added, 'so let's make a start.'

Sherlock Holmes carried a bull's eye lantern to light our way as we clambered down from the high tor, skirted a dangerous mire, and pushed our way through low bushes and stunted trees that had been twisted into bizarre shapes by the wild winds of Dartmoor.

'There, Watson,' whispered Holmes as he grabbed my arm. 'Just ahead.'

Ahead of us was a clearing in the bushes, and in that clearing stood a circle of standing stones. In the very centre of that circle, crouched over a crackling fire of bracken and twigs stood the gipsy woman, Mina Zak.

Her lips were moving, and, as Holmes and I huddled in silence behind a twisted tree trunk, her voice was carried to us on the cold, damp wind.

'Come fire, come rain, come dark spirits, come again,' she was chanting in her strange voice. 'Curse the ground and curse the sky, and curse the one who has cursed I.'

She threw a handful of something into the fire and the flames leaped up and flashed bright yellow. As the fire died down again, Mina resumed her chant, 'Curse the night and curse the day, and curse the woman Alice Grey.'

'What does Alice Grey have to do with this?' I whispered to Holmes.

'Sshh, Watson.'

'Curse the work she has begun, curse the woman who stole my son.' The chanting ended in an eerie cackle that had a ring of anger and cruelty about it.

At that moment Holmes stepped forward into the red glow of the firelight.

'This will not bring back your son, Mina Zak,' he said sternly.

'Who's that? Who's there?' she demanded. 'Who are you, and how do you know these things?'

'My name is Sherlock Holmes—and it is my business to know.'

I stepped to Holmes' side, my hand firmly gripping the revolver in my pocket.

'I came here tonight,' continued Holmes, 'to have my suspicions verified—and you have done just that. Your son Robbie has eloped with Alice Grey, hasn't he?'

'Yes, he has!' She spat out the words. 'He should have married a good gipsy girl, but he wouldn't. And now he has brought shame upon my husband and me among all the Romany tribes—for he has married outside the clan.'

'He has made his choice and he has gone. If you accept that and forgive him you may see him again, and he may still become the comfort of your old age. But rage against him in unforgiving anger and you and your husband will grow old alone, as if you were childless.'

The woman sank down onto the ground and sobbed.

'And you would do well,' Holmes continued, 'to forget this dark and dangerous nonsense of casting spells. If you wed yourself to the occult you will be wed forever. You are inviting an eternity of torment in the grip of the dark spirits you summon. Much better to make your peace with the great God who made you and all the world around you.'

Slowly, Mina Zak raised her head and looked at Holmes.

'Do you know where I can find my son?'

'Yes. I tracked their footprints on the night they eloped. By now Arthur Grey will have received a letter from his daughter telling him that she could not face marriage to a man thirty years her senior, and that she has secretly married the man she loves.'

'But where are they?' asked Mina pitifully.

'Do you promise to forgive?'

'Yes, yes, I will forgive.'

'They have not gone far. Your Robbie is working for a blacksmith in the town of Lydford. If you and your husband go to them with smiles, they will welcome you.'

'I will go with blessings,' said Mina, smiling a wide toothless grin.

'Come, Watson,' Holmes said as he turned to me. 'Our work here is done, but there is more work for us to do this night.'

The clock on the church tower was chiming eleven pm as we walked back into the village of Little Meldon, and let ourselves into the front door of the inn.

We found Arthur Grey sitting in the deserted tap room reading a letter.

'Ah, Mr Holmes, Dr Watson—you won't have heard my sad news.'

'That Alice is now married to the gipsy boy?' said Holmes.

'I don't understand how you know these things, Mr Holmes—but it's quite true. A letter arrived by hand this evening. I've read it over and over. I can't believe what she has done to me.'

'What do you mean?' I asked.

'Doppler is a rich man. Alice, and Teddy, and me, all of us, could have been comfortably off for the first time in our lives. Is that such a bad thing to want? And he being so much older than she, she wouldn't have had to put up with him for long. Then, once he had died, she could have married a young man of her own choosing—she would be rich enough to pick and choose.'

'Was that a fair sacrifice to ask your daughter to make, Mr Grey?' asked Holmes solemnly. 'Was your request to her one that God could approve of?'

'Don't talk to me of God!' snapped the innkeeper angrily. 'I believe in no God. I am an atheist—I make my own rules. You are a man of science, Mr Holmes—surely you agree that God is just a childish myth?'

Holmes did not answer immediately. Instead he walked over to one of the tables on which there was a vase of fresh picked roses.

'There is nothing in which deduction is so necessary as religion,' said he, taking a single rose from the vase and leaning back against the table. 'It can be built up as an exact science by the reasoner. One of our highest assurances of the goodness of God seems to me to rest in the flowers. All other things, our powers, our desires, our food, are really necessary for our existence in the first instance. But this rose is an extra. Its smell and its colour are an embellishment of life, not a condition of it. It is only *goodness* which gives extras, and so I say again that we have much to learn from the flowers.'

With that Homes replaced the rose in its vase and turned his back on the innkeeper as he said, 'Goodnight, Mr Grey.'

16

First thing next morning, after a hot breakfast, we set off down the village street.

'First I must call at the post office to send a wire to Prague,' said Sherlock Holmes, 'and then we shall call upon Constable Potter.'

I waited in the pale sunshine in the street while Holmes went into the village store and post office to send his telegram. The sound of hooves attracted my attention, and, looking up I saw a pony trap trotting into Little Meldon from the direction of Okehampton. The passenger I quickly recognised as James McArdle, the reporter from the *Daily Gazette*.

'McArdle!' I called out. 'What are you doing here?'

'If Sherlock Holmes is here,' said he, leaping lightly from the back of the cart with a suitcase in his hand, 'then there is a story here. And I've persuaded my editor to let me come down and find out what it is.'

'I take it I must have rather spilled the beans over lunch the other day,' I mumbled, feeling somewhat embarrassed.

'Rather,' agreed McArdle with a cheerful smile. 'Where can I get bed and breakfast around here?'

'There's only one inn—Chequers, just down the street.'

'You staying there?'

'Yes, we are.'

'Excellent.'

At that point Holmes emerged from the small stone building that was the village store and post office.

'Ah, McArdle—hot on our tracks again, I see,' observed the detective.

'Would you care to give an interview to the *Daily Gazette*, Mr Holmes? Tell me what it's all about?'

'I am in no position to do that, McArdle. You will have to use your own ingenuity.'

'If you say so, Mr Holmes. I'll book a room and start asking questions around the place.'

With a cheerful smile and a nod of his head McArdle set off towards the inn.

'Sorry about that, Holmes. I appear to have peeked the fellow's interest, and he followed me down here.'

'Not to worry, Watson. Now, you and I should call upon Constable Potter.'

We found the village constable in his front garden pruning his roses.

As we stood there Holmes began to brief Potter on the investigations he had conducted during his two days on the moor, and what he had discovered. This was interrupted by the clatter of a cart and a voice calling out, 'Bert! Bert!'

A farm cart came to a halt in front of the policeman's cottage and a young farmer leaped down from the driver's seat.

'You got to come and see, Bert,' he said, breathlessly.

'Now, just pull yourself together there, Ned Hope,' said the constable. 'Take a deep breath and tell me what's been going on that's got you so fired up.'

'It's been around our farmhouse, during the night,'

replied the farmer, and then he dropped he voice to almost a whisper to add, 'the werewolf is what I'm talking about.'

'Nonsense is what you're talking about. That there "ghost wolf" what I saw has turned out to be nothing but a big dog, all painted up with phosphorescence so as it would glow in the dark. Mr Holmes here shot the animal last night. So, you can forget about all this nonsense.'

'Nonsense is it? Well, let me tell you. In the early hours of this morning my dogs started barking and the hens were making a racket, and when I went out at daybreak to take a look there were footprints.'

'What sort of footprints?'

'I already told you,' said Hope in a harsh whisper, 'the prints of a gigantic wolf!'

'I would like to see these footprints,' said Holmes.

'And so you shall, Mr Holmes, so you shall. If you three gentlemen would like to hop into my cart I'll take you out there straight away.'

Ned Hope's farm was not far from the village, and we were soon there.

'This way,' cried Ned, leaping out of the cart and beckoning us to follow him, 'around behind the barn.'

The farm house was a pleasant cottage surrounded by vegetable gardens and fruit trees. Behind the house was a wide expanse of moorland where we could see sheep grazing. We followed the agitated Ned to the back of the farm house where there was a barn and a hen house.

'Now, take a look at that!' he said, pointing towards a broad open area of muddy ground. Sure enough, the mud was heavily imprinted with paw prints—but prints like no paws I had ever seen before. They were enormous.

'Well, just take a look at that, Mr Holmes,' said Constable Potter, scratching his head. 'Now, this is something I don't understand. What do you make of it?'

Holmes said nothing, but taking his lens out of his pocket he dropped down on one knee and began examining the closest set of pad marks very carefully.

'These marks were certainly not made by any domestic, or wild, dog with which I am familiar, and I have trained myself to recognise fifty seven different types of dogs by their paw prints.'

'There you are then,' said Ned Hope triumphantly. 'It must be the shape-changer.'

'And the size, Holmes,' I said. 'Whatever made those pad marks must have been a gigantic hound ... or, possibly, I suppose ... wolf.'

'What is your conclusion, Mr Holmes?' asked the policeman.

'I don't draw conclusions, Potter, until I have all the data,' Holmes replied, as he stood to his feet. 'However, what I have just seen has told me exactly what I must be looking for.'

'And what's that?'

'If we go to the gipsy camp, I think I'll be able to show you.'

Ned Hope took us in his cart to the edge of the village where the footpath began that led across the moor. Holmes, Constable Potter and I were about to set off when a shout attracted our attention.

'Mr Holmes! Dr Watson!'

It was McArdle, the reporter, and he was running down the street towards us.

'Oh, I'm glad I caught you,' he puffed, trying to catch his breath. 'I've questioned the folk at the inn—and I know what it's all about.'

'What what's all about?' I asked.

'No need to play coy with me any longer, Dr Watson. You dropped a few hints over lunch, and now I know that it's true.'

'That what is true?' demanded the policeman. 'Do talk sense young man!'

'That you are hunting a werewolf!' he announced triumphantly.

'Where did you get that idea?' I demanded.

'From the hints you dropped over lunch.'

'I didn't drop any hints!'

'Well, perhaps not deliberately, but, well I read between the lines. And then when I asked at the inn they told me all about the "ghost wolf", or shape-changer, or werewolf.'

'But,' I protested, 'Holmes shot the dog last night that had been ...'

McArdle dismissed my objection with a wave of his hand. 'Just a practical joke in bad taste that someone has been playing. It doesn't explain the dead sheep, and the shape-changer the Bennetts saw at Moorgate farm.'

'You have succeeded in gathering a lot of information in a short space of time,' Holmes said.

'Thank you, Mr Holmes, I'll take that as a compliment. I am a good reporter. And I've done my research. Checked out werewolves in the newspaper library before I came down. I found out all about the *lycanthrope* or wolf-man. In French they are called *loups-garous*. They are men who hide beneath the mask of the beast, and beasts who kill with the tortured soul of a man. Country folk believe there have always been some men who could turn themselves into wolves. Some become wolves by rubbing their bodies with a wolf's skin, some by drinking water from a wolf's footprint, and some—the tragic cases—cannot help themselves. They suffer from the ancient disease of *lycanthropy* and change into wolves at regular intervals whether they want to or not.'

After this long speech, he paused to catch his breath. Then he resumed, 'You see, I've done my homework. So, now can I come with you, and watch the investigation?'

'No,' snapped Constable Potter at once. 'Not a chance. This is police business, and you are to stay away.'

'I'll file a story with my newspaper any way.'

'You can fly to the moon for all I care,' the constable said irritably. 'Just don't hang around us.'

17

And so it was that McArdle stayed in the village while Holmes, Constable Potter and I set out together for the gipsy camp on the slope of Vixen Tor.

When we reached the solitary caravan only Hugo Zak was in sight.

'Here's trouble,' he growled as we arrived. 'What do you lot want from me?'

'A few answers, Mr Zak—truthful answers,' said Holmes firmly.

'Ask any question you like,' replied the gipsy belligerently. 'I'll answer 'em all right!'

'I think, constable,' said Holmes, turning to Potter, 'that we might search before we question. After we have concluded our search, Zak, I warrant that your answers will be a good deal more truthful.'

'You can go through my caravan from top to bottom—I couldn't care less.'

But instead of the caravan, Holmes walked across the clearing beyond the camp fire, climbed a small slope, and began taking apart a pile of stones.

'Hey! What do ya think you're up to?' demanded Hugo Zak.

'Just watch him, Potter,' Holmes said severely. 'When

I've finished here, he'll have a lot of explaining to do.'

As Holmes removed the last of the stones in the pile a small treasure trove was revealed: there was a canvas sack, a large knife with a curved blade, and a pair of boots.

'What a strange mixture of things,' I remarked, feeling puzzled.

'Now, Mr Zak,' Holmes remarked as he carried these things back to the camp and laid them next to the fire, 'shall we begin with this canvas sack.'

'Begin where you like for all I care,' snarled the gipsy.

Onto the ground fell a collection of small objects, mostly silver from their appearance, when Holmes up-ended the sack.

'I think you'll find, constable,' explained the detective, 'that these are the items stolen from Professor Doppler— some from the site of the dig up on High Barrow, and the rest from the professor's home.'

'What have you got to say to that, Hugo?' demanded Constable Potter, looking as pleased as punch.

'I ain't sayin' nothin', and that's a fact.'

'But what are the rest of these objects, Holmes?' I asked. 'This knife, for instance?'

'Take a close look at it, Watson—a razor sharp blade, curved like a hook. This is the blade that Hugo Zak has used to maul, kill and mutilate sheep.'

'So, there's been no wild animal attacking sheep, it was this man all along?' asked the policeman.

'Exactly, Potter.'

'But how do you know, Mr Holmes?'

'Because I followed him on his rounds, the night before last.'

'You followed me?' squeaked Zak, sounding genuinely

alarmed. 'But I saw no one.'

'That is what you may expect to see when I follow you,' replied Holmes.

'I confess that I still don't understand, Holmes,' I said. 'Why did this man butcher sheep in this horrible fashion? Why did he hack the carcasses to pieces, and pretend they were the victims of some powerful animal?'

'To disguise what he was really doing,' explained my friend as he strolled over and leaned against the gipsy caravan. 'He was stealing meat. A little, no doubt, was consumed here at this camp, but most of it was sold to a butcher in Tavistock.'

'You must be the devil himself, Sherlock Holmes, if you know all of this,' snarled Hugo Zak.

'No supernatural power was involved—just observation and deduction. There was a family of gipsies in the area, but they were not offering their services as tinkers, nor were they offering to tell fortunes or any of the other tricks that your people get up to, to earn a living. So, I asked myself, how does this family survive? If sheep are being slaughtered out in the wild, any missing parts of the carcasses would be assumed to have been eaten by the animal that made the attack. Under that cover you carted away whole sheep and sold them to your friend at Tavistock. But not satisfied with a little sheep stealing, the whisper of silver objects dug up by the professor sent you thieving from him as well.'

Suddenly all the fight seemed to go out of Hugo Zak. The big man's shoulders sagged, he sat down on the ground, and, as he buried his head in his hands, he said, 'I know when I'm beaten.'

'But there is more to the story, isn't there, Zak?' continued Holmes, 'for on the night you raided the professor's cottage you also drugged his hound, released the animal's chain, and smeared blood around its mouth, in an attempt to shift suspicion on to that innocent animal.'

'But what about the "ghost wolf" that Dr Watson and I saw?' asked Constable Potter. 'I mean the dog, Hannibal.'

'Hugo couldn't leave well enough alone. He kept embroidering his plan, making it more and more elaborate. When his method of sheep stealing caused the local villages to talk about a "ghost wolf" he decided to give them one—a further step to keep suspicion away from himself. So he painted his dog, a large German Shepherd, with luminous paint, and turned it loose on the moor each night. It had the desired effect.'

'It frightened the life out of me,' admitted Potter.

'Still not able to leave well enough alone, Mr Zak decided that the beast should leave paw prints as well.'

'The prints we saw at Ned Hope's farm?'

'Precisely, constable. When I examined them this morning I knew they had been faked. The huge pad marks had been very carefully made, but the distance between the steps was the distance of a man's stride, not a dog's. And the depth of each impression was too even to have been made by an animal as it shifted its weight between its four legs. On top of which, there was a slight indentation around each paw print.'

'I saw those paw prints myself,' remarked Potter, 'and I missed all that.'

'But I did not. Some elementary deduction added to those observations and I concluded that the prints had been manufactured by something like these boots.'

As he said this Holmes turned over the pair of boots he had found hidden with the silver and the knife. On the sole of both boots were carefully carved wooden impressions of the giant paw marks we had seen in the mud.

I was struck by how ingenious this all was—both Zak's original scheme, and Holmes' unravelling of that scheme. But some pieces of the puzzle still did not seem to fit.

'What about the howling that was heard?' I asked, 'and the "shape-changer" that was seen at Moorgate farm? Was that Zak as well?'

'No, Watson, it was not. It fitted in nicely with Zak's plans, but I think it puzzled him as much as it puzzled us.'

'Then what is the answer?'

'That, Watson, I believe I can show you tonight.'

18

It was late in the afternoon when Edith Doppler and Trevor Franklin met with us in the front parlour of the inn—in response to a note that Sherlock Holmes had sent.

'Do you have news for us, Mr Holmes?' asked Miss Doppler.

'Yes, I have. First, allow me to return this to you.' So saying, Holmes handed over the young woman's diary.

'Thank you, Mr Holmes. Was it of any use to you?'

'A great deal of use. In fact, the information from that diary plays a key role in bringing this matter to a conclusion. By studying the dates on which your father exhibited his strange behaviour it became clear that there is a regular pattern. Tell me—has he received any mail today?'

'There was a letter and there was a small packet,' said Edith, 'each with the small cross under the stamp which warned me not to touch them. There has been nothing else.'

'Just as I thought. Now, Miss Doppler, Mr Franklin, we shall, I think, come to some conclusion tonight. If my deductions are correct we should have an opportunity of bringing matters to a head. In order to do so it is necessary to hold the Professor under observation. I would suggest, therefore, that you remain awake and on the look-out,

Mr Franklin. Should you hear him pass your door do not interrupt him, but follow him as discreetly as you can. Dr Watson and I will not be far off. By the way, where is the key to that little wooden box you told us about, Miss Doppler?'

'Upon his watch chain.'

'I fancy our researches must lie in that direction. At the worst the lock should not be formidable. Have you any other able-bodied man on the premises?'

'There is the coachman, Halifax.'

'Where does he sleep?'

'Over the stables.'

'We might possibly want him. Well, we can do no more until we see how the thing develops. Good-bye—but I shall expect to see you before morning.'

It was nearly midnight before we took our station among some bushes immediately opposite the hall door of the Professor. Fortunately there was no rain or mist, but the wind blowing off the moor was bitter, and we were glad of our warm overcoats. The breeze drove thick clouds across the sky, obscuring the half-moon from time to time.

It would have been a dismal vigil were it not for the expectation and the excitement which carried us along, and the assurance of my colleague that we had probably reached the end of the strange sequence of events which had engaged our attention.

'If the time cycle holds good, then we shall have the Professor at his worst tonight,' said Holmes. 'The facts are that the strange symptoms began after his visit to Prague, and that he is in secret correspondence with a shady dealer in London, who presumably represents the contact in Prague, and that he received a packet from him this very day. What he takes and why he takes it is still beyond our knowledge, but that it emanates in some way from Prague is clear enough. Look out, Watson! Here he is! We shall have the chance of seeing for ourselves.'

The hall door had slowly opened, and against the lamp-lit background we saw the tall figure of Professor Doppler. He was clad in his dressing-gown. As he stood outlined in the doorway he was erect but leaning forward with dangling arms.

Now he stepped forward into the drive, and an extraordinary change came over him. He sank down into a crouching position, and moved along upon his hands and feet, skipping every now and then as if he overflowed with energy and vitality. He moved along the face of the house and then around the corner. As he disappeared Franklin slipped through the hall door and softly followed him.

'Come, Watson, come!' whispered Holmes, as we stole as softly as we could through the bushes until we had gained a spot whence we could see the other side of the house, which was bathed in the light of the half-moon.

The Professor was clearly visible crouching at the foot of the ivy-covered wall. As we watched him he suddenly began with incredible agility to ascend it. From branch to branch he sprang, sure of foot and firm of grasp, climbing apparently in the mere joy of his own powers, with no definite object in view.

With his dressing-gown flapping on each side of him he looked like some huge bat glued against the side of his own house, a great square dark patch upon the moonlit wall. Presently he tired of this amusement, and, dropping down from branch to branch, he squatted down into the old attitude and moved towards the stables, creeping along in the same strange way as before.

Blaze, the wolfhound, was straining at the end of his

chain, barking furiously, and more excited than ever when he caught sight of his master. He was quivering with eagerness and rage. The Professor squatted down very deliberately just out of reach of the hound, and began to provoke its in every possible way. He took handfuls of pebbles from the drive and threw them in the dog's face, prodded him with a stick which he had picked up, flicked his hands about only a few inches from the gaping mouth, and endeavoured in every way to increase the animal's fury, which was already beyond all control.

And then in a moment it happened! It was not the chain that broke—it was the collar that slipped, for it had been made for a thick-necked Newfoundland. We heard the rattle of falling metal, and the next instant dog and man were rolling on the ground together, the one roaring in rage, the other screaming in a strange, shrill voice of terror.

It was a narrow thing for the Professor's life. The savage creature had him fairly by the throat, its fangs had bitten deep, and he was unconscious before we could reach them and drag them apart. It might have been a dangerous task for us, but Franklin's voice and presence brought the great wolf-hound instantly to reason.

The uproar had brought the sleepy and astonished coachman from his room above the stables.

'I'm not surprised,' said Halifax, shaking his head. 'I've seen him at it before. I knew the dog would get him sooner or later.'

The hound was secured and together we carried the Professor up to his room, where Edith Doppler helped me clean and dress the wound to his throat. The sharp teeth had passed dangerously near the carotid artery, and the bleeding was serious. I did everything my medical knowledge allowed me to do for him, and in half an hour the danger had passed. Once I knew he was safe I gave him an injection of morphine and he sank into a deep sleep.

'Thank you, Dr Watson,' said Miss Doppler, 'you've saved my father's life.'

Then, and only then, were we able to all look at each other and take stock of the situation.

19

"Will it be possible to keep this matter to ourselves?" pleaded Edith Doppler when we four were seated before the fire in the parlour. 'At present the scandal is confined to our own household. If it gets beyond these walls it will never stop. Father will lose his position at the university. He will be the laughing-stock of London.'

'Consider poor Edith's feelings,' interrupted Trevor Franklin.

'Quite so,' said Sherlock Holmes. 'I think it may be quite possible to keep the matter to ourselves, and also to prevent its recurrence now that we have a free hand. The key from the watch-chain please, Mr Franklin. Halifax will guard the patient and let us know if there is any change. Let us see what we can find out in the Professor's mysterious box.'

There was not much, but there was enough—a small, empty bottle, another nearly full, a hypodermic syringe, several letters in an untidy handwriting. The marks on the envelopes showed that they were those that had disturbed Edith's routine as her father's secretary, and each was addressed from the Commercial Road and signed "W. Sprague." They were mere invoices to say that a fresh bottle was being sent to Professor Doppler, or receipts to acknowledge money. There was one other envelope, however, in a more educated handwriting and bearing an Austrian stamp with the postmark of Prague.

'Unless I am much mistaken,' cried Holmes, 'here we have our material. This should be from a gentleman named Lowenstein.'

'How can you possibly know that, Holmes?' I asked.

'I have received a reply to my telegram from the head of the Prague police. I was able to assist him in a difficult matter some time ago, and he was very willing to help. "Lowenstein" is the name he suggested.' With these words Holmes removed the letter from its envelope. A quick glance told me that Holmes was quite correct—that the signature at the bottom was indeed Lowenstein.

'What does it say?' asked Franklin. 'Read it aloud please, Mr Holmes.'

'Honoured Colleague,' read Holmes. 'Since your esteemed visit I have thought much of your case, and though in your circumstances there are some special reasons for the treatment, I would none the less enjoin caution, as my results have shown that it is not without danger of a kind.

'It is possible that the serum of Anthropoid would have been better. I have, as I explained to you, used black-faced Langur because a specimen was accessible. Langur is, of course, a crawler and climber, while Anthropoid walks erect, and is in all ways nearer.

'I beg you to take every possible precaution that there be no premature revelation of the process. I have one other client in England, and Sprague is my agent for both.'

'Weekly reports will oblige.

'Yours with high esteem,

'H. Lowenstein.'

'I still don't understand, Mr Holmes,' said Edith, a look

of puzzlement on her young face.

'From the light that I see dawning in Dr Watson's eyes,' Holmes replied with a smile, 'I think that he may be able to provide more details.'

'Yes, Miss Doppler,' I remarked, 'I believe I can fill in some gaps. You see, the name Lowenstein is notorious in medical circles. I read about him in the correspondence columns of *The Lancet*. He is an obscure medical scientist who has been striving in some unknown way for the secret of rejuvenation and the elixir of life. His patients are older men and women. He promises them—quite unethically—that he can restore their youth and extend their life.'

I shook my head in disgust as I went on, 'Lowenstein of Prague! Who would have thought it? Lowenstein with his so-called wonderful strength giving serum, banned by my colleagues in the medical profession because he has refused to reveal its source.'

While I was speaking, Franklin had taken a book on zoology from the shelves. 'Here is the entry,' he said, 'let me read it to you: *Langur—the great black-faced monkey of the Himalayan slopes, biggest and most human of climbing monkeys.* Hhmm, it goes on to add many details. Well, thanks to you, Mr Holmes, it is very clear we have traced the evil to its source.'

'The real source,' said Holmes, 'lies in the untimely early death of your mother, Miss Doppler, the Professor's wife. He had a not-uncommon reaction of lapsing into a morbid fear of his own death. Initially this showed itself in his deep depression. However, the discovery of Viking relics in his archaeological dig at High Barrow revived his interest in life—and Professor Doppler decided to fight death in every way he could.'

'Which is why he courted a young wife in Alice Grey?'

'Precisely, Miss Doppler, and, more to the point, it is why he pursued this dangerous "monkey gland" treatment. He had the idea that he could turn himself into a younger man—and so push death off into the far distance. He may even have clung to a hope of defeating death altogether.'

For a while Sherlock Holmes sat looking at the small, glass bottle in his hand filled with its clear liquid, and then he said, 'When one tries to rise above God's plan one is liable to fall below it. The highest type of man may revert to the animal when pride leads him off the straight road of obedience to God.'

Suddenly the philosopher disappeared, and Holmes, the man of action, sprang from his chair, 'I shall send a second wire to my friend, the chief of police in Prague. I think Herr Lowenstein shall find himself held to be criminally responsible for the poisons which he circulates—and we shall have no more trouble.'

'Mr Holmes,' said Edith Doppler, reaching out to take my friend's hand, 'You are the one man in England who could have cleared up this puzzle, and saved my father from his own foolishness. I thank God that you could be here to do so.'

Even Holmes' vanity was a little embarrassed by her warmth and sincerity.

'I think there is nothing more to be said, Miss Doppler,' he responded. 'The various incidents will now fit themselves easily into the general scheme. The dog, of course, was aware of the change far more quickly than you. His smell would ensure that. It was the monkey, not the Professor, whom Blaze attacked, just as it was the monkey who teased Blaze. Climbing was a joy to the creature, and it was mere chance, I take it, that the pastime brought him to your window.'

'And the other incidents on the moor, Holmes?' I asked.

'The Langur, if I recall correctly, Watson, is a howling monkey. Thus it was the Professor who was the source of the terrifying howls that helped to spread the superstition of "werewolves". And it was the Professor the Bennetts saw at Moorgate farm, and whom they took to be a "shape-changer". It is from incidents such as these that superstitions arise.'

20

'There is an early train to town, Watson,' said Sherlock Holmes, 'but I think we shall just have time for a cup of tea at Chequers Inn before we catch it.'

Holmes' words were interrupted by a terrific crash just outside the parlour window. When we rushed out to investigate we discovered McArdle, the reporter from the *Daily Gazette* lying sprawled on the ground, the fragments of a wooden barrel, that he had been standing on to see in through the window, scattered around his feet.

'How long have you been listening, Mr McArdle?' asked Holmes as he helped the young man to his feet.

'For the past half hour.'

'Then you have heard everything?'

'Everything.'

'Do you intend to publish?' asked Holmes sternly.

'Oh, please, please, Mr McArdle,' Edith Doppler pleaded earnestly, 'you will ruin many lives if you do.'

'Edith is quite right,' added Trevor Franklin. 'You will not only ruin Edith's life, and that of her father, you will damage his valuable work in archaeology, and who knows where the damage may end.'

'Well ...' said the reporter reluctantly. 'It is never the intention of a journalist to hurt anyone. But a story is a story.'

'If you report this particular story,' Holmes said sternly, 'you will lose my good will. And that may cost you many more far better stories in the future. Which do you want? This particular "human interest" story? Or my good will, and the many stories of crime in London that may come with it?'

'You leave me no choice, Mr Holmes,' McArdle responded, as he opened up his notebook and tore out half a dozen pages. These he handed to Edith Doppler.

'Oh, thank you, Mr McArdle—thank you,' she gushed. 'And thank you, once again, Mr Holmes—our lives would have been ruined without you.'

As Holmes, McArdle and I walked back down the chilly, moonlit street through Little Meldon to Chequers Inn, I asked the reporter, 'How will you square this with your editor? He sent you down here for a "werewolf" story and you won't have one. What will you tell him?'

'I still have a good story to tell,' said the reporter cheerfully. 'The story of Hugo Zak the gipsy, and of how he frightened the locals while carrying on with his thieving—and how he was unmasked by Sherlock Holmes. That's a good story.'

'Quite true,' I remarked, 'but you will not be able to explain some points—such as the howling on the moor, and the "shape changer" seen by the Bennetts at Moorgate farm.'

'True, but then it does not hurt to leave a few things unexplained. I might even suggest to my editor that I could do a series of stories about strange happenings, parts of which cannot be explained. These stories we could label "X" for the unknown. I have a file of them in my desk drawer.'

And so the privacy of Edith Doppler, her unwise father,

and Trevor Franklin her fiance, was protected.

Later that morning, as Holmes and I sat in a railway carriage being carried swiftly back to London, I asked, 'Do you think anyone will ever invent a safe serum to prolong human life?'

'I hope not,' the great detective replied gravely. 'There is a danger there—a very real danger to humanity. Consider, Watson, that the material people, the sensual people, the worldly people would all prolong their worthless lives. The spiritual people would not avoid a call to something higher. It would be the survival of the least fit. What sort of cesspool may our poor world then become?'

'And then another question I have, Holmes, is about Professor Doppler's fear of death. I have seen it before in other people. They become obsessive about exercise and diet, far more than it is healthy to do so, in order to preserve their youth and delay old age and death. What causes this reaction?'

'I don't think the people concerned even understand this themselves, Watson. At a deep level, perhaps an unconscious level, what they fear is not death, but judgement. Judgement cannot be avoided. One day each one of us will stand before the great Judge who made us to give an account of how we have made use of his gift of life. It makes more sense to prepare for that moment, rather than to—fruitlessly—attempt to avoid it.'

Afterword

Well, how did you go in identifying the references to the original Conan Doyle stories in *The Wolfman of Dartmoor?*

The easiest references to identify are those to the short story entitled "The Creeping Man". *The Wolfman of Dartmoor* is based on incidents in that story.

There is a reason for that, by the way. Many Sherlockians regard "The Creeping Man" as one of the poorest stories Conan Doyle ever wrote, even though it is based on an excellent idea: I aimed to put that original idea into a rather better tale.

Please don't think I am being presumptuous in saying so. "The Creeping Man" is a late story (published in 1923), and towards the end of his writing career Conan Doyle (great writer though he was) had come to regard the Holmes stories as potboilers and did not always give them the attention they deserved. (Even Homer nods.)

But "The Creeping Man" is just the beginning, of course: given my aim there are many more cross-references. For instance, I have reproduced Sherlock Holmes' famous "rose speech" from "The Naval Treaty".

Then again, the dog in this book—the Irish wolfhound called Blaze—was named, so Miss Doppler explained, after a famous race horse. That racehorse was, of course, Silver Blaze, and he features in Conan Doyle's short story with the eponymous title. On the subject of dogs—this tale also refers to that gigantic and dangerous animal *The Hound of the Baskervilles.*

And that's as much information as I intend to give you. The rest of the cross-references you can hunt out for yourself. (Well, you are a serious Sherlockian, aren't you?)

By the way, the geography of Dartmoor in this tale is accurate (or as accurate as research on a map can make it). Which is more than can be said for Conan Doyle's Dartmoor geography in *The Hound of the Baskervilles.*

People who know the moors well tell me that the distances are all wrong in that, the greatest of the Holmes adventures.

But then, who cares about geography when the mystery is as puzzling and bizarre as the tale that Conan Doyle weaves so superbly in *Hound?* ("They were the footprints, Mr Holmes, of a gigantic hound!") Give me a mysterious spectral hound any day of the week, and geography be blowed!

OTHER BOOKS BY
KEL RICHARDS

Something strange is walking in the darkness!
Professor Soames Coffin has spent his life studying
the secrets of ancient Egypt—and as he lies, dying, in
his dark, old mansion in Scotland he believes the old
magic of the Pharaohs will bring him back to life. Soon
the creature who is "The Walking Dead" is stalking the
living … including Sherlock Holmes!

THE HEADLESS MONK

The ghost is after the gold! The legend from the Dark Ages has come to life—the monk that has no head—and it's hunting for the missing treasure of 40,000 gold coins. A terrified lighthouse keeper and his family call upon Sherlock Holmes—the world's greatest detective—to protect them from deadly danger.

THE VAMPIRE SERPENT

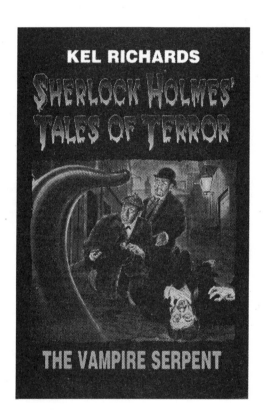

The legend of the vampire has come to life—and is stalking the streets of London. Another dead body has been found—drained of every last drop of blood! Inspector Lestrade of Scotland Yard is baffled. Only Sherlock Holmes—the world's greatest detective—can solve the mystery.

THE CASE OF THE VANISHING CORPSE

The world of Ben Bartholomew is a world of standover gangs and armed terrorists, a world in which a P.I. for hire must carry a gun if he wants to live beyond lunch time. It is a world of religious fanatics, petty tyrants, spies and nightmares, which explodes with intrigue and danger when a corpse disappears from a sealed tomb. In *The Case of the Vanishing Corpse* Romans in togas

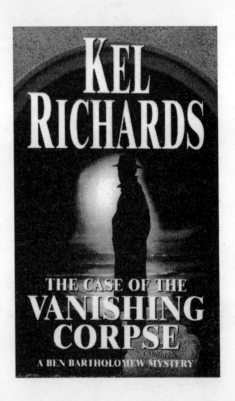

mingle with gun toting private eyes in sports cars. When Ben Bartholomew begins investigating how and why the body of Jesus the Nazarene disappeared from a solid, rock tomb guarded by armed soldiers, he finds that he has stumbled onto the ultimate locked-room mystery!

AN OUTBREAK OF DARKNESS

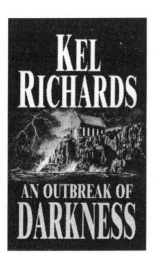

Out of the darkest pages of history comes a black shadow to threaten the present.

On a remote uninhabited island an ancient stone monument to evil is mysteriously rebuilding itself.

Creatures from your worst nightmares attack the small team investigating the island.

It is as if the gates of hell themselves have been opened.

It is—*an outbreak of darkness!*

DEATH IN EGYPT

An ancient Egyptian tomb sealed from the outside world for centuries deep inside solid rock—the sarcophagus is opened—inside is a freshly murdered corpse. Impossible? Legendary detective writer G K Chesterton investigates the mystery—and reveals the amazing solution—but not before there are more deaths and deadly danger.

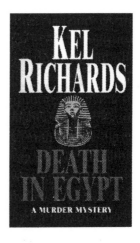

Kel Richards' Books

are available from:

Beacon Communications Pty Ltd
PO Box 1317
LANE COVE NSW 2066
AUSTRALIA

Visa, MasterCard and Bankcard accepted

Phone: 02 9427 4197
Fax: 02 9428 5502

Internet www.gospelnet.com.au/holmes

Email beacon@planet.net.au

Catalogue Available